PRAISE FOR

"A gritty, compelling, and altogether engrossing novel that reads as if ripped from the headlines. I couldn't turn the pages fast enough. Chad Zunker is the real deal."

—Christopher Reich, *New York Times* bestselling author
of *Numbered Account* and *Rules of Deception*

"*Good Will Hunting* meets *The Bourne Identity*."

—Fred Burton, *New York Times* bestselling author of *Under Fire*

THE TRACKER

CHAD ZUNKER

THOMAS & MERCER

Published by Thomas & Mercer, Seattle

www.apub.com

Amazon, the Amazon logo, and Thomas & Mercer are trademarks of Amazon.com, Inc., or its affiliates.

ISBN-13: 9781503943230 (paperback)
ISBN-10: 1503943232 (paperback)

Cover design by Faceout Studio

Printed in the United States of America

To Katie, my wife,
for taking the crazy ride with me;
to Nancy, my mother,
for two decades of support and prayer;
to Anna, Madison, and Lexi, my daughters,
the inspiration behind my dreams.

ONE

Saturday, 1:18 a.m.
Boerne, Texas
Two days, twenty-two hours, forty-two minutes till Election Day

The cheap motel-room ceiling was stained. Like muddy yellow clouds.

A smoker's room. I'm not a smoker. But I'd have lit up just about anything if it would have calmed me down. My heart felt like it was going to explode. I stared at the ceiling. I should have been asleep. The motel bed was comfortable enough, but every limb of my body felt rigid. I was unable to relax. Unable to breathe easy. Unable to slow my mind. The room temperature was a pleasant seventy degrees, yet beads of sweat dripped down my neck onto the hard pillow. There was no noise from other motel rooms. No wild teenage party down the walkway. No loud snores from a traveling salesman next door. Just the unsteady rattle of an old air conditioner in the ceiling, the squeak of rusty pipes in distant walls. But I could hear the clear banging of my own heartbeat in my ears.

Twenty-five. A few months away from grinding out a degree from Georgetown Law, finding a decent job, and finally making a real living after a lifetime of getting my butt kicked over and over again, in and out of foster homes, having to prove how tough I was every six months. Finally, I would put the years of living on the streets behind me. But now, I was going to have a heart attack in a filthy motel room in the middle of nowhere.

I thought about my mom, tried to catch my breath and calm down.

I told myself everything would be OK. I was having a hard time believing it.

I'd made two phone calls. One to my boss. He was on his way.

The other call was to the only calming presence I'd ever had in my life. She didn't answer. She hadn't answered in more than five months. I didn't leave a voice mail.

I checked my phone again. The text from my boss was from eighty-six minutes ago. Eighty-six of the longest minutes of my life. What was taking him so long?

Stay put. On my way. Don't say a word to anyone until we talk!

The drive west from Austin proper to Boerne could take an hour and fifteen minutes. Maybe a few more if you got caught behind an 18-wheeler on one of the area's countless one-lane country roads. Rick knew this was urgent. I'd texted him back twice already. Where are you? Hello? No reply. Cell-phone signals sucked out here in the Texas hill country.

I pushed myself up onto my elbows. Two lamps were on in the room. One in the corner. One on the nightstand. The cheap kind you'd find at Walmart for thirty bucks. The blinds were cracked, so I would be able to spot headlights in the parking lot. Nothing. I stared across the room into the mirror above the flimsy dresser, surprised I couldn't see my heart flitting up and down under my shirt. I was still fully dressed. Blue jeans; dark-blue flannel button-down; old, gray Nike running shoes. Common law-school student attire. Crap I wore every day to class. But I'd been skipping classes for three weeks for this job to earn some quick cash—a little for rent and books, and everything else to help with my mom's escalating medical bills, trying to beat the cancer somehow. I wasn't sure there was enough money in this job to win that battle.

Leukemia sucked.

I wouldn't really call it a job. I was what you call a political tracker.

My job was to follow our opponent from small town to small town on the campaign trail and record with a video camera every word that came out of his mouth every single time he stepped into public. And sometimes in private. I had no business card. Nothing that said *Samuel W. Callahan, Political Tracker, Esq.* And I doubt there was ever a job posting. But there were others like me hiding in the crowds of every political contest going on around the country right now. Eager young law students or government majors looking to make a name for themselves in their own political party, jockeying for position, already climbing the powerful and influential DC political ladder.

In my opinion, both sides of the political fence sucked. Otherwise, there wouldn't be thousands of kids who were lost in a broken and crooked foster-care system, as I had been, and getting abused in every city in America. I was only out for a buck. The only politician I cared anything about at the moment was Benjamin Franklin, simply because his pretty, old face was plastered on hundred-dollar bills. And I hoped to have a very nice roll of them in my back pocket when this deal was all over in four days.

My apathy toward any specific political party didn't change the fact that I was still good at what I did. My street skills translated well. I knew how to blend into a crowd, stay under the radar. I had quick hands, quick feet, and an even quicker mind. But there was more to it than that. I had something extra. A special gift. Something that even I couldn't fully understand. My mind seemed to work differently than others. I could oftentimes see things before they happened. Like an anticipation reflex. My mind allowed me to view events differently, almost in slow motion, especially in really stressful situations. I had the odd ability to look around corners—not like a freaky superhero or anything—but like I'd memorized Google Maps. I could visualize a full escape route within seconds. I'm not really sure why. I'd never been to a doctor about it. Never had a CAT scan done on my brain. I figured that maybe my mom had been on a serious acid trip when she was pregnant with me and some wires got crossed.

This unique ability really used to freak out my street gang as a teenager. It also made me the best thief in the bunch. When I was eleven, it meant easily stealing wallets in crowded bus terminals. Or purses from oblivious women in grocery stores. In and out within seconds. Never even close to being caught. Not even with security cameras. By the time I was fourteen and living on the streets full-time, it meant jacking expensive cars from gas stations in affluent Denver neighborhoods when unsuspecting victims thought they had two minutes to rush inside with the car running and grab a Snickers and a Diet Coke. You had to have a certain temperament and skill set to ease behind the steering wheel of a Mercedes sedan, unnoticed from only twenty feet away, and calmly drive out of a parking lot.

I'd put that life behind me after a brief juvie stint, straightened up my act, finished my GED, and smoked my SATs. Got a perfect score on the math section. That got me accepted into the University of Colorado. Started putting together consecutive semesters with a 4.0 GPA. No more hustling. No more scams. I had no desire to live on the streets again, so I went clean. Basically. If you don't count the time I snagged a classmate's credit card from his wallet freshman year and had forty large pizzas delivered to our government class. Or the unapproved joyride junior year in the dean of students' new Camaro. To me, it was more borrowing than stealing. I put the car back completely unnoticed.

Josh, my old roommate at CU, was a government major who'd gone on to work at a powerful lobbyist firm in DC. He was doing well and making a name for himself. He called me a month ago, said he needed someone like me for a few weeks; they were in a pinch, had one of their guys back out midcampaign, could really make it worth my while. He knew about my mom, knew things had gone from bad to worse, knew we really needed the money.

Quick cash. Easy job. Three weeks. In and out. Those were his exact words.

I wish I'd never answered the call from Josh.

Where was Rick already?

Being a tracker was mostly mind-numbing, tedious work. The role had become more prominent nearly a decade ago when George Allen, the popular incumbent senator out of Virginia, lost in a stunning upset after calling a guy just like me, a young campaign tracker of Indian American descent, a *macaca*, right there on the tracker's video camera. The video went viral, and Allen's campaign collapsed under the weight of it. One word. Caught on video. Viewed a million times on YouTube.

Tens of millions of dollars have been poured into tracker organizations with very generic patriotic names like America Cares, the American Right, and Bridges Over America, which was the name of my group. After all, no legitimate politician's campaign would employ its own trackers. Too sleazy, right? So, I just worked for an organization with certain political leanings. I didn't care. Just pay me in cash when I'm done.

The campaign was for a coveted seat in the US House of Representatives from the Twenty-First District of Texas, a territory that covered parts of Austin down to San Antonio and then hundreds of small towns to the west. Like Boerne. Population 10,471. Pleasantville,

America. My so-called campaign target, whom I guess was technically supposed to be my opponent, was in a heated battle with the popular incumbent, and he'd been hitting several towns a day with his rally cry for change, reform, and government accountability. He'd held a rally for a few hundred locals on the steps of the Kendall County courthouse a few hours ago, followed by a barbecue on the vast lawn. It was the same in each small town. Empty promises. Charming smiles. One-line political zingers. Fake rallying cries. Planted audience clapping. Kissing babies. Hugging old folks. And flashing those perfect, pearly-white choppers for any camera in sight.

In most years, my campaign target would not have had a chance in this district. The incumbent, Congressman Leonard Mitchell, had held the seat for more than a decade. But this was not most years. And my target was no ordinary politician. Lucas McCallister. Thirty-five. Good-looking. Charismatic. Beautiful wife with Texas roots. Two precious elementary-age kids: one boy and one girl, of course. Harvard Law grad. Currently held the position of Commissioner of the Texas General Land Office. A rising star with the perfect lineage. Lucas McCallister was the only son of John McCallister, current US senator from Virginia, and the man who'd nearly won his party's presidential candidacy last round. Lucas McCallister's grandfather had also been a US senator from North Carolina. Lucas was part of a powerful and distinguished political legacy.

It was clear there were extraordinary stakes for District Twenty-one. It was not just about representing the good people of Texas. Lucas McCallister was being groomed for the presidency. His party had him on a ten-year track for the White House. He was their number one draft pick, and they were being strategic about his steps along the path. This was the first big test. McCallister had been planted specifically in this district in Texas to take down Leonard Mitchell, who'd been a powerful and vocal thorn in the side of the opposing party for the past decade. This was a heavyweight battle. They wanted Mitchell out. And they chose Lucas McCallister to be the one to throw the knockout punch.

Having significantly more media coverage than other congressional campaigns in the country made it much easier for me to blend into the crowd. But harder for me to catch my target off guard. McCallister was already a seasoned pro who rarely slipped up in public. Sure, we'd caught him stretching the truth here and there, exaggerating numbers to make a point, incorrectly quoting famous philosophers or key Scriptures from the Bible, and even tripping over a sidewalk curb and scraping his knee. But nothing that was going to erase his sudden three-points-and-climbing lead.

I again swallowed the knot in my throat. Nothing until tonight.

I pushed off the bed, walked to the front window, cracked the dusty blinds with a finger.

I was on the first floor of a two-story motel. Not one of the major chains. Most likely the cheapest in town. A mom-and-pop deal where a pimple-faced nephew ate Cheetos behind the front check-in desk. I was being paid a daily travel stipend with this gig, so it was up to me to save money where I could on food and lodging, which meant cheap gas-station sandwiches most days and staying overnight in dumps like this one. But I'd slept in much worse. Park benches. Under bridges. Concrete steps outside of churches. This was plush coming from that world.

My '96 black Ford Explorer with balding tires was parked right in front of my room door. My ride had more than 213,000 miles on it. It sputtered for five seconds each time I turned the ignition before eventually coughing to a start. It was on its last legs two years ago. I hoped it could somehow make it back to DC.

The orange Chevy truck that was here when I arrived was still parked three spots down. Same with the red Honda Accord with the two dents on the front next to it. And the white Toyota minivan beyond that. But there was a new car in the parking lot that surprised me. A dark-gray Oldsmobile sedan. Parked in the second row facing the building on the edge of the lot, next to an open pasture that led to the woods. I was certain it hadn't been sitting there when I arrived. Maybe I was wrong. But I think I would have noticed headlights as it pulled in. I squinted, thought I noticed movement inside. It was dark, and the parking lot wasn't well lit. My eyes narrowed even more. Then I saw a wisp of smoke leak out the window. Cigarette. Someone was sitting in that car, smoking.

A flash of new headlights suddenly splashed across the window.

Rick Jackson. My boss. Speeding into the parking lot in his blue Altima. He jerked the car into a spot right next to my Explorer, quickly got out. I unchained the door and let him inside.

"Where the hell you been?" I asked, chaining and locking the door behind us.

He dumped his bag on the bed. "Sorry. Phone died, or I would've called. I got ten minutes out of town, realized I didn't have my laptop, and had to double back."

"I've been going nuts here." I checked the blinds again, studied the Oldsmobile.

Rick was thirty-five, skinny, black hair, pale skin, solid black glasses. Tan Dockers and a white button-down. A nerd, but a decent guy. He was trying to grow a goatee, going after the tough-guy image. But it just looked desperate. He'd been doing this tracker thing for eight years. He was good. Really good. Not so much at the slip-in-and-out-of-crowds-unnoticed thing. Not like me. Rick was clumsy. But he was a genius at analyzing data quickly and pulling out anything that could be damaging to the campaign. Rick would catch things I'd flat-out missed. Even while being up close and personal. I would upload my videos and logs to our server every night, and I was always surprised when Rick found valuable nuggets by six the next morning. The guy had no life. No one in politics had a life. Especially during election season.

Our organization would feed the info to political blogs and news hot spots, send out some tweets, and by the time said politician had showered and shaved to face the cameras, he'd have to spend the whole morning clarifying or backtracking the misstep rather than pushing forward his own message. It would dominate the day. And each day not focused on his own agenda was a day lost on the campaign trail. Rick had developed a solid reputation, and most opposing politicians feared him.

"Let's see it," Rick said.

I pulled my phone out of my pocket.

"You didn't use the camera?" He glared at me as if I'd slapped his grandma.

I shook my head. As a tracker, it was critical that we captured video footage ready-made for television, because there was always a chance that our video would be cut and spliced and made into a commercial within hours in an effort to crush the opposition. And we needed the audience to see every last wrinkle on the politician's face when he put his big foot in his even bigger mouth.

"I had no time. My camera was here in the motel room. I was done for the day. I was out at a bar when the text came in."

"And you have no idea who sent the text?"

"Not a clue."

Rick unpacked his laptop on the bed. He powered it up.

"Have you uploaded the video yet?" Rick asked.

"I haven't done a thing but sit here sweating, man."

"OK. Let me have it."

"You sure you want to see it?"

He didn't flinch. "You're damned straight."

I tapped a few times on my phone screen, loaded the video, and handed it to Rick. It was five minutes and twenty-seven seconds long. I'd watched it a half dozen times already, still not able to comprehend the magnitude of it all. Rick held my phone in his bony fingers like it was so fragile it might break if he squeezed it too hard. He pressed the screen.

The video on my phone began to play. I hovered close to Rick.

My heart felt jittery again.

This suddenly felt very real. Another human being was watching what I'd just witnessed.

A man killing a woman. And not just any man.

TWO

Friday, 11:32 p.m.
Boerne, Texas
Three days, twenty-eight minutes till Election Day

The text that landed me in this mess arrived halfway through my second bottle of beer.

I'd been watching college-football highlights on a boxy, old-school TV perched behind the bar. I glanced at an oil painting of Willie Nelson, looking only slightly like the country singer and a lot more like Jesus, which I thought was maybe how he was viewed in these parts.

I'd driven around town for more than twenty minutes looking for anyplace that stayed open past ten to grab a few beers and watch some sports. I only noticed Reggie's—according to a faded sign above the battered front door—when I pulled into the dirt parking lot to gas up the Explorer. It was connected to the back of an old Shell gas station in a crumbling white building. I doubted the joint made the local Chamber of Commerce list. It was a dump. But this wasn't Austin, so I couldn't complain too much.

There were two dusty pool tables, an old jukebox playing Johnny Cash, some pinball machines in the corner, and enough cigarette smoke from a half dozen rednecks to give me a full case of lung cancer by morning. I sat at the end of the bar, the only place I'd spotted a semi-clear bubble of air amid the smoky haze. Just me and Willie, watching ESPN. Not a bad way to end the night. I was sick and tired of being on the road.

It was an unknown phone number. The 212 area code indicated New York City.

Sam Callahan?

I stared at my phone for a moment. New York City? I mentally scrolled through the short list of folks I knew in the Big Apple, but these were all numbers I already had stored in my phone. It was unlikely a friend. I responded: Who is this?

A new message came thirty seconds later.

Be at this address in fifteen minutes. 35150 IH 10 West, Room 113. Stay hidden but be ready.

I squinted at my phone. *What?* I quickly checked on the address. Sure enough, it was legit. My phone pulled up a Rolling Hills Inn right there in Boerne. The map showed it as only 4.2 miles from my barstool. Stay hidden but be ready.

I responded again. Ready for what?

I waited a full two minutes. Nothing. I typed again. No, really, who is this? I sat there and waited for another minute or two, studying my phone. No reply. Whoever it was clearly wasn't interested in explanations. But did they really expect me to head there with no explanation? The crew from NFL Live was about to do an inside look at my beloved

Broncos' matchup versus the Saints next Sunday. I looked up at my famous pot-smoking, ponytailed friend, shook my head.

Downing the rest of my beer, I threw a wrinkled ten-dollar bill on the bar, grabbed my keys, held my breath as I crossed through the cancer ward, and headed for the front door.

On the road again, Willie.

Room 113 was in the very back corner of the motel property, completely hidden from the highway, on the first floor of a two-story building. It was actually the very last motel room in the building. I wondered if that was intentional. The edge of the Rolling Hills Inn hugged several wooded acres behind it. I parked near the front of the parking lot, walked toward the back, hands in pockets, casual and cool, scanning the room numbers. The parking lot was only a third full. It was definitely a more popular overnight stay than my cheap digs. There were no cars parked in the spots directly outside Room 113. The nearest was a black Camry, four spots over. The lights were off in the room, as they were for most of the other rooms. It was a few minutes past midnight on a cool, late-October evening. The town was asleep. Except for my new friends over at Reggie's.

Without trying to be too creepy or conspicuous, I walked up close to the door, paused, listened, but heard nothing. Then I crossed by the window with a quick glance, unable to see much inside the darkened room through the tiny crack in the curtains. I doubted anyone was inside. Should I knock? The message said to be ready and stay hidden. I sighed, annoyed with the text. I checked my phone again. It had already been seventeen minutes since the first message had arrived.

OK, now what? This was ridiculous.

I started to wonder if my new pal, Derek, was playing a joke on me. Derek was another young tracker on my campaign trail, only he was working for the opposition. Our paths had intersected early and often as we crisscrossed the Twenty-First District following the candidates. He was a good guy. A first year at Duke Law. He'd played a little shortstop at Virginia Tech. Most of the other trackers I'd met took themselves way too seriously, like they were political superheroes donning capes, trying to save this great country, and they were nearly aghast when they found out that I had no true party affiliation.

Derek wasn't a hard-liner or a patriot like the others. He was more like me, simply trying to pick up some extra cash, get through law school with a little less debt. But he was also a serious prankster who'd gotten me good a few times in the past ten days. A couple of days earlier, I'd found the air had been let out of all four tires on my Explorer outside Fredericksburg. Both candidates had stopped at a diner at the same time for a pie-eating contest. He also stuck me with the bill at a Denny's restaurant outside San Antonio by somehow convincing the waitress that we were brothers—even though he was black and I was white. He'd slipped out when I went to the restroom. And then there was a prank call at 2:00 a.m., claiming to be the Secret Service.

But this felt different. Still, I typed a quick text to Derek's cell number.

Room 112 or 113?

He texted right back. Is this a trivia question? I'll take 112, Johnny. What do I win?

I texted again. An old Denny's receipt. What are you doing?

The usual. Partying with the Saudi prince. You?

I grinned. Partying with the Saudi princess.

You need something, Callahan? It takes at least six hours of sleep for me to look as pretty as you.

Nah, sorry. Just bored.

Only a few more days of this. Cya.

So, it wasn't Derek. I would have picked up on something in the exchange. I was about to head back to my car when an SUV pulled into the parking lot. On instinct, I jerked back into the shadows, behind the corner of the building near the stairwell, out of view. A black Cadillac Escalade eased through the parking lot, its thick tires crunching across the pavement, coming toward me. It turned into the parking spot directly in front of Room 113. The door opened. A tall blonde with seriously long legs got out of the driver's seat. She was probably in her early thirties, very attractive, hair and makeup ready for the runway. Her short, black dress and stiletto heels accentuated her every curve. I didn't recognize her. She hadn't been on the campaign trail; I was certain of that. However, I did recognize the man who stumbled out of the passenger seat.

Lucas McCallister.

He was still wearing the sleek, dark suit from his event earlier, only the tie was now missing. His black hair that was normally plastered perfectly in place was disheveled. He was clearly intoxicated. He bumped into the front of the vehicle, nearly fell down, caught himself with a hand. I was suddenly on hyperalert. Before I could even whip out my phone, McCallister had his hands on the blonde, pulling her in close, wanting to prop her up on the hood of the Escalade. She giggled, pushed his hands away, and said, "Not here. In my room. Come on, cowboy!"

"Giddy up!" McCallister slurred. He was hammered.

My fingers were shaking as I pressed the Record button, caught one last passionate kiss between them. Then the blonde led McCallister by the hand into her room. He was groping her all along the way, the blonde continuing to fight him off playfully as she unlocked the door. They fell inside onto the carpet together, giggling like teenagers. McCallister managed to kick the door shut behind them. I was stunned. I had just caught the candidate on video kissing a woman who was not his wife. But who was she? And who had sent me the text? I suddenly felt exposed and very uncomfortable. There was another person out there somewhere who knew this was coming. Someone who had wanted me to be here to catch it firsthand. Who? Were they out there watching as well? Watching me? My eyes scanned the other cars. I didn't see anything unusual.

The light went on in the motel-room window. I saw the curtains tug open slightly, saw the woman at the window. She seemed to be looking around for someone outside. Was it me? McCallister was behind her again, kissing her neck. She turned away, moved back into the room, leaving the curtains a foot apart. I wasn't sure what to do. I had no desire to watch anything more intimate between them. But I couldn't pull myself away. The man was four days from winning the election. He was up by nearly four points. What was he doing, risking this? It didn't make sense. There were rumors in certain circles that Lucas McCallister was a player, always had been with the ladies, in spite of the perfect public portrait of a devoted husband and father, but I had yet to see any signs of a loose zipper on the trail. I figured if it were true, then he was smart enough to do it outside of campaign season. Guess I'd given him too much credit.

I was about to text Rick when I heard a sudden scream come from inside the motel room. The woman. I felt panic rip through me. Instinctively, my feet moved quickly toward the window. I had a clear view through the gap in the curtains, my breath hitting the glass. The lamp was on by the dresser. I could see white powder in neat lines on the small table. They were both at the foot of the bed, half-disrobed, but McCallister had the woman by the hair in his right hand. She was slapping at his face, screaming at him. Were they just messing around? No, she looked genuinely pissed. And he seemed startled by her actions. She punched, and connected near his crotch. He let go, crouched over, moaned. Then she was on top of him, attacking him, hitting him with her fists on the back of his head. She jumped on his back, hooking her right arm around his neck as if to choke him.

McCallister spun around, yelled, "Get off me!"

He flung her loose with an arm thrust. She let go, stumbled, a high heel catching on the carpet, and her face smashed directly against the corner of the TV cabinet. It was loud and violent. Then she fell limp to the carpet. McCallister cursed, wiped blood from his lips, and examined it for a moment on his fingers. Then he seemed to notice she wasn't moving. He bent down, turned her face up. Blood was pouring from her head and covered half her face. He grabbed her cheeks in his thick fingers, shook her face. She didn't respond. He grabbed both shoulders and shook more violently. Nothing. She just lay limp, blood now soaking into the carpet.

McCallister instantly sobered at the sight, stepped back.

For a second, I couldn't move. Was she dead? She looked dead. I'd seen a couple of dead people on the streets. One had frozen to death on the cold streets of Denver, another overdosed. This was different. There was blood. Lots of blood.

I looked down at my phone. It was clutched in my fist three inches from the window and aimed directly into the room. I'd recorded the entire thing. It had never stopped recording. It had become automatic. My hand was shaking. I didn't know what to do. Should I go into the room? Should I call 911?

McCallister didn't seem to know what to do, either, as he sat on the end of the bed and turned ghost white, like he might pass out. Instead, he leaned forward suddenly and vomited all over his dress shoes and onto the tan carpet. Seconds later, McCallister heaved again and emptied his stomach. I turned away, so as to not vomit myself.

When I turned back, McCallister was standing at the window, staring directly at me.

I jerked back, startled. We were inches apart. Separated by only a thin glass windowpane.

This was the closest I'd ever been to the candidate.

I'd never seen more hollow eyes.

THREE

Saturday, 1:39 a.m.
Boerne, Texas
Two days, twenty-two hours, twenty-one minutes till Election Day

Rick slowly exhaled, shook his head. It was clear by the look in his eyes behind those thick black glasses that the video shocked him. The footage was more than a campaign game changer. A person was dead. I could hear the drip of the faucet in the bathroom as I waited for Rick to process what he'd just watched.

"What happened next?" Rick asked.

"Are you kidding me? I ran my ass off. Got out of there as fast as I could. I've been sitting here hiding in my motel room for more than an hour, trying not to have a panic attack. Waiting for you so we can figure out what to do next."

"Do you think he recognized you? Does McCallister know you?"

"I don't know. I've never dealt with him directly. And it was dark outside the motel room. It was only a split second, man. We locked eyes, then I hauled it out of there. Never looked back, so I'm not sure."

Rick kept shaking his head, a slow and rhythmic back-and-forth swing. A tic to help him somehow absorb the magnitude of it all. He seemed to be getting his feet beneath him. His fingers were already pecking away furiously on his laptop. He began messing with my phone and a cord, plugging things together, typing. I assumed uploading the video somewhere secure. However, I didn't recognize the website he currently had open on his laptop. It was not our normal server. He was sending it somewhere else.

"What should we do, Rick?" I asked him. "Do we call the police or what?"

"I don't know yet. Are you sure she was dead?"

"Well, no. I didn't check her pulse or anything. But it looked like it to me. There was enough blood to fill up a swimming pool. If I'd have thought there was any chance she was still alive, I would have called 911 right then."

"Right, sure. This is incredible."

"I think *horrible* is a much better word."

"Right." He typed away. The video was uploaded.

"It was weird, man. It was like McCallister looked right through me. Like I wasn't even there. Just stared off with such sad eyes."

Rick slammed his laptop shut, stood. "We need to call Ted."

Ted Bowerson was the CEO of Bridges Over America. Rick grabbed my phone, punched in the number, and began to pace around the room in a tight circle. I fell back on the bed again, rubbed my face, stared at the filthy clouds on the ceiling. I felt better now that Rick was in this with me. He now shared the burden. I was no longer alone. If he was bringing Ted into play, maybe the weight of it all wouldn't be so unbearable. Together, all of us could figure out what to do next. I wanted to grab my backpack, jump into my Explorer, and head back to DC. Return to my simple life as a law-school student. Screw it. No amount of money was worth this.

Rick was standing by the front window, leaving a voice mail for Ted, when I heard the odd noise. It was a loud and sudden pop, like when the car in front of you kicks up a small rock that smacks your windshield, leaving a tiny dent and a crack that eventually spreads from east to west. I had three of those jagged cracks in my windshield right now. But it was weird to hear that sound in my motel room.

I pushed myself up, looked over to the window. That's when I noticed that one of the blinds had a hole in it and was dangling. It wasn't like that before. Another loud pop. Exact same as before. I saw the blinds move again. Rick jerked. Then he spun toward the bed and fell face forward. Rick smashed into the edge of the bed and slid to the carpet, my phone bouncing from his hand. I jumped out of bed, turned Rick over. There was a hole in his forehead, and blood was pouring down his neck. Bullet hole. His eyes were still open, his mouth parted, but he was completely limp. Rick was gone.

The gray Oldsmobile. The shadow smoker I'd spotted before Rick arrived.

Another pop. I felt something whiz right past my ear, like a wasp buzzing within an inch, heard a thump in the wall behind me. I was next. I dove for the lamp on the nightstand, shoved it against the wall, shattered it to pieces. The light went off. Then I crawled quickly to the corner, yanked the tall, freestanding lamp over to the carpet, ripping the cord from the wall. The room was now dark. The only light coming in was from the parking lot through the blinds. I crawled over Rick, reached up, and grabbed the string to the blinds, yanking them closed. I grabbed my phone off the carpet, stuffed it in my back pocket. What now? I couldn't escape out the front door. There was no back door. I was a sitting duck.

Then my mind flipped a switch. My focus sharpened. The noise was sucked from the room. I looked down, remembered seeing the small hole in the bottom of the wall right beside the bed. Like some guest had inadvertently put the heel of his boot through the Sheetrock in the wall, and no one had bothered to repair it. Earlier, I had dismissed it as part of the charm of this dump. But now, I was thinking a lot about that hole. I scooted along the carpet and found it. Fear rushed through my veins, but my mind was already two steps ahead. I stuck my hand inside the hole in the Sheetrock, felt around. I couldn't find any wood or steel studs. That was good. I tried to rip away at the Sheetrock with my bare hands. I needed something more forceful. I stood, spun around once, then lifted the heel of my shoe and thrust it at the wall. Chunks of Sheetrock broke away at the edges. The hole grew bigger. I kicked hard again, and my shoe went all the way through to the other side.

I felt a sudden vibration in my back pocket. My phone.

I reached around, stared at the screen, thinking it might be Ted Bowerson. It wasn't. It was her. Calling me back. I was stunned. After all this time. Five months. She was calling me back at a moment like this? Sweat dripped down my forehead and into my eyes. I wiped it away with a sleeve. I couldn't answer it. Not now. Not when I could hear the doorknob rattling outside my room. I'd locked the door, but it wouldn't stop them for long. I reared my leg back again, then drove it with all my power at the hole in the wall. Another huge chunk collapsed. There was a smash against the front door. It sounded like someone was putting a shoulder into it. Another kick of my shoe. More Sheetrock gave way on both sides of the wall. There was a crawl hole now. I heard the front door splinter at the hinges. I dove headfirst into the hole. As I wiggled my body through, I found another motel room exactly like mine on the other side—empty. I heard the door crash open in the other room.

I rushed to the front window. I didn't spot anyone on the walkway. I reached over, unlocked the door. Looking back, I saw light penetrate the hole in the bottom of the wall behind me, and I knew I had a matter of seconds. I said a prayer as I sprinted into the parking lot. There was nowhere to hide. I was thirty yards from the protection of the woods, completely exposed. As I ran, I looked over and spotted the gray Oldsmobile empty, with the driver's door wide open.

I was ten feet from the edge of the woods when I heard feet behind me in the parking lot. I dove forward into the grass and heard a pop hit a tree two feet to my left. I rolled farther into the grass, heard another pop right above me, the splitting of bark. I was behind a tree now, up, running again, unable to see much. Tiny branches from bushes and small trees slapped against my arms and face. I found a small clearing with several large piles of brush. I moved behind the largest pile and lay on my stomach. There was enough moonlight to make out shadows and figures. I felt small cuts and scrapes all over my face. Had I been shot? I felt fluids on me, but I thought it was just sweat. Not blood. At least, not my own blood. My adrenaline was pumping so fast I wasn't sure I could tell if all my limbs were still intact.

I heard a snap like a foot stepping on a branch. Then I saw a shadow move past. It looked like he was dressed in all black. It was easy to see the shine of the gun with the long barrel in his right hand. Five feet away. I held my breath, tucked my chin low. He paused, turned. The moonlight splashed over his face. He had short hair, almost a buzz cut. Midthirties, my guess. Strong, square jaw. There was something familiar about him, but I couldn't place him. He scanned the clearing, looked over and around me, then took several steps forward. Past me now. Five feet. Ten feet. Twenty feet. He moved into the next set of wooded acreage. Then he disappeared into darkness.

When I could no longer see the shadow of his figure in the moonlight, I crawled out from the brush. Then I took a deep breath and sprinted back the way I'd come. I hit the parking lot but never slowed down. It wasn't until I was running through a ditch beside the highway that I realized I no longer had my phone. It had fallen from my pocket somewhere in the frenzy of the chase. I'd lost it. And the video. But there was no turning back. I had sidestepped death once already. I wasn't going to push it.

It wasn't my first near-death experience. That came much earlier in life, when I was ten.

SAM, AGE TEN

Denver, Colorado

The tiny closet was completely empty. Just tattered carpet and walls. No shelves. No other items. And scary dark. Not even a hint of light creeping in from the bedroom under the door. My angry foster dad wanted this place to be scary, which was why he'd completely sealed the cracks in the door and nailed plywood to the walls. You couldn't see your hand six inches in front of your face. He called it The Hole—the cramped space he dragged me into when he wasn't happy, either with me or with life. Unfortunately for me, he was unhappy a lot lately, and he'd become more violent in the past two weeks. Mainly when my foster mom was out working the late shift.

I was used to the violence. The system was full of violence. They couldn't stop it. I'd already gone through eight different foster parents, mostly crummy adults who knew how to work the system, scam cash from the state, and somehow make me look presentable enough when workers from Child Protective Services were scheduled to stop by and check on us. Sometimes they didn't get away with it. Like the last couple. It was hard for them to hide the cigarette burns on my arms or my two black eyes, although they'd certainly tried. The mom made me wear makeup. I was glad to say good-bye to those losers. The Hole felt like a resort hotel compared to my foster dad three rotations ago, a military man who'd put out four different leather belts on the bed, some embedded with stones or metals, and asked me to choose one for the whooping that night.

My current foster mom, Judy, wasn't so bad. I don't think she knew what her husband, Carl, did with us when she wasn't around, which was usually when he took too heavily to the bottle. We dreaded Monday, Wednesday, and Friday nights. There were two of us. Amy was eight. A shy blonde.

I was wearing only my white underwear. Carl made me sit in the dark in nothing but my tighty-whities for up to ten brutal hours at a time. The carpet beneath me was worn and smelled like wet dog. I placed my hand on the back of my head, massaged it. Carl had grabbed me by the back of my head with a thick fistful of hair after his eighth beer (I always counted), dragged me down the hallway, and practically lifted me off the floor when he tossed me into The Hole. I think he took out chunks of my hair.

But that's not what concerned me the most. I was tough. I could survive Carl.

It was the girl, Amy. She had stopped talking a few days ago. She just went numb.

Something was terribly wrong. And I had a feeling it had to do with what was happening with Carl while I was locked in The Hole and Judy was working the late shift.

I had a plan tonight. I'd been working it out in my mind throughout the day.

I reached into the corner and felt around until I found the lump where I'd placed it. My escape. I peeled off the duct tape and grasped the small knife I'd hidden a few days ago. Then I stood and began feeling around the walls in the dark. The closet was five feet deep and five feet wide. I opened the knife to reveal the blade, stuck the knife in between my teeth, put my hands up on one wall, then lifted one bare foot to the wall behind me. I secured that foot, held both hands firmly in place, then lifted the second foot until I had lifted my body up off the carpet. Then I began to work my way in the dark toward the ceiling, parkour-style. One hand sliding up six inches, then the other, then one foot, then the other.

Within a minute, I was pressed up against the ceiling. I secured myself with my left hand and held firmly with both feet flat against the other wall, my muscles shaking from the stress. I reached up with my right hand toward the corner, completely blind, and I felt along the ceiling. Just as I expected. Carl hadn't nailed plywood to the ceiling. It was regular Sheetrock. I worked quickly, grabbing the knife from my teeth, holding it in my tight fist, and while still secure with one hand and two feet, I jabbed the blade into the ceiling and worked it back and forth, slicing and cutting. I began to sweat. It was hot as hell in The Hole. There was no circulation. I got a few inches cut out and then slowly descended to the carpet to take a breather. Then I was back up and working again. Up and down.

It took me ten minutes, but I finally pushed a square of Sheetrock up and out of the ceiling. A humid and dark attic was above me. The knife back between my teeth, I was able to get a hand up and through the hole. I grabbed a board somewhere, then swiftly reached around with my second hand to the board as my bare feet dropped. My legs swung and banged up against the closet wall with a thud. I felt a twinge of panic. Could Carl hear that? I dangled from the ceiling for a second, listening, then I quickly pulled myself up into an attic crawl space.

My heart was racing. I crawled in the dark around boards and insulation until I found what I was looking for ten feet away. A ceiling attic door from the other closet in the second bedroom. I quietly slid it open, seeing my first sign of light from the bedroom. I dropped my feet into the closet, set them on shelves, and quickly worked my way down to the carpet. I stepped around the bed and raced to the bedroom door, cracked it open. I hoped I wasn't too late.

Peeking out, I saw Carl standing drunk in the living room. A baseball game was on the TV. He was yelling at it, his words slurred. He was bare-chested in jeans, his belly hanging over the front of them, a beer can in his hand.

I crawled on all fours. Hid behind one of the couches. Carl and Amy were on the other side. I could hear Amy softly crying. I felt sick to my stomach. I wanted to kill this man. I moved quickly, crawling on the floor to the table in the corner next to the greasy recliner. The phone was on the table. I carefully reached up, took it off its cradle, and dialed 911. A police lady answered. I said nothing. Instead, I set the receiver down on the carpet so that the recipient could hear into the room.

Then I saw Carl drop his beer to the carpet, turn, and move toward Amy on the couch. When Amy let out a loud whimper, something erupted in me. I sprang up over the couch, lunged at Carl, and drove the knife blade straight into his back.

Carl let out a gasp, stumbled forward. He reached around, pulled the knife out, stared at it and the dripping blood in disbelief. Then his red eyes connected with mine, and I could tell he was going to try to jab it in me. He was a crazy man. He took a step toward me, knife in his angry fist, swung wildly. I ducked out of the way. Carl was woozy and wobbled to a knee. We had to get out of there or I was dead.

I grabbed Amy's hand, yanked her from the couch.

We ran straight out the front door, across the street to Margie's house, the nice old lady who often gave us chocolate. I pounded on the door with my fist. Amy was crying. I wrapped my skinny arm around her to protect her.

I was still in my underwear. It was embarrassing and terrifying.

Carl was on the front sidewalk now, cursing at the top of his lungs, searching for us.

Margie opened the door. Before she could say anything, we rushed inside.

I could hear a siren a block away. We hid in the corner of the kitchen. Margie quickly covered us both with blankets. We were trembling.

Amy was stuck to my side. She wouldn't let go.

FOUR

Saturday, 2:06 a.m.
Boerne, Texas
Two days, twenty-one hours, fifty-four minutes till Election Day

I stared at myself in the cracked mirror. I now had dozens of tiny cuts from running through the woods; salty beads of sweat stung like hell as they rolled down my face. Then there was the blood, and not just my own. On my right cheek, on my ear, and all the way down the right side of my neck. I couldn't stop thinking about the look in Rick's eyes. I began to splash cold water on my face. Ran my wet fingers through my hair. Slowly cleaned myself up the best that I could. Tried to get my bearings.

The restroom was in the back of a convenience store that was currently closed. I had picked the restroom lock with a thin shard of metal I'd found near the Dumpster. A few tugs and scrapes of the shard in the keyhole, and I was inside. It all came back so easily.

I'd run probably two miles along the highway before finally feeling safe enough to peel off somewhere and try to regroup. Catch my breath. Formulate a new plan of action. I was alone again, and now there were two dead. I was supposed to be dead body number three. They'd made that very clear, whoever they were. Someone on McCallister's security team? I hadn't had a moment even to think about that yet. However, I knew they'd keep coming. I couldn't slow down, no matter how physically and mentally exhausted I was.

The restroom stunk something fierce. I finally gave up on cleaning, sat on the dirty floor, back against the metal door. I had nothing. My phone was gone. My wallet was in the motel room along with my bag and backpack. I had the clothes on my back and a few dollars in my pocket. That was it. There was no way I was ever going back to get anything. Surprisingly, I was breathing easier. Either my body had gone into complete shock, or I had shifted into survival mode. Probably the latter. If nothing else, I was a survivor. Always had been. I'd faced a couple of attempts on my life. It had been a long time, but I'd felt that familiar surge of adrenaline and fear before. You don't live on the streets as a teenager without a gang member trying to stick a shiv in you at some point. But this was a different rodeo altogether.

This was a man dressed all in black with a gun and silencer.

Had I been set up?

I had to think. I had to focus. I had to rest.

I closed my eyes, put my head back against the door.

This wouldn't have been the first time I got screwed in a setup.

SAM, AGE TWELVE

Denver, Colorado

The siren woke me first. Just a quick wail, then it shut off.

Then I saw the red-and-blue flashing lights through the window.

The Denver Broncos clock on the nightstand said it was eleven thirty.

I peered through the cheap blinds. Andrew and Jenny, my foster parents for the past nine months, were outside standing in the cracked driveway. Two policemen in uniform were standing next to them. I saw neighbors staring out their front doors from across the street in our low-income neighborhood. I turned around, dropped my head over the edge to the bunk bed below me. Jet was still gone. I hadn't seen him all day. I knew it was trouble. Jet was always getting in trouble. Although only twelve, like me, Jet had a mean streak. I had my own anger issues, no doubt, but Jet was different. He'd flipped a switch a long time ago. Jet was ruthless. He would slap an old lady in the face on the sidewalk just to steal two bucks out of her pocket, and he wouldn't even feel bad about it. He'd gotten pissed at Jenny a few weeks ago, even took a swing at Andrew in the kitchen.

I didn't understand why Jet was trying to blow this deal for us. It was the best situation either of us had ever experienced in the system. Hell, I'd already bounced through ten unstable foster homes. But Andrew and Jenny McGregor were different. They seemed like honest and good people. They were kind, warm, and present. To a cynical kid like me, who'd seen and experienced the cruelty of the system over and over again, they seemed too good to be true. They told us early on that they could not have their own kids, even though they'd tried for more than ten years. Now, in their midthirties, they felt like God was calling them to foster those of us in the so-called aged-out category. Lately, the conversation had shifted toward adoption. I resisted at first. Of course, I wanted it to be true, but the system had a brutal way of repeatedly yanking the hope out of your hands.

The adoption talk really rattled Jet. He started lying, stealing, and provoking them however he could the past few weeks. I didn't understand it. I'd been amazed at the level of patience Andrew and Jenny had shown to my bunkmate. But I knew it wouldn't last forever. Everyone had a breaking point. I tried to talk some sense into Jet, but he wouldn't listen to me. Kept telling me to get my head out of the clouds, that this wasn't real, that kids like us don't ever get a *real* family. Might as well get it over with now before it's an even bigger disappointment. Screw that, Jet said. He was getting out. He even threatened to put a knife in me while I slept if I didn't shut up about it and leave him alone.

I wasn't scared of Jet, but I believed he would try. I felt bad for him. I knew he'd been at the wrong end of some bad things. Much worse than me. He'd wake up screaming from some awful nightmares, then try to pretend it was nothing. Just the same, I'd slept with one eye open every night for the past month.

I stared out the blinds again. Something was wrong.

This wasn't about Jet missing or running away. This was about Andrew.

Andrew held out his wrists. One of the police officers actually put handcuffs on him, led him over to the back of the police car. Jenny was crying hysterically. I was getting pissed. I knew Jet was behind this. I could tell lately he was up to something. He didn't take discipline well. I'd seen him playing on Andrew's computer, sneaking in and out of their bedroom.

I felt sick to my stomach. I wanted to punch Jet in the face.

The next day, my suspicions were confirmed. Jet was still gone, but a lawyer was sitting at the small kitchen table with Jenny. I overheard most of it. The police had received an anonymous tip, secured a search warrant, and found something on Andrew's home computer.

I thought of Jet. He'd set Andrew up in a big way, then bolted.

I sat in the living room playing video games. Jenny was crying again.

The lawyer was completely incompetent. I could already tell. He had thin, greasy hair combed poorly over to the side and wore a brown suit that looked like it was twenty years old. He was giving Jenny horrible advice. I'd been around enough lawyers to have a good grasp of how it all worked, and this guy was talking out of his ass. He must have gotten his degree from a community college. But I knew Andrew and Jenny couldn't afford a real lawyer. Andrew was a history teacher at a small private high school and barely made enough. Drove a beat-up fifteen-year-old Toyota truck. Jenny had worked part-time at a day-care center before quitting when we arrived to make sure she invested as much as possible in us. The house was falling apart. There was no money to fix broken windows or bad plumbing.

This was bad. Really bad. I was screwed. I felt it all slipping away.

An hour later, the social worker showed up and took me away.

Jenny cried again and hugged me tightly. She promised that it was only for a day or two, that they'd be coming to get me soon enough.

The lawyer was going to handle all of it for them. She felt very confident in that.

"Don't worry, Sam," she said, hugging me, tears in her eyes. "Everything will be cleared up in a few days, and we'll get back to being a family again."

As I drove off in the back of that car, I had a hardened pit in my stomach.

Maybe Jet was right. Kids like me don't ever get a family.

Because I knew I would never see Jenny or Andrew again.

FIVE

Saturday, 3:06 a.m.
Boerne, Texas
Two days, twenty hours, fifty-four minutes till Election Day

I dozed off and on in ten-minute spurts. My back still pressed against the cold restroom door. I needed some rest and allowed myself the luxury. But it was difficult. I kept waking at every shift of the wind or dog bark or random truck driving by in the distance. Rick's face right in front of me, alive one moment and dead the next. Dreaming of the blonde woman looking out her motel window, wondering if she was searching for me, then seeing her lying in her own blood on the carpet. Flashes of the man with the square jaw hunting me down in the woods. I kept jumping up and cracking open the bathroom door, expecting to find that same man outside with a gun.

By five in the morning, I'd decided what to do. After making sure there was no alarm or security cameras, using the same metal shard from before, I picked the lock to the back door of the convenience store, found a phone on a desk in a tiny back office, and dialed 911. I could not let this go any further on my own. It would be an absolute zoo, a media circus, and I would be in the very middle of it. My life would be flipped upside down. But Rick was dead. And so was the woman. I would not be next without someone else knowing about it. I would not let the trail end with me.

The phone rang once, and then an emergency dispatcher was on the line.

"Nine-one-one, what's your emergency?"

"I need to see a police officer right away."

"What is your location?"

I gave her the name of the convenience store.

"Sir, what is your emergency?"

"Just get someone here fast."

I hung up. I had no desire to explain myself over the phone. I'd wait to speak with a police officer in person. I considered what I would say. Where would I start? I decided I would begin with the woman at the motel and work my way forward from there. Let the chips fall where they may.

A standard white police car with *City of Boerne* painted on the side arrived two minutes later. This was a small town. Probably not a lot of 911 calls during the middle of the night. By now, I'd made my way to the front of the convenience store and was just waiting outside the dark front door. A short, squat man in police uniform got out, ambled toward me. He had curly brown hair, looked to be in his forties, and was about fifty pounds overweight. His gut hung over the front of his uniform belt. But he was a cop. And for maybe the first time in my life, it was good to see a cop of any shape or size.

"You call nine-one-one?" he demanded.

"Yes, sir," I said.

"What's your emergency?"

"I may have seen something. I did see something."

"Something? Like what? UFO? Ghosts?" He smirked.

"No, sir. A murder."

He furrowed his brow and studied me for a moment. "A murder, huh? Where?"

"Up the road. Rolling Hills Inn."

"What are you doing here?"

"It's a long story, sir. I ran. Can I just go show you what I saw?"

He nodded. "Yes, son, you'd better."

I rode in the passenger seat of the Boerne patrol car. Officer Barker— according to his name badge—kept a close eye on me. I couldn't blame him. I was being sly with information, shifty. But I wondered if there was still a way to get the police involved and somehow get myself out of this mess as well. I had not yet mentioned a word about Lucas McCallister. I wasn't ready to throw that hand grenade just yet; I mentioned only being at the motel and seeing a man and a woman struggle in the room. I tried not to make eye contact with Barker. I wondered if he noticed the blood on my shirt. Or the dozen scrapes on my face.

As we pulled into the parking lot, I felt my heart begin to race again. The Escalade was gone. This made me uneasy. We pulled up into the parking spot directly in front of Room 113.

"Stay here," he ordered. I was fine with that.

Barker got out, circled the police car, approached the front door. A motel clerk was waiting for him. A dispatcher had called over in advance. I could see that the curtains were now fully closed, and the lights were out in the room. Again, this made me feel uneasy.

Barker and the motel clerk exchanged brief words. I saw the motel clerk shrug, and then Barker used a fist to knock firmly on the door three times. No answer. He glanced back at me. Three more firm raps. No response. The motel clerk pulled out a set of keys and opened the door for the officer. Barker pulled out his revolver, took a slow step inside. The motel clerk waited outside. I saw the light come on inside the room. Ten seconds later, Barker stepped back out and motioned with a firm wave of his hand for me to join him.

I climbed out of the vehicle, took hesitant steps toward him.

Barker didn't look happy.

"You've got some explaining to do."

He opened the door, led me inside. The room was completely clean. I mean, spotless. Like no one had been in it in weeks. The bed was made perfect, the pillows perfect, the furniture all in perfect place. Even more stunning, the carpet was scrubbed completely clean. Not a spot on it. There was no sign of blood or vomit or any of it. They had somehow scrubbed the room clean in a matter of hours. In the middle of the night. I stood right over the spot where the blonde had lain motionless. But there wasn't even a hint of a stain on the tan carpet beneath my shoes. Not a nick on the TV dresser where her head had collided so violently.

"Have you been doing drugs, son?" Barker asked me, filling up the doorway with his substantial girth.

I turned. "No, sir, I swear it all happened just like I said."

"In this room? Earlier this evening?"

I nodded. "Yes, sir. This is the room."

For a second, I wondered. Had I lost my mind? Was it a different room?

I suddenly felt the urge to run again. They'd cleaned the room spotless in a matter of hours. There was no blood. No body. No sign of any struggle.

"Go wait for me in the car," Barker said. It was an order and not a request.

I stepped past him, and with unsteady legs, I slid into the front seat of the police car again. I hunkered down low, wondered about my next move. I was sure Barker would drive me directly down to the station now. I'd be asked a lot of questions. Should I take him by my motel room? Show him what happened there first? I wondered if we'd even find anything. Had that been scrubbed clean, too? Perhaps I should just say I *had* taken some drugs and needed to sleep it off. Maybe they'd let me sober up for the night in the safe confines of a city jail cell. Or was anywhere safe?

I watched as Barker stood in the doorway of the motel room, taking notes on a small pad in his chubby hand. Suddenly, the radio squawked inside the police car. A police dispatcher, reporting a new crime. I heard something about a dead body, so I perked up.

"Suspect is twenty-five-year-old Samuel Callahan of Washington, DC. Last seen on foot in blue jeans and dark button-down shirt."

It took my breath away. Had the dispatcher really just said my name?

I leaned over, tried to find a volume knob, to hear more of what was being announced across the police scanner. And that's when I noticed my driver's-license photo flash in full and vivid color on the computer screen that faced the driver's seat. I quickly put it together. Rick must have been found in my motel room. I was a suspect? And then I thought of what I was suddenly up against, how Room 113 had been wiped clean, how I'd been found so quickly, and there was no doubt in my mind that my new enemy had set multiple courses of action to find me and bring me down. Including framing me for the murder of my friend.

Barker stepped inside Room 113 again, out of view. The motel clerk had walked up to the front of the motel. I knew it was time to go. Time to run. The police were no longer an option for me. I slid out of the police car, shut the door silently behind me, made sure Barker was still inside the room, then for the second time in five hours, I sprinted through the motel parking lot.

SIX

Saturday, 6:01 a.m.
Boerne, Texas
Two days, seventeen hours, fifty-nine minutes till Election Day

My new ride was a plain '87 Chevy Silverado, light gray, nothing fancy, to avoid any unwanted attention. I didn't even have to hot-wire it. The driver's door was unlocked, and the key was in the visor. This was Boerne, Texas, after all, where people still left their front doors unlocked. Kids played on the sidewalks unmonitored.

I was ten minutes outside of town at a convenience store, spending my last few dollars on coffee and a couple of granola bars, when I suddenly saw my face splash across the TV screen behind the front counter. It was the six o'clock early-morning NBC newscast out of San Antonio, reporting an overnight shooting in a motel room in Boerne. The first slaying reported in the city in eight years. Fortunately, the young clerk looked half-asleep and wasn't paying too much attention as I dropped down my five, but I felt the wind knocked out of me.

My photo was gone seconds later, and the TV flashed to a young female reporter standing outside my motel room in front of yellow crime-scene tape. It was still dark out. Crime-scene investigators were moving about behind her. Police were reporting that drugs had been found in the room. Drugs? Whoever was involved had eliminated evidence of the woman's death and then framed me for Rick's murder. All my belongings were inside that room. My bag filled with my clothes, my underwear, my socks, my books, my toothbrush, my laptop. I wondered if they'd find my phone. Or was it in other hands now?

I got my change, turned, and noticed a red-haired woman who reeked of cigarettes standing behind me. She looked to be in her midfifties, and she seemed to take a double glance at me. I desperately tried to look casual, gave a half smile, and headed for the door. I took several deep breaths, kept a calm pace, and made my way to the truck. I slid the granola bars into the pocket of the tan hunting jacket that I'd found inside the truck. The box of hair dye I'd stolen was in the other pocket. I was on my most serious crime spree since my teenage years.

I started up the Chevy and backed out of the parking spot. I noticed the redhead watching me through the front glass doors. She seemed to be saying something to the store clerk.

From that point forward, I needed to be more careful.

I had to go off the grid, completely underground.

Fortunately, I'd done it before. Hell, I'd spent most of my youth off the grid.

SAM, AGE THIRTEEN

Denver, Colorado

I stared through the bushes at the shiny red Corvette. A kid's dream car. I'd spotted it several times driving around the block near the Jeffreys' dump the past month. My fourth foster home in three years. A dozen foster homes overall. I should get a set of steak knives or something. How was a kid like me supposed to find any stability in life or trust anyone when bounced around like that? There were three other kids in the home with me, all younger. Two were brothers. All abandoned. Since I was the oldest, old-man Jeffrey made me do all the housework by myself. I swear, he'd taken me in just to have his own personal slave. But he'd hit me only once, which wasn't bad compared to some of the other homes.

I was counting the days until I could go out on my own. I'd met several other guys a few years older than I was who seemed to be just fine living on the streets. Hustling and making it happen. No one bossing them around. Free to do what they pleased. My time was coming soon. Maybe tonight.

The Corvette was parked outside a duplex, next to a brown Jeep Wrangler. There was a light on in the duplex window. It was nearing eleven o'clock. I had bounced out of the window in the bedroom I shared with the three other boys an hour ago. A man on a mission. I felt like a man tonight. A guy three years older than I was named Mickey had given me instructions, tools, and had even shown me how to do this properly.

I watched the street for a few more minutes. Traffic had crawled to a stop. Everyone in the neighborhood seemed settled down for the night. I knew my time was nearing. I'd been casing this for weeks. Then I noticed the light go out in the duplex window. Right on time. I made sure the laces were tied tightly on my worn black Nikes, a pair a size too small. I'd cut open the ends and wrapped them with duct tape. I pulled the black hood of my ratty sweatshirt up over my head. I felt surprisingly calm. I inhaled deeply, exhaled. Then I stepped out from around the bushes and walked straight up the cracked sidewalk to the driveway. The Corvette was sparkling. The big dude with the mullet and handlebar mustache washed it, like, every day. I couldn't blame him. It was a beautiful ride.

In my right sweatshirt pocket, I felt my fingers grip around the homemade snake-rake lock pick made out of a small hacksaw blade that Mickey had given me. He encouraged me to start small, like in the junkyard, get some practice. But that had never been my style. I stood five feet behind the sports car for thirty seconds, one last gut check, one last stare into the dark window of the duplex. Then I stepped around the back bumper, squatted by the driver's door, and pulled out my tools.

With my left hand, I lifted a small metal circle that I'd use to balance the lock pick while inside the lock. I worked swiftly. I knew the car alarm wasn't set. This was my sixth time hiding in the bushes in the past two weeks. The first five times, mustache guy had beeped the alarm. Tonight, he had not. I was determined that he'd pay for it.

I pressed the metal circle to the door, encompassing the lock. Then I stuck the lock pick into the hole and began raking it back and forth, just like I'd been taught. I could visualize the mechanics inside the lock. I had the door open within forty-five seconds.

My adrenaline was pumping. I slipped inside the vehicle and dipped under the dash. Mickey had to show me how to do this only one time. I'd always had some kind of weird photographic memory. I popped the plastic covering under the steering wheel and quickly pulled down the bundle of electrical wires. My hands were so steady, I almost freaked out. I separated the correct wire bundle for battery, ignition, and starter. I stripped the bundle with another tool, pulled the wires apart, then took another breath and sparked two wires together. Again, I could see Mickey in my mind, showing me exactly how to do this. It took three sparks, then the Corvette suddenly started.

Now, my heart was hammering double time. It was loud. The engine rumbled.

I was in the driver's seat, one hand on the wheel, the other on the shifter.

I'd never driven a stick shift, but I'd watched a video online. I'd actually driven only twice in my life. But neither of those cars was stolen. And neither time did I have an angry-looking, bare-chested man chasing after me, as I did now. He was in the doorway of the duplex in nothing but boxers, yelling a string of curse words.

I hit the clutch, shifted into gear, hit the gas. The Corvette exploded in reverse, nearly causing me to knock myself out on the steering wheel. Then I shifted into gear again and raced the 'Vette down the neighborhood street, the man chasing after me with bare feet. But I was a goner. The sports car was everything I'd hoped. So powerful. Like sitting in the cockpit of a fighter jet, I imagined.

I turned the steering wheel, hit the gas again, burst down a side road.

I had no plans from there. I just wanted to see if I could do it. Just wanted to test myself. See if I was ready to go on my own. But I was definitely going to have as much fun as possible in the process. I turned down more streets. I was a bit clunky with the clutch and gears at times and jerked myself around a bit, but when I got going, it was the thrill ride I'd dreamed about for two weeks. I found the main road, a long clearing with nothing but blinking yellow lights, and I pushed the pedal down to the floor. I was nearing eighty in a thirty-five zone when I saw it parked at a gas station. It was a blur, but I clearly spotted two men in uniform in the front seat. The red-and-blue lights exploded with a siren a second later.

Now I was scared. This wasn't part of the plan. I was only going to go for a spin, drop it somewhere. No harm, no foul. I wasn't looking for a car chase. I spotted the string of warehouses up on my left and yanked the wheel into an empty parking lot. I slammed on the brakes, left the car running, hopped out. The police car with its lights blaring was right behind me, tearing down the street. I ran toward the buildings. They looked abandoned. A faded sign said something about steel manufacturing. The glass door to one building was unlocked, so I raced inside.

I could hear the police car slide to a stop right outside. Two doors opened and slammed, then I heard feet on gravel. I darted through what looked like a former front office—though it was empty now—through two more metal doors down a long hallway and into a giant warehouse. It was dark. The lights were out. But there were a few windows at the top that let in some light from outside. I could tell there were more than a dozen tall rows of massive metal industrial shelves, some still filled with abandoned wooden crates.

I sprinted down a row in the middle, zigzagged my way to the very back wall.

I heard the door to the warehouse open and shut. Then the sound of one of the officers.

"Police! Step out now if you don't want to get shot!"

I saw two powerful flashlight beams. The officers separated and took opposite rows. They headed in my direction. It was darker in the back of the warehouse. I was having a difficult time finding my way around, but I spotted a metal exit door. When I got there, I saw it was locked with a thick chain. I turned around. The beams from the flashlights were getting closer. They had me surrounded. I was about to be busted. Sent to juvie. I couldn't believe it. Right when I was about to gain my freedom. Screw that. I think I would've preferred to be shot than go through the court system.

But then something happened. It was odd. I felt everything suddenly go silent around me, as if I'd put in earplugs. I could tell one of the officers was yelling again, but it sounded muffled. I could hear only my own heartbeat. It had seemed to slow down to a very steady thumping. My vision felt more focused. I looked over, spotted the metal ladder. Fifteen feet away, attached to the third row away from me. It went straight to the top of the metal catwalk. Twenty feet up. From there, my eyes followed a trail to the left of that catwalk. It stopped five feet from a metal balcony. Looked like an upstairs office suite or something. Suddenly, I could visualize a hallway to an emergency exit out back. I wondered if I were tripping on a drug or something. It was so weird. Like an imaginary mapping system in my mind. But I hadn't done any drugs the past two weeks. I'd wanted to be clearheaded for this.

The cops were getting closer. It was time to go. I stepped away from the wall, found the ladder, began to climb. Quickly. Quietly. I'd reached the top when the beams of light hit the back wall. I looked down below me. The cops seemed to stare at each other for a moment, confused. I turned, crawled across the top of a few wooden crates, reached the edge of the catwalk. The jump to the metal balcony was at least six feet. I didn't even take a moment to consider. I just jumped. I landed awkwardly, flipped over the railing, banged to the floor. I spun around, blinded by a flashlight beam. I had no time to waste. I pivoted, pushed through a metal door. Just like I'd envisioned, there was a hallway with six offices. I could see a split in the hallway. One way led back into the warehouse. The other out the back of the building.

I raced to the back. The metal door wasn't locked. It pushed open easily, and I found what I was looking for. An emergency-exit stairwell on the outside. I hit every third step on my way down, then jumped for the gravel.

Thirty seconds later, I was lost in the industrial park. No signs of cops.

I felt strangely exhilarated and yet weirded out by what had just happened.

That was the first time my mind had done something like that.

But I'd accomplished my mission.

I'd stolen my first car ten days before my fourteenth birthday.

I was ready to be my own man. Time to get lost from the system.

SEVEN

Saturday, 6:56 a.m.
Johnson City, Texas
Two days, seventeen hours, four minutes till Election Day

I drove forty-five minutes down the road from Boerne and parked the Chevy truck next to a silver Toyota Camry behind a small grocery store that was still closed. The car probably belonged to the grocery-store manager who was getting the store up and running. I could see some lights on in the windows. Perfect. The Camry owner likely wouldn't be coming back anytime soon. I needed to create space and distance, to get a head start. The Camry's doors were locked. It slowed me down for maybe twenty seconds. I scrambled inside the car and quickly removed the access panel on the steering column, then grabbed the electrical wires. Like I'd done a hundred times, I connected the ignition and battery wires and sparked the starter wire. The engine started. I unlocked the steering wheel by pulling hard in both directions. A couple more revs of the engine, and I was on my way.

The boys from my old street crew would be proud. There had been four of us. All the guys were a bit intimidated by my uncanny ability to think on my feet. Especially if we were pulling a con.

A shady guy named Kenny had offered us a sweet deal one night. Kenny would strip stolen vehicles in his ghetto garage and sell the parts for cash. Two hundred fifty a pop for low-end rides; five hundred or even more if the cars met a certain standard of luxury (Mercedes, Lexus, BMW). In my three years of stealing cars, I could practically do it in my sleep. That night, I pulled seven cars in under four hours. All high-end. All without breaking a sweat. My closest competitor from our group got three. But I wasn't satisfied with that. I was bored and wanted to push myself. Target number eight was a sweet black Bentley that I knew cost a quarter of a million dollars. Kenny said he'd give me three grand.

I stole it from a secure restaurant parking lot.

I was halfway down the street with a big smile on my face when I saw the first set of flashing lights. Then I quickly spotted four or five more sets of lights. Police sting. I'd been set up. Someone had squealed. Long story short, I felt the tight grip of metal cuffs on my wrists. With the quick pummel of a judge's gavel, I was sentenced to twelve months in juvie. I served three of them and fought off the unwelcome advances of a three-hundred-pound bear of a kid named Nard who was supposedly sixteen but looked more like thirty-five. That was the end for me. I swore I'd never go back to that kind of life.

At least two from my crew were in prison right now. I wondered if I'd be joining them soon.

I pulled onto the road and continued on my journey.

Next stop, Austin. I had no identification, no money, and my name and face would likely be plastered everywhere within hours. I needed a friend. Quick. Someone who really had the power to help.

I needed to see Ted Bowerson.

EIGHT

Saturday, 7:28 a.m.
Austin, Texas
Two days, sixteen hours, thirty-two minutes till Election Day

I'd only met Ted twice. Once in DC when my old roommate, Josh, and I were invited to some fancy political shindig at a popular nightspot. And then again two weeks ago when I'd sat down with Rick in the Austin office of Bridges Over America to get my marching orders. Ted seemed like a decent guy. About forty, short brown hair beginning to gray, thin build of a marathon runner. He spoke with his hands, moved constantly, pacing like he downed a case of Red Bull every morning. He was a powerful man with powerful connections. I'd done enough research on Bridges Over America to know that. Ted had been involved in politics his entire career. He was on the senior staff of several prominent US senators, had success as a lobbyist, and now made a very nice life for himself bouncing back and forth between DC and Austin.

Bridges Over America had a small but exquisite office suite with about ten staff on the fourth floor of One Congress Plaza in the heart of downtown Austin, a block north from the Colorado River and ten blocks south of the pink-granite splendor of the Texas State Capitol building. Most employees parked in a garage right next door and took an underground tunnel into the main lobby. I'd done the same when visiting the office two weeks ago.

Once I was in the main lobby, right inside the tunnel from the garage, I stopped behind a planter. It was seven thirty. I'd left the Camry on the fifth level of the garage. I needed to keep swapping out vehicles, just to be safe. I also needed a shower and some new clothes in the worst way. But I'd managed to clean myself up again in a truck-stop restroom on the way to Austin. My hair was now dyed dark black, and I'd chopped off the waves, which was painful. Girls loved the waves. But there were no girls in prison. My hair was really short now. I hadn't worn it this short in more than ten years. I barely recognized myself in the mirror.

I still had on the tan hunting jacket. It was buttoned up near the neck, covering my blood-soaked shirt. I had to get out of this shirt already. That was next up on my to-do list.

I hung around by the planter, out of view, head tucked low. I wondered how many of these men and women who were working this Saturday morning had watched the national morning news, how many had seen my face on their TVs while they ate breakfast or worked out at the gym. I wondered how many of my friends and classmates and professors had seen the news. What were they thinking? Had Sam Callahan lost his mind? I wondered if my mom had watched the news. I really needed to call her and tell her the truth. Make sure she was OK and knew that I was safe. However, everything on my to-do list kept getting pushed down by priority number one: stay alive.

At two minutes to eight, I spotted Ted Bowerson. He looked all business, as usual, wearing a sharp, pin-striped, dark-blue business suit, red tie flapping, very patriotic. He was clutching a black briefcase, hustling from the walkway toward an elevator up to his office. I knew he'd be at work on Saturday, this close to Election Day. I stepped into the flow of traffic, sidled up right beside him.

"Ted," I said, as low as possible.

He turned, slowed, as if he didn't know me. Then it seemed to register. He stopped, turned fully toward me. His eyes flashed for a second. "Sam? What are you doing here?"

His tone told me he wasn't startled to see me. He was *frightened* to see me. He must have gotten the news about Rick. I had to defuse this quickly.

"I didn't do it, Ted. I swear. I'm not a drug dealer. I was set up. I need your help."

Ted was head of an organization trained to track and read people. He studied me for only a moment before grabbing me by the elbow.

"Come on, we've got to get out of here."

NINE

Saturday, 7:42 a.m.
Austin, Texas
Two days, sixteen hours, eighteen minutes till Election Day

We huddled over coffee in the back corner of a diner nearby.

"What happened?" Ted asked me. He hadn't touched his coffee. "This morning I check my voice mail first thing, and there's an urgent message from Rick. He says he's sitting in a motel room with you. To call him immediately on your phone. That you guys have got something big to share with me. Then I turn on the TV to news that Rick is dead, and they're saying that you're the main suspect. They found drugs in your motel room. And now you show up with this new look, and you smell like death."

Death felt like the right word. I took a swig of hot coffee, considered where to start. There was no use cloaking any of this in mystery. Someone needed to know the whole truth, every detail. As I said, I needed help. So, I started at the very beginning with the anonymous text and laid out the whole nightmare that followed. Recounting the whole thing out loud in vivid detail made it seem even more surreal. It had been one hell of a night. But I couldn't get a good read on Ted. He was just sitting there, watching me.

"You get a good look at the guy who tried to kill you?" he asked.

"I don't know. I caught a glance."

"It wasn't one of McCallister's security guys?"

I shook my head. "No, I know all those guys. He wasn't one of them. Unless he was brand-new to the team. Like, added that day."

Ted was drumming his fingers on the tabletop. I could practically see his mind processing the information. "No texts since then?"

"Nothing. I searched for the phone number and found nothing. I think it was one of those cheap temporary cell phones you can buy anywhere."

"New York City?"

I shrugged. "Was a two-one-two area code."

"And no idea who the woman was?"

I shook my head again. "But she definitely had McCallister's attention."

"Do you think he knew her?"

"Maybe. I mean, they certainly seemed to be comfortable with each other. Look, I'm not sure who sent me the text. But it seems pretty clear to me that once I got there and saw what I saw, someone from McCallister's team wanted to make sure I didn't share it."

Ted continued to tap the tabletop with his fingers. He couldn't stop moving for two seconds. He was making me nervous. I also found it odd that there was no talk about Rick, about informing his family, about the fact that the man who'd worked with Ted for almost five years was dead. These political guys were callous. Ted couldn't take one minute to mourn the death of a friend?

"Have you talked to anyone else, Sam? Who else knows about this?"

"No one."

"You're certain?"

"Yes, of course, I'm certain. I talked to Rick; he's dead. Now you." This didn't seem to faze him.

"We need to somehow find where Rick sent that video," Ted said.

I took another swig of coffee, thought about where Rick might have uploaded the video. I vividly remembered spotting a small cartoon pig-skull-and-crossbones logo on the screen of his laptop. But there was no name or any other distinctive characters. Even though it was only a split second, I was sure. I was usually able to catch things at a glance and log them away. We used to hold contests at a diner when I was a teenager and put each other to the test. You'd walk in, sit down in a booth, and have five seconds to scan the room. Then you'd get peppered with questions. No one could touch me. I could tell you the lipstick color on the waitress behind the counter, the color of Nikes on the man by the checkout, whether the little girl sitting with her mom had green eyes or brown eyes. It was the only way to pull a con clean. To make sure there were no wandering eyes. No loose ends. No off-duty cops out of uniform. No mistakes. I kept the info about the pig logo for the server to myself for the moment.

I felt uncomfortable every time the door jingled and a new customer entered the diner. I watched eyes to see who returned my stares. So far, no one seemed to have any interest in me. I'd already spotted the back door to the kitchen, where I was sure there was a rear door to the diner. I'd already put together a mental map. I could be in the back alley in ten seconds, if necessary. Gone in twenty. But I was tired of running.

"What do we do?"

Ted rubbed his forehead. "I don't know. I'll call my lawyer. See what he has to say. You need to hide out for a few hours."

"Hide out where?"

"I'll go get you a room next door, at the Four Seasons. You can hide out there, get yourself cleaned up, get some rest. Take a shower." He pulled a thick roll of cash from his pocket bundled together inside a shiny gold money clip. He quickly counted off about five hundred-dollar bills and slid them across the table. "Just in case you need it. You can charge whatever you want to the room. I'll put it on my card. But wait for me to come get you. You understand? Just be patient and trust me, Sam."

I guess Ted didn't understand something about me. I trusted no one.

But a hotel room, a hot shower, and some new clothes sounded perfect right now.

TEN

Saturday, 8:53 a.m.
Austin, Texas
Two days, fifteen hours, seven minutes till Election Day

The room was on the third floor of the plush Four Seasons Hotel, with a private balcony and a view of the river and the running trails. I was grateful for a hot shower in a luxury hotel room with strong electronic bolts and a thick metal bar securing the door. I soaked for probably thirty minutes, letting the scalding water punish my skin, trying to wash out every remnant of the night before. But the expensive shampoo could only do so much. The stink of sweat and dirt and blood and tissue were gone, but the vivid images were locked in my memory.

I found deodorant, toothpaste, and a toothbrush on the bathroom counter. I'd picked up a few clothing items at store nearby. A black T-shirt with *Keep Austin Weird* printed in white on the front, blue jeans, gray cotton pullover, and a black ball cap with the familiar burnt-orange Texas Longhorns logo. I laid out the items neatly on the bed. After shampooing, I examined myself in the mirror. My short hair was now a mix of splotchy colors, all shades of black and brown, as I was no professional stylist. I changed into my new clothes and threw on the ball cap to hide the botched color job.

I sat at the small desk in my room, picked up the hotel phone, and punched for an outside line. Then I dialed the number from memory. I anxiously waited as the phone rang several times. My mom answered on the fifth ring. I felt a wave of relief. She sounded weak. We now talked a couple of times a day, usually once in the morning and once in the evening. I could always tell how she was feeling right away by the level of strength in her voice.

"Hello?"

"Mom," I said, almost a whisper, even though I was alone.

"Samuel? Thank God. Are you OK? What the hell is going on?"

She must have seen the news. I was hoping that maybe she'd slept in later than usual, that I would catch her before she got worked up about it. I could picture her in her cramped room, staring in bewilderment at the small TV in the corner. Sneaking cigarette puffs, even though it was against the rules, quickly spraying afterward with a deodorizer. Her gray-brown hair pulled up in a tight bun. The quilt her lady friends from the church up the street had given her pulled up snug to her neck. She was always freezing in that place.

"I'm fine, Mom. I promise. And whatever you saw on TV this morning, it's not true. You have to believe me."

"I do believe you. I knew that man was lying."

That man? "Mom, who are you talking about? What man? On TV?"

"No, the man who came by to see me an hour ago. He said he was with the FBI. He said he needed to find you right away. For your own protection."

"Did this man show you identification?"

"No. I didn't think to ask for it. Plus, he was handsome. And I never get company around here, so I let him talk. He just wrote down a phone number on my pad. Asked me to call him immediately if I heard from you."

"What did he look like?"

"Like I said, really handsome. Like Sean Connery. Probably in his sixties, with a gray beard. He wore a black sport coat, gray slacks, I think. He was really warm and pleasant. And he had the prettiest clear-blue eyes. Reminded me of yours."

The FBI? I seriously doubted it. Which did not make me feel any better. I'd rather it be the FBI than whoever else was out there hunting me down right now. They'd already found my mom. They'd been in the room with her.

"Listen, I don't want you talking to this man again. Or anyone. You have to trust me. Do not call that number back, and do not talk to anyone else who comes by asking you questions. Not until you hear from me again. Do you understand? I'm serious."

"OK. But what's going on?"

"I don't know yet. But I'm going to be OK. Don't worry. I just need some time to figure this out. And don't watch the news. You just need to focus on getting better. Did Dr. Wilson come back with the test results?"

"Yeah. Last night. They don't look great. They're running more tests. I'm not sure any of these doctors knows what the hell they're doing."

This made my heart sink. We had desperately hoped the latest treatment would work. "We'll figure something out. We'll get through this. I promise."

"Oh, I know. I'm tough. You know that. I didn't survive the last forty years to get taken down by a few bad cells in my body."

"OK, I've gotta go now."

"Please be careful. Call me soon."

I hung up, stared at the phone. Then slammed my fist down in anger at the thought of a possible murderer sitting in the cracked brown-leather chair next to my mom's bed. I found the TV controller, flipped on the flat screen inside the TV dresser at the foot of the bed. I found a local news station. Within five minutes of watching the news, I found myself staring once again face-to-face with Lucas McCallister.

I was startled by how good he looked. No red lines in his eyes. No sagging cheeks. Hair perfect. As if nothing had happened the night before. As if his fingers hadn't been all over the blonde. Had they made her disappear altogether? Again, I thought about that text message. Stay hidden but be ready. McCallister's wife, Lisa, stood innocently beside him. I wondered how much she knew about her husband's extramarital affairs. She was obviously clueless about the events of the previous night or there was no way she'd be standing by in support of her man. Had he come home to their hotel room at midnight, all cleaned up, as if his late-night "campaign meeting" had simply run long?

McCallister was giving a statement in front of a throng of microphones, saying he was as shocked as everyone else about the horrific events that had transpired in Boerne overnight while they were campaigning there. When asked about the suspects being connected to his campaign, McCallister said that he knew neither man involved; he reiterated that they were not men on his team. He trusted that the authorities were properly handling the matter. He and Lisa were praying for the family of the victim. They had plans to continue with their regular campaign stops and were not at all concerned with his security. I couldn't believe how calm and cool McCallister sounded. Just ten hours ago he'd been standing over the body of a dead woman in a puddle of blood, his own vomit at his feet.

Seconds later, the news segment cut away to a video clip of McCallister's opponent, Congressman Leonard Mitchell, a distinguished-looking, gray-haired gentleman of fifty-five, standing behind a podium at a rally from the previous night in San Antonio. The reporter was giving an update on the campaign race, saying that McCallister's lead over Mitchell had grown to four points, according to the latest polling. And that Mitchell's team had become much more desperate in their efforts to somehow close that gap in the final few days before Election Day. I was about to turn off the TV when I saw him. I walked up really close to the TV. It was him. I was sure of it. Standing directly behind Mitchell, wearing a black suit, with an earpiece in his right ear. Midthirties, prominent, square jaw, short hair, small eyes. Yes, it was him. The same man who'd put a bullet into Rick's forehead and chased me through the woods. One of Congressmen Mitchell's security guys. The assassin. I was positive.

I sat on the edge of the bed, stunned.

The assassin was with Congressman Mitchell. Not with Lucas McCallister.

I felt a chill rush through me, as cold as the familiar bite of winters spent on the street.

SAM, AGE FIFTEEN

Denver, Colorado

It was the most frigid night I'd ever experienced in Denver.

It was certainly the coldest I'd tasted since I'd chosen to live on the streets two years ago. The weather guy on the TV at the gas station said it might be even worse than the blizzard of 2003 that dumped about thirty inches of snow over two days. That put the city on lockdown. I remembered. I'd had a warm bed at the time and watched it through a window. The temperature was supposed to drop to fifteen below zero tonight. With the wind, it could easily reach twenty-five below.

For the past week, I'd been sleeping on the second floor of a two-story office building with a buddy and about twenty other guys—a building that had been abandoned halfway through construction. Sheetrock was up in parts of the building, so some of us had our own tiny makeshift efficiency apartments. There was no plumbing or electricity, but it wasn't too bad. Felt much safer than an alley or under a bridge. There was a roof over our heads. And it was certainly cheaper than the weekly rate motels. They extorted kids like me. Three hundred a week? For a dump that had a lumpy mattress, a gross toilet, and a grimy shower?

I was huddled under two heavy blankets when I heard the commotion.

It was a familiar noise. One I heard too often on the streets at night. Cops. A whole group of them. Entering the building a few minutes after ten o'clock to shake us down and scatter us like rats. I knew this place was too good to be true. I was used to it. Word got out fast, and then too many guys flocked to it. That's when they usually shut us down. I heard cops telling everyone to head over to Rachel's place, the worst shelter in the city. I couldn't believe this was happening on a night like tonight. The other shelters were packed, the motels booked. They were going to have several human Popsicles all over the city in the morning. The mayor might have promised to clean up the city, but did he really want to kill street kids like me in the process?

I quickly grabbed my gear, rolled it up, stuffed it in my bag. I hit the road before a cop could lay close eyes on me and ask me why a fifteen-year-old was on the streets. I didn't need that tonight. Everyone was quickly scattering, not wanting trouble, just trying to make it to the next day. We were all too cold even to curse the cops. I found the stairs in the back, briskly moved up the sidewalk. Once I'd cleared the building, the wind hit me right in the face and took my breath away. I knew some of the old guys were headed straight back to the woods. They would put up tents, try to build a fire, and somehow weather this ice storm. I couldn't do the woods.

I began to roam the frozen streets. Alone. Snow pounding me. No one was out. I mean, not a soul. No people walking around, no cars driving. It was too cold even to get into a car. The gas tanks were probably blocks of ice right now. My toes were so numb, and I felt the bite working its way up my legs above the knees. My lips were trembling. My eyes watered so badly that I could hardly see. And I was starving. The places I usually went to grab food on the cheap had been on lockdown all day. This was the first time I thought I might literally die on the streets. The first time I wondered if I'd made a huge mistake going out on my own. Maybe the beatings and abuse weren't such bad trade-offs to have a hot bowl of soup and a warm bed, even if I had to share it with someone else.

The chill was above the waist now. My legs weren't working right. And I felt faint. I was feeling pretty desperate when I turned onto Twenty-Fourth Avenue and spotted Zion Baptist Church. There were no cars in the parking lot. No lights on in the building. I followed a snow-covered sidewalk around to the side, then I quickly stepped up to a back door. It was locked. Not that this mattered to me. I just hoped that God wouldn't strike me dead for breaking into a church. With barely any feeling in my hands, I managed to pull a tool out of my bag and work the lock. I pushed the door open a moment later and nearly fell inside, out of the wind and snow.

I shut the door behind me, the heat inside embracing me like a thick thermal jacket. I sat there on the carpet in the hallway for ten minutes, just thawing out. I took my shoes off, tried to massage my toes. They were rock solid. Finally, I got up and began exploring. Thank God there was a kitchen. I immediately found a box of crackers and a jar of peanut butter. I stuffed my face, finished the whole box, then emptied the full container of peanut butter with a spoon. I drank some milk from the refrigerator to wash it all down. My stomach started to settle. The feeling was returning to my fingers again. But I wasn't sure my toes would ever recover.

I moved to a hallway that led to the massive sanctuary.

All the lights were off except for a few in the ceiling that focused on the stained-glass windows. One of the windows showcased Mary with baby Jesus. I studied the image. At least he had a mother.

I sat on the first wooden pew. It had a nice cushion on it. Comfortable. I set my bag down beside me, untied my blankets, shook off the ice as best I could. I felt bad about bringing my mess into this nice church, but what choice did I have?

I was beat. I collapsed over onto the pew, pulled my feet up, and covered myself.

I would live. And that's all that mattered that night.

SAM, AGE SIXTEEN

Denver, Colorado

The child-welfare office was inside a monstrous four-story rectangular building. The last time I'd been inside their second-floor offices was three years ago while sitting at the desk of my caseworker, a nice-enough fiftysomething woman named Ms. Jeanetta, who checked on my well-being as I awaited another foster-home assignment after being yanked out of yet another really bad situation. Story of my life.

That was three months before I bolted from the system altogether.

I was back outside the building now, standing in the cold snow. It was after ten. The building was locked down for the night, but I was still determined to get inside. Today was my sixteenth birthday. Not a soul knew about it. No one. It had admittedly been weird not having any birthday mentions the past three years. Like I hadn't publicly aged. Like I wasn't even a real human being. Even the worst foster parents usually had stuck a candle in a crummy cupcake and sung the stupid song. But that was life on the streets, life without family, life on your own. I told myself I'd gotten used to it.

That's a lie. You never get used to it.

Today felt different. Something had stirred inside of me.

Three years ago, Jeanetta had let it slip when looking through my official file that I'd been abandoned on my actual birthday. Not *around* my birthday. But on the actual date of my birth. I'd heard her whisper, "How cruel" under her breath while reviewing my paperwork and adding new reports. I'd let it slide at the time. I was thirteen. I didn't care, didn't want to know.

But I cared today. For some reason, I'd been thinking about it a lot the past week. For the first time, I wanted to know more about what had really happened. What did my file actually say about me? About the details on the day of my abandonment? Did it say anything about my mom? My dad? Any family at all? Who the hell was I, really?

The side door from the parking lot for employees had a security system. You had to have an electronic key card to access the building. I'd easily snagged one from an unsuspecting office worker near her minivan earlier that evening as I helped her load up two boxes into the back of her vehicle before she headed home for the day. The badge said Dorothy Jenkins.

The parking lot was nearly empty. I sidled up to the employee door, flashed the badge at the security box, heard the door click open. I was inside a second later. The hallways were well lit, the office suites dark. I found the stairs, scooted quickly up a level, poked my head into an empty and silent hallway. I knew exactly where I was going. I found the right office suite a few seconds later, used the badge one more time, and was inside. I left it dark. I didn't want to turn on any lights and draw unwanted attention. I didn't need to steal my file. I technically could walk in during broad daylight and have access to it. I had rights. But I didn't want to deal with people, deal with the system, deal with Ms. Jeanetta.

I liked being "missing" and planned to keep it that way.

I slipped around three metal desk cubes and spotted the familiar desk of Ms. Jeanetta near the corner of the room. The same pictures of her grandkids were on the desk. I could smell her fragrance, a mix of flowers and chocolate. I'd always liked Ms. Jeanetta. She really seemed to care about me. Everything on and around her desk looked exactly the same as when I'd sat there three years ago. I pushed in behind her swivel chair, stood in front of the two plain gray-metal file cabinets. My mind began flashing back. I knelt down to the third drawer on the left cabinet and pulled it open. Bingo. I found the *C* files exactly where I expected to find them. I began to skim.

A few seconds later, I had my thick file. I used my phone as a light, did a quick scan inside to be sure it was me. I immediately spotted pictures they'd taken from all over my body. Evidence of abuse. Stuck to detailed reports.

There were a lot of pictures, a lot of reports. Yep, it was me.

For a second, I hesitated. Did I really want to open Pandora's box? Did I really want to know more? Maybe my hell was already big enough. Did I really want to relive every cigarette to the back, every lash of the belt, every punch to the face? Did I want to see images of large finger imprints around my skinny neck when I was nearly choked to death as an eight-year-old? Did I really want to know the sordid details about the day I'd been so cruelly abandoned?

My file suddenly felt heavy in my hands.

I swallowed the thick ball in my throat, shut the cabinet drawer, and found the hallway again.

An hour later, I stood on the sidewalk outside of Saint Luke's Medical Center.

It was snowing again. Light flakes. Nothing heavy. But they floated down out of the night sky and blanketed the medical vehicles parked right outside the doors of the emergency room. I watched as an ambulance with lights spinning raced around a street corner and up to the glass doors. It jerked to a quick stop. Emergency staff hustled out from the building to help pull a patient out of the back on a stretcher. Looked like a middle-aged man, all strapped down to the bed, pale skin but eyes open. Moments later, a middle-aged woman showed up in a separate car along with two boys my age, teenagers, probably the man's family. All concerned, holding one another, reassuring the dad. They all rushed inside the glass doors together.

I watched these types of scenes for nearly a half hour, eyes on those glass doors.

The file said fifteen years ago to the day, at exactly eleven forty in the evening, a woman claiming to be my mom had dropped me at those exact glass doors, screamed for help, told medical workers she thought I might already be dead from frostbite, that I'd stopped breathing and my lips were blue. They'd ushered me quickly inside and had taken care of me.

But my mom had walked away. Forever.

Orphaned on my first birthday.

Not much at all was known about my mom, according to the file. I didn't arrive at Saint Luke's with any official paperwork. The young woman gave them my name, and that was it. But the night was accurately detailed by medical staff once social workers showed up.

I blew warmth into a fist. It was cold. But nothing like that night fifteen years ago.

My file said it was ten below that night.

I had pored over my file for an hour in a corner booth at a McDonald's up the street. It was like an emotional torture session. I relived every foster home, every swing of a fist, every weapon of abuse, every vicious verbal lashing. So many names, so many faces, so much rage. Even thinking back on the McGregors brought up so much dashed hope and pain.

And it had all started on the night of my very first birthday.

I'd already hated my mom before that night. But that was an ambiguous and generalized hate. Now, my hate was more specific. Hell, the word *hate* wasn't a strong enough word. It was something that ran much deeper in me than that.

I pulled my phone out of my pocket, watched it for a few minutes until the digital numbers on the screen finally turned to eleven forty. Felt tears form in the back of my eyes. Then I quickly shoved them away, gritted my teeth, shook my head.

Happy friggin' birthday, Sam.

SAM, AGE SIXTEEN

Denver, Colorado

This night, I chose a middle pew for sleeping inside Zion Baptist Church.

The old church had become my new home this brutal winter.

The plaque in the hallway called it the oldest African American church in the western Rockies. All I knew was that they kept the temperature warm at all hours, always had plenty of extra food they wouldn't notice was missing in the church kitchen, and left the back door unlocked most nights. Not that this would have stopped me. But it somehow made me feel better about being there. Like maybe someone was intentionally leaving the door open for me. I'd been sleeping there for nearly two weeks, slipping in around ten most nights and out before dawn the next day without anyone ever noticing. Until today.

I heard a voice before I ever saw anyone. I was in dreamland.

"Hey, friend, time to get up."

I felt a nudge on my shoulder. My eyes fluttered open, confused. Then I saw the face of a twentysomething black man standing above me. I shot upright, startled, looked around me for all my things, ready to make a run for it before the cops got there. But the man in the dark suit and green tie put up a friendly hand.

"Hey, take it easy. You're not in trouble."

I looked at him. Was he serious? He had a nice face, with big brown eyes, a perfectly trimmed goatee around a solid chin, small round spectacles.

"It's bitter cold out," he said. "I get it. Worst winter I've seen. I'm actually sorry to wake you up, but we have a six o'clock prayer meeting in here twice a month."

I looked at my phone. Five forty. My alarm was set for six thirty, which was when I would usually grab my things and hit the cold sidewalk. I stopped panicking but still began packing up my bag. I wasn't going to hang around. This jig was clearly up. That sucked.

The man was hovering and watching me.

"How long you been staying here?" the man asked.

I shrugged. I wasn't in the mood for small talk. Just needed to get moving.

"My name is Pastor Isaiah. I'm one of the associate pastors here at Zion."

I rolled my bag, stood. Time to go.

"You got a name?" asked Pastor Isaiah.

"Nope."

Pastor Isaiah smiled. "OK. You want some breakfast?"

I paused. I was starving.

"I got fresh bagels and doughnuts," he offered. "Straight from the bakery. And coffee, orange juice. I'll make you a trade. I get a name—you get breakfast."

"Charlie. My name's Charlie."

He nodded. "OK. Come on, Charlie."

We walked through a hallway into the small kitchen. As the pastor mentioned, there were three large boxes of bagels and doughnuts on the counter. They looked and smelled incredible. Pastor Isaiah told me to help myself. He said they always had plenty of food left over after prayer breakfast, and he usually took it over to the shelter. I immediately stuffed three warm doughnuts into my face without even taking a breath. Then poured a large cup of orange juice and nearly downed it in one gulp.

"You a Broncos fan?" he asked me, nodding at my sweatshirt.

I shrugged. "Yeah, guess so."

"I like the Cowboys," he said. "Grew up in Ashdown, Arkansas, near the Texas-Arkansas border, not far from Dallas."

"I hate the Cowboys," I offered.

He laughed. "Yeah, most people either love them or hate them. There is no in-between. You ever been to a Broncos game?"

I told him about a game I'd gone to last year when the Seahawks were in town. I left out the part about how I'd pickpocketed a man outside the gate for his tickets, sold them to a scalper, and then purchased other tickets in case the police tried to find who was sitting in the stolen-ticket seats. The pastor and I talked a few more minutes about football as I worked my way through a half dozen doughnuts and two cream-cheese-covered bagels until I could barely put another bite in my mouth. Pastor Isaiah didn't seem to care that I was cleaning out an entire box all by myself. He was an easy conversation. I immediately liked him.

"How old are you, Charlie? Sixteen?"

I nodded. "How old are you?"

He smiled. "Twenty-seven. You living on the streets?"

I shrugged. "Sometimes. When you lock the church up."

We exchanged an easy grin.

"Right. No family around?"

"No, sir. Not a soul."

"Sorry to hear that. You're not in foster care?"

"You sure do ask a lot of questions, Pastor."

He chuckled. "Yeah, I guess I do. But the gospel compels me. Can't get to the heart without getting to know you first."

"Well, no offense, but you can save your breath and your gospel. I don't need to be saved, OK? If God was going to save me, he should have done it a long time ago. I can take care of my own self. I have been my whole life."

"I understand. But everyone needs the gospel. Everyone needs hope."

"Not me. Just doughnuts." I sighed. "Look, you seem like a real nice man, Pastor Isaiah, and I appreciate this food and you not turning me in to the police and all for staying here overnight. So please don't take this the wrong way, because I really don't mean any disrespect. But you don't know a damn thing about me or the hell I've been through in life."

"That's true, I don't, Charlie." He leaned against the counter, sipped his coffee, considered his next words for a moment. "When I was five, my father used to burn me and my brother on the backs of our legs with a scalding cattle iron, when he'd had too many beers. I have scars all up and down both legs. My father got life in prison for murder when I was six. My brother drowned in the neighbor's pool when I was seven. My mother overdosed on crack when I was eight. Found her cold, dead body myself in the bedroom. I went to live with an uncle in Little Rock, who used to pass me around to his drug-addict friends, if you know what I mean. Then he skipped town on me, and I lived on my own in his apartment for a month until the landlord took issue with no rent coming in. I bounced around the streets for three months as a ten-year-old, living secretly at different friends' houses, sometimes sleeping under the bleachers in the gym at school by unlocking the door before leaving. Until the school found out and called in child welfare." He took a sip of his coffee. "But you're right, I don't know you. And I certainly don't know anything about your hell."

I was chewing slower, studying him.

"So, you went into the system?" I asked.

He shook his head. "No, avoided it. They found a great-aunt living here in Denver who agreed to let me come live with her. She brought me into this church. That sweet angel of a woman had a heart attack and went to be with Jesus when I was sixteen. Your age. I didn't have anyone outside of that. No other aunts or uncles that I knew about or who would at least offer to take in a kid like me. Maybe a bunch of half brothers or half sisters scattered across Arkansas. I was basically homeless again."

"You seem to have turned out OK."

"Not without help. And a lot of grace. It could have gone really bad for me. But the senior pastor here took me in and gave me a second chance."

"That's nice. Good for him. Good for you."

I finished my doughnuts and bagels, wiped my hands with a napkin. Then stood.

"Nice to meet you, Pastor. Thanks for the doughnuts."

"Sure. You're welcome here anytime. I mean it."

"Thanks."

"Hey, before you go, son, can I get your real name?"

I smiled. "It's Sam."

ELEVEN

Saturday, 11:56 a.m.
Austin, Texas
Two days, twelve hours, four minutes till Election Day

My plan was simply to rest.

Just take a few minutes, lay down, and close my eyes.

I needed it and had nowhere to go, anyway. I was supposed to just hide out and wait for Ted to call. See what his lawyers had to say. But the king-size luxury hotel bed was so comfortable and my body was so exhausted that I slipped off into a deep sleep. The body was capable of only so much.

I was startled awake by a knock on my hotel door.

I turned, stared at the digital clock.

Another firm knock. I pushed myself up. Who was at the door? Ted? I hadn't heard the phone ring. Maybe I'd slept through it?

I quickly planted my shoes on the carpet. I was already fully dressed.

A third firm rap, followed by a deep voice. "Sir, hotel security. We need a word with you, please."

Hotel security? I pushed myself up, walked to the door. The security bar was locked at the top. I placed my eye on the peephole. There were two men. The man right in front of the door wore a brown blazer with the Four Seasons logo emblazed on it. Looked legit. He was probably in his late twenties, slick black hair, buff, slight scar on his chin that looked like a check mark. He also had black sideburns that reminded me of a young Elvis. The second man standing behind him to his left sent a charge of adrenaline straight through me and cleared the fog in a second. The man from the woods. The security guy on Mitchell's team. Right there, four feet away from me, separated only by the hotel-room door. He wore a matching blazer with the Four Seasons logo, black slacks, no tie. A few frantic thoughts ran through my head. Had they wired my mom's phone, waiting for me to call her?

Or had Ted Bowerson set me up?

I didn't have time to have this conversation in my mind. They knew I was in the room. I heard a key card hit the slot outside my door, the electronic bolt unlock, the door push open an inch, only to be stopped by the metal bar at the top. My heart pounded.

I stumbled backward, my shoulder bumping the wall, alerting them to my actual presence in the room. The door was cracked an inch, but they couldn't see into the room, only at an angle toward the wall by the bathroom.

"Sir, open up. We just need a few seconds."

Yeah, a few seconds to kill me. I spun around and spotted the private balcony. I rushed to the glass door, slid it open, stepped onto the balcony. It was maybe a fifty-foot drop to a grass lawn with sidewalks. Probably wouldn't kill me. But I could break both legs if I landed wrong. I whipped my head around when I heard a metal clanging sound. They had a tool, like a miniature crowbar. I knew they would have the door open within thirty seconds. I'd done this kind of job myself. The clock was ticking. I rushed back to the king-size bed, yanked the covers off, ripped the top sheet away. I ran back onto the balcony and tied the sheet to the metal railing. I pulled it tight and tossed it over, letting it flap in the breeze.

I was tracking the time in my mind. Ten. Nine. Eight.

I pulled off one of my gray running shoes. Dropped it at the edge of the railing, right next to the knot in the white sheet. Then I darted back inside the room. The thick burgundy curtains on both sides of the balcony's glass doors hung floor to ceiling. I chose the corner tucked behind a brown-leather reading chair, ducked behind it, felt sweat drip onto my upper lip.

Three. Two. One.

As expected, they were inside. I heard the metal bar slide, and the door was open.

I could hear shoes on the carpet.

"The balcony!" one of the guys said.

The men raced toward me, hitting the concrete balcony.

"You see him?"

"No, come on. Let's get down there."

They ran back through my hotel room. I heard the opening of the door, then it clicked closed. Silence. I held my breath for twenty more seconds, listening. Nothing. I finally exhaled, slowly pulled the curtain back. They were gone. I stepped cautiously over to the balcony and retrieved my running shoe, put it back on my foot. I swiftly gathered my new belongings. A quick peek into the hallway outside my hotel room. No sign of Elvis or Square Jaw. With luck, they were racing down to the ground level and out the back, looking for me.

Rushing out into the hallway, I found the stairwell. Maneuvered down. Carefully. Quietly. Stepped into the busy lobby and tried to go unnoticed as I located a side exit from the hotel lobby and stepped out onto a crowded sidewalk.

I quickly got lost in downtown foot traffic.

TWELVE

Saturday, 5:47 p.m.
Austin, Texas
Two days, six hours, thirteen minutes till Election Day

Every major city has a secretive underground network. Young men stuck somewhere between adolescence and adulthood. Guys mostly my age, midtwenties, with beards and bellies or all skin and bones, no real care for their physical appearance, slackers who trust no government authority or corporate entity, and who mostly operate under goofy computer code names like Czar12, TheEmperor, Mongoose87, and Sukafudawg. They're rarely found without their head mics on, sitting in front of their hub of computers, where they're constantly connected to a vast network of other techies just like them around the country. They operate in dark basements and garages, back rooms of tattoo parlors or video-game shops, maybe living with their parents because they have no real careers, so-called legitimate jobs, or even girlfriends. They have everything they need right in front of them. They are some of the most powerful players on the planet, feared by most governments, the military, and major corporations because no online network, server, or computer system in the world is safe from their reach.

I was connected to that underground network in DC. I'd become friends with Tommy Kucher. He was twenty, skinny as a rail, spiky black hair, tattoos everywhere, and he was already head of a ruthless online blog called *The Watchers*—a group of renegade teenagers, really—whose mission was to expose every possible US government conspiracy around the globe. According to Tommy, there were thousands of conspiracies going on around us all the time. I used to be slightly skeptical, but after the past twenty-four hours, I was becoming a full-fledged, card-carrying believer.

I'd met Tommy, code name Maverick, playing Texas Hold'em on one of the online poker sites. Something I dabbled in here and there late at night to pick up a quick hundred bucks when needed. Which was all the time. Fortunately for me, Tommy talked a big game but actually sucked at it, and after a head-to-head battle at the digital table one night, he ended up owing me a good amount of money. In a private chat session, I mentioned that I was playing cards to earn extra money to help with my mom's bills. He looked me up and realized that I was legit. I really did have a mom with cancer living in a facility nearby. Tommy felt like a jackass, admitting to hacking into the poker system and depositing a decent amount of fake cash into his online poker account. But Tommy was an honorable guy. Crazy or not, he actually had a conscience. He had no problem cheating crooked corporations and the government, since they'd made billions cheating us every day, but he had no interest in stealing from a regular guy like me. He swore to make it up to me.

So Tommy started doing me small favors. Harmless stuff. Like courtside seats at Wizards games and front-row concert tickets. A few clicks of the keyboard and Tommy could really do magic. He even managed to get me and a law-school buddy inside the Redskins' owner's suite for a game against the Broncos last year. No one knew for sure who I was, but no one really questioned it because my VIP badge was legit. I landed in the box right next to Jon Bon Jovi, of all people, who was taking in the game as a special guest of the owner. Tommy thought it was hilarious to put my legal name down as John Wayne. I got a few skeptical looks about that, but my new driver's license confirmed it right there. I had no choice but to roll with it. It was totally worth it to see my Broncos win 34–28 at FedExField. Tommy started to call me The Duke thereafter.

Soon, Tommy and I actually became friends. He admitted he would probably need a good lawyer one day if the Feds finally got lucky and found his private lair. Before he escaped to Switzerland.

Tommy and I rarely spoke by phone. He didn't trust phones. He said the government owned AT&T, Verizon, Sprint, pretty much all of them. They were puppet corporations created so that the NSA could spy on people. There was a secure chat room buried deep inside a science-fiction movie website called Leia's Lounge, named after Princess Leia of the *Star Wars* movies. Tommy set me up with a private account and had me go to the chat room each time I needed to communicate with him.

I was very thankful for that now. I no longer trusted phones, either.

After getting lost for a few hours, I found myself eight blocks north of the Four Seasons Hotel, in the middle of downtown Austin, on the second level of the Faulk Central Library. I found a free desktop computer in the corner, next to a man and a woman at nearby stations who looked like they might be homeless. This was where you'd go if you didn't own a computer, which I did not at the moment. I owned almost nothing. There was my tiny studio near campus in DC, but who knew what kind of activity had already blown through there in the past few hours? Was any of my stuff still there? Not that I had anything too valuable or worthwhile that mattered to me.

I logged into Leia's Lounge, typed in my username (The Duke) and password (TrueGrit12087). Then I pinged Tommy with a phrase from an old Western movie that he required to authenticate that it was really me: *You can't serve papers on a rat, baby sister. You gotta kill him or let him be.* I waited. Ten seconds later, I was being pulled into a private and secure chat room. Tommy was home.

Maverick: Dude. You really kill that guy?

The Duke: Of course not.

Maverick: Yeah, didn't think so. Wassup with all that?

The Duke: Conspiracy at the highest levels.

Maverick: I hear ya. What do you need?

The Duke: New ID. New face. To start. ASAP.

Maverick: The full works?

The Duke: Yes, anything and everything. And a secure phone and tablet, if possible.

Maverick: Hold on. Give me a few minutes.

I waited, glanced around me. A portly old security guy walked through our area on the second floor. I kept my eyes buried behind my black ball cap. The Longhorn logo on it probably made me look like a local college student. I watched, waited. Tommy was back online five minutes later.

Maverick: OK, be at Affinity Tattoo on 6th at ten o'clock sharp tonight. Ask for The Hog. We go way back. He'll take care of you.

The Duke: You're a lifesaver.

Maverick: What else?

The Duke: Can you trace a license plate number?

Maverick: Shouldn't be too hard. Send it over.

I typed in the plate number for the blonde woman's Cadillac Escalade.

The Duke: Also, have you ever seen an online server with a cartoon pig skull and crossbones in the logo?

Maverick: Doesn't ring a bell. But there are tens of thousands of servers all over the world. What are you looking for?

The Duke: An account that a guy named Rick Jackson has access to.

Maverick: The dead guy?

The Duke: Yes.

Maverick: Let me get on it. Could take some time. Needle in a haystack.

The Duke: I owe you big already.

Maverick: You know where to find me, Duke. Don't get shot.

I signed off, let out a deep sigh.

I noticed the security guy eyeballing me. Made me uneasy. While I didn't want to end up dead, I certainly never wanted to see the inside of a jail cell again, either.

Been there, done that, don't ever want to wear the T-shirt again.

SAM, AGE SIXTEEN

Denver, Colorado

The yellow jumpsuit was two sizes too big.

YOUTH DETENTION was printed in bold black letters on the back. This was the uniform they put on me and my two buddies after they arrested us three days ago. I'd been sitting in a jail cell for more than seventy-two hours, waiting for my time in juvenile court. It was brutal. Not that I was getting worked over by other inmates or anything—I was actually in my own cell—but I was bored out of my mind and ready to get the hell out of there. Especially when Bobby and Casper had been released almost forty hours ago. Lucky jerks.

Today was finally my day. My adjudicatory hearing in front of the judge. I was ready. I just wanted to stand in front of the judge, say that I was sorry, beg for forgiveness, swear it would never happen again, promise to be an upstanding young citizen, get slapped with standard probation, and be on my merry way. I knew the routine. I'd known plenty of guys on the streets who went through the same juvie-court process. No one gets harsh treatment on the first round. The juvenile jails were already overcrowded.

Bobby was a fifteen-year-old runaway who'd been hanging with us for only a month. After being processed, he'd called his distant father, who I guess had some money, and who got a lawyer down to the juvie center for him ASAP. The lawyer got him released during the initial detention hearing. No lawyer would be showing up for me. Because of that, I had to spend an extra two days in that jail cell being psychoanalyzed by callous adults in the juvenile-rehabilitation process who acted like they cared.

Moments later, I finally got ushered into a small private courtroom in front of an angry-looking old woman in a black robe wearing glasses, sitting behind the judge's bench. I tried to look as innocent as possible, but the judge barely looked at me. Her eyes were on the papers in front of her. A bailiff with a menacing scowl and a mullet stood near me. He smelled like barbecue. The prosecutor, a guy named Jordan who looked like he'd just graduated from college, stated the official court case against me, my name, some of the other parameters. I glanced over at the bailiff. His eyes were slits. His arms were crossed and bulging. I remember thinking he'd love for me to make a mad dash for freedom just so he'd have an excuse to throw me against the wall.

I wasn't paying too much attention, just waiting for my chance to say I was sorry to the judge, when I heard Jordan mention something about Bobby and Casper (whom he called Mr. Nedders and Mr. Lighton), submitting a certified letter from their attorney stating that I was the true instigator and brains behind the whole car-theft operation. That they would testify against me. And that they'd offered up a separate list of other theft endeavors that were clearly made up on the spot. I was stunned. First, that Casper would sign such a thing. We'd been together for almost a year. He seemed loyal. Second, that this lawyer would work to manipulate the juvenile system in such a way to ensure clearing his own clients. I know I shouldn't have been stunned; after all, no one trusted lawyers. But we were still just teenagers. I was technically still a kid.

"That's a lie," I blurted out.

The judge glanced up suddenly, peering over her glasses, looking even angrier than before. "Quiet, Mr. Callahan. Keep your mouth shut until I ask you to speak. Do you understand? This a courtroom, not a basketball game."

"But they're lying, Judge, I swear it."

"That's enough out of you. Keep quiet or I'll have you hauled back to your cell."

The bailiff inched closer to me. I gave him a quick glance, gritted my teeth, felt my blood pressure boil. I was defenseless. The prosecutor continued with his assessment of me, stating that I had no known family or relatives, no current foster situation, no current address, and that I'd apparently been living on the streets for the better part of three years. Although I had no prior arrest record, it was pretty clear from the sworn testimony of two of my streetmates that I'd made breaking the law a daily practice. While that may have been true, I certainly didn't like how a lawyer had manipulated the system against me. I was furious.

The prosecutor finally finished. The judge turned to me.

"This doesn't look good for you, Mr. Callahan. What do you have to say for yourself?"

I tried to stay calm. "Look, Judge, I'm not going to stand here and tell you that I'm completely innocent. I'll admit that I've done my share of dumb things just to survive on my own. I have, Judge. I don't deny it. But I've never hurt anyone. And I promise I'm not the ringleader of a grand-theft operation. I'm just a kid who's made a mistake and who wants another chance. What Bobby and Casper are saying about me is not the truth. I swear."

Her small eyes glared at me. "You expect me to believe you, son, over the offerings of these other two boys? And the account given by the police?"

"Yes, because it's the truth. Just give me a second chance, Judge. I've learned my lesson. I promise you. The past three days have been scary enough. I'm a good kid. I don't belong in jail." I tried to offer my best innocent smile.

My desperate plea seemed to hang out there for ten minutes. But it was only ten seconds. The judge stared me down. Then she seemed resolved on the matter.

"Mr. Callahan, it's in my judgment that more time with us would do you good. Might help wipe that smirk off your face."

My heart sank. I couldn't believe it. "Wait, are you serious? How much more time?"

"We'll determine that at your disposition hearing, son. You're dismissed."

I was panicking. "Wait, Judge. Please. It's that lawyer. Bobby's lawyer screwed me!"

The judge was already done with me. "Please take Mr. Callahan back to his room."

The beefy bailiff put his strong hand on me. It felt like he might rupture my arm with his tight squeeze. Then he nearly yanked me off my feet.

SAM, AGE SIXTEEN

Denver, Colorado

The juvie correctional officer opened the door to my tiny room, stuck his head inside.

"Let's go, Callahan. You got a visitor."

I set the book down beside me on the uncomfortable bed. A visitor? I'd been in juvie for three months without a single visitor. I wasn't expecting anyone. It wasn't like one of my street buddies was going to set foot in this jail. Not a chance.

"Who is it, Chucky?" I asked the officer.

"Hell if I know, kid. Some black guy. Come on."

I followed Chucky down the hallway. He was one of the only decent juvie guards in this place. Most were jerks who were looking to use their batons any chance they could get. I couldn't blame most of them, though. Many of the kids in this hellhole were destined for violent crimes and real prison one day. The guards were regularly spit on and accosted. I'd done my very best to keep a low profile and stay out of trouble. Just counting down the days, grinding it out. It was horrible.

Chucky led me through two secure doorways and then opened the door to a holding room. He ushered me inside and shut the door behind me.

I was shocked at the face waiting for me. Pastor Isaiah.

He was sitting on the opposite side of a square table in one of his nice gray suits.

"Sam," he acknowledged. He stood, and we quickly shook hands.

"What are you doing here, Pastor?"

"Have a seat, OK? Let's talk."

I pulled out a chair and sat across from him. "How did you find me?"

"When you disappeared on me, I started asking around. Took a few months, but I finally found someone who knew you, could tell me what happened, and I was able to connect the dots from there."

After our first meeting that morning at Zion Baptist, I'd visited Pastor Isaiah several more times at the church. Usually in hopes of free food, which he always happily delivered. There was a lot of food and conversation. Pastor Isaiah did most of the talking. I enjoyed listening to him. And I missed it. I missed a lot of things now that I'd been locked away in a small, sterile room for three long months. I even helped Pastor Isaiah unload church donations at the homeless shelter down the street from Zion several times. We'd started to build a decent relationship over the course of the month that I knew him. But I hadn't seen him since that fateful night that found me in handcuffs several months ago.

"It's good to see you, Sam. In spite of the circumstances, you look good."

"Believe it or not, I eat better in here than on the streets."

"I believe it. But it's not a diet plan I would ever recommend."

"You got that right. This place sucks. I'm going crazy in here."

"You got twelve months?"

"Yes, sir, nine more long ones to go. Two hundred seventy-two days, unless I can get some time off for good behavior, but I'm not counting on that. The days go by so slowly in here, Pastor. It's rough. A whole year of my life down the drain."

"What do you think you'll do when you get out?"

I shrugged. "I don't know. Hard to think about that when it feels like a decade away. But avoid places like this, that's for sure."

"You mean that?"

"Absolutely. I'm never coming back to a place like this."

Something was up, I could tell in Pastor Isaiah's serious face.

"Why are you here, Pastor?" I asked.

"I have a proposition for you."

I tilted my head, waited.

"How would you like to get out of here right now?" he asked me.

I stared at him. "What . . . what do you mean?"

"I spoke to the judge. Pastor Gregory knows her well. I personally vouched for you. She's agreed to release you on strict probation if you'll remain under my direct supervision and care."

"Are you serious?"

"I'm serious if you're serious, Sam. My wife and I have a spare bedroom. You could stay with us for a little while. You'd have to agree to meet the terms of your probation and stay out of trouble. No more stealing cars. No more scams. No more hanging with the wrong crowd. You'd work for me and help around the church. You'd study and finish your education."

"I don't understand. What's the catch?"

"No catch. I told you, we're all in need of a little grace sometimes. You're a talented kid with a good heart. I believe in you. I think you just need a second chance."

I felt numb. No one had ever offered me grace before. The term felt foreign.

"I don't even know what to say, Pastor."

"Just say yes. And let's get the hell out of here."

I smiled. "Yes, sir."

Pastor Isaiah and his wife, Alisha, lived in a tiny three-bedroom home within walking distance of Zion Baptist. Alisha could not have been more openly gracious to me. I still didn't really understand how this young married couple with a newborn baby in the house could invite an incarcerated street kid like me into their home. Were they crazy? But I just kept following Pastor Isaiah forward with each step. I had nothing to lose. He had just legally sprung me from jail. I'd do whatever he told me. I desperately wanted a second chance and a fresh start. I wanted to put my street life behind me. I definitely never wanted to see the inside of a jail cell again for the rest of my life. To ensure that, I knew I had to change direction. But this was surreal.

Although small, the home was well decorated and smelled incredible. Alisha was baking cookies in the kitchen. The baby, Grace, was sleeping in a swing in the living room. The biggest bedroom—which wasn't saying much—belonged to them. There was a bassinet where Grace slept at night next to the bed. They'd actually given me Grace's nursery. I couldn't believe it. One of the other bedrooms was a makeshift office for Pastor Isaiah, who said he used it for church work and to study for his sermons. I'd sat in on two before juvie. He was a good speaker. Very relatable. Like he was in our one-on-one conversations.

Pastor Isaiah opened the door to the third bedroom.

"Welcome home, Sam."

That word *home* hit me like a ton of bricks. I couldn't make sense of it. I knew it would take me a long time to believe it, but I was glad to hear it. The room had a twin bed in the corner, a row of empty bookshelves along one wall, and a small wooden desk against another wall. It was warm and perfect. I felt overwhelmed with emotions.

"Make yourself comfortable here," said Pastor Isaiah. "You're welcome to rearrange the furniture to your liking, put up whatever pictures you want, as long as they are respectable, and do whatever you need to do to make this feel like your space."

I nodded.

"The guest bathroom is just down the hallway. Please keep it tidy, OK?"

"Yes, sir."

"I have to head over to church for a meeting. Dinner is at six p.m. every night. You don't want to miss it, I promise. Alisha is an amazing cook."

"I won't miss it. Ever. You can count on that."

He smiled, put his arm around my shoulder. "You OK?"

"I don't know. It's just so hard to believe I'm here. I woke up this morning in a tiny jail room. I showered awkwardly with other guys. Put on my uncomfortable prison uniform. Got yelled at by guards. Just like the past eighty-nine days. And now I'm standing here."

"That's over now, Sam. Time to make a new life, if you really want it."

"Yes, sir. I do."

Pastor Isaiah connected me with a job at the homeless shelter, said the church would pay me a small monthly stipend to serve there several hours a day. I'd work in the kitchen, stock shelves, run errands to pick up donated items, work with the guests, and whatever else the director at the shelter needed. Then we would look into getting my education back in order. I just kept doing what he encouraged me to do, step-by-step, one foot after another, tried not to overthink it, and it felt like my life was slowly and unexpectedly changing.

It was the first time in nearly four years I had an actual schedule and a rhythm to my day. Like regular breakfast, lunch, and dinner. No more wandering around, wondering about meals, scheming how to get my hands on some quick cash. I was reading a lot. Pastor Isaiah kept giving me books that I usually devoured in one night. I was a sponge. I served every single day at the shelter, whether on the clock or not, and made a lot of new friends with people on the streets, men and women with shaggy hair and missing teeth. Some of them I already knew. I studied hard to get my GED, which was easy for me, got my driver's license, and I was eating so well from Alisha's cooking that I'd packed on ten healthy pounds.

After several months, Pastor Isaiah sat me down in his home office one day.

"Let's talk about college, Sam."

"College?"

"Yeah, have you thought about where you might go?"

I was baffled. "I've never once in my life thought about going to college."

"Well, that's ridiculous. You're going to college."

"But . . . how?"

"Just like everyone else. By taking the right entrance tests, talking to the right people, applying for the right grants. Making it happen. That's how."

"I'm not like everyone else, Pastor."

"You're right. You're special. You're smarter than any teenager we've ever had at Zion."

He swiveled his chair toward his desk, grabbed a stack of folders. Then swiveled back to me. "I've taken the liberty of getting material from different colleges around the state. I want you to look through them and see what stands out to you."

"OK."

"You might want to even consider law school."

I laughed. "What? That's absurd."

"Why not? Nick at the shelter says you've been helping a lot of the guys with their legal paperwork. He said you've got a knack for it and even wrote a letter for one of the guys using a lot of legal language that even he didn't understand. Said one of the lawyers at the street clinic has been trying to recruit you to work at their place."

"That's true. But that's a long way from law school."

He leaned forward on both elbows, moved closer to me. I knew when he did this, it was time for a life lesson. Time to get serious. And I was OK with that.

"Listen, Sam, you have way too much potential and too many incredible gifts to not pursue them all to the very highest level. You're one of the smartest kids I've been around. You're brilliant, really. You can read a book a night. Books that take me at least two weeks or more, you just plow through them like they're comic books. Who can do that? And you have this amazing charisma with people. I see it all the time at church and at the shelter. Alisha sees it in you, too. You need to start seeing it in yourself. You can do anything you want in life. College would be the first step for you, if you want it. From there, who knows where God will take you? To me, it seems clear from watching you at the shelter, and speaking with the director, that a life of service to others might be in your future."

"I don't know what to say. I honestly don't feel worthy of any of this."

"It's not about being worthy. It's about being grateful. And letting that gratitude help you maximize the new opportunities you're getting."

"I am grateful."

"Let me tell you something. And I had to accept this for myself several years ago when I felt called into ministry. I know you got the short end of the stick in life. Mom dumped you. That sucks. Dad was never around. And you've been through some horrible experiences. Things I wouldn't wish on any kid. You probably have every right to be pissed off at God. No one would deny you that. But you have to let go of it when given the chance to move forward. Your past doesn't have to define you. While I don't believe any of that pain you experienced was God's plan for your life, I absolutely believe He is in the redemption business. I've experienced it myself. You think I, for one moment, feel like I deserve Alisha, or Grace, or any of this life I now get to live? No way. But I've come to not only accept but to embrace that God often likes to take the pain of our past and turn it into the fuel for our ministry future. You understand me?"

"Not really."

He smiled, patted me on the shoulder. "I mean, your past can be used for good, if you'll allow it, Sam. So stop running away from it. Check out these college pamphlets, and let's talk more by the end of the week. We need to get your applications started."

"Yes, sir."

THIRTEEN

Saturday, 8:04 p.m.
Austin, Texas
Two days, three hours, fifty-six minutes till Election Day

Ted Bowerson lived in a 3,200-square-foot home just south of the river near downtown Austin, in an exclusive old neighborhood overlooking the skyline near Zilker Park and Barton Springs. According to the public property records, Ted had purchased the home two years ago. He had obviously done very well for himself. I knew he also owned a luxury condo in Adams Morgan in DC. The cabbie dropped me on the corner of the quiet street. Earlier, I'd called Ted several times from an old-school public pay phone outside a Stop-N-Go near the library. I never left a message. I wasn't interested in more trails. As the radio silence grew between us throughout the day, I was becoming more suspicious of Ted. What would Ted have to gain by giving me up? Was he connected to this thing somehow? He was the only one at the moment, other than my mom, who knew some version of the truth. Unless he'd already shared it with others.

I was somehow still alive. Much to the chagrin of whoever was trying to do away with me. Twenty-four hours ago, I was a simple political tracker covering a barbecue and campaign rally at the courthouse in Boerne, Texas. Then the text arrived.

Why had they chosen me?

A question I couldn't stop asking myself. One of many questions.

A black Range Rover was parked in the driveway. The outside security lights were on by the massive glass front door. I could spot a light on in an upstairs window. After watching for fifteen minutes, I didn't notice any shadows of movement inside.

I would not use the front door. I had no intention of walking straight up to the house, giving the doorbell a ring with, "Hey, Ted, Sam Callahan here. Yep, I'm still alive. Disappointed? Can we talk about that for a sec?" Staying in the shadows, I hopped the short fence protecting his property, crossed his well-manicured lawn, and kept my eyes and ears open for any dogs, though I did not take Ted for a dog person. He seemed too tidy to want a dog around messing up his stuff. Plus, he traveled too much. But I would still be careful. The last thing I needed right now was a mutt to jump out from nowhere and bite me in the ass.

Behind the house, I found a metal stairwell that led me up to multi-level decks that displayed views of the downtown skyline. I eased up the metal stairs to the first deck. My eyes gazed from the skyscrapers over to the renowned tower on the University of Texas campus, just north of downtown. The tower was lit up in burnt-orange lights.

A million-dollar view. Or two point four million, to be exact.

A security light was on above the impressive oversize glass doors in the back. I cupped my hands to the glass, peeked inside. A light was on in the kitchen above the sink. I also noticed a light on beyond the railing on the second level, along with a flicker. Maybe a TV? But no other lights. There were no signs of life inside. It sure didn't look like anyone was home. I wondered about the Range Rover in the driveway. I supposed Ted could easily own two or three cars. Perhaps he was out in the Porsche right now. My eyes surveyed the walls by the doors inside, looking for an alarm keypad. I spotted one near the kitchen. It did not appear as if the house alarm was armed. Shutting down a complicated alarm system was not completely beyond my scope of experience, but I was rusty. Technology had advanced so much in the few years since my last go-round. So that would save me a little stress. I pulled out the new compact tool set from my back jeans pocket. A tiny kit I'd purchased at a pawnshop downtown that held miniature screwdrivers, various-size paper clips, some wire, a pair of scissors. It was amazing what you could do with a few simple tools.

Turned out, I didn't need any of them. The glass door was unlocked. I paused. This made me uneasy. Yes, it was a high-dollar neighborhood. There was a general feeling of safety and security. I'd even noticed a neighborhood rental cop drive slowly by in a Mazda earlier. But I also knew that rich people liked to protect their very expensive stuff. I pushed the glass door open a few inches, leaned in, listened, counted slowly to twenty. No sirens. No sudden loud wails from a hidden security system that had evaded my eyes. And maybe even more important, no charging Rottweiler coming from a back hallway.

I could hear a TV now. Upstairs and around the corner. The flicker. I was sure of it, as the volume was loud, and I could make out the distinct voice of George Clooney engaged in banter. *Ocean's 11*? There were no other sounds coming from the house.

I slid inside, shut the door behind me. Something didn't feel right.

Without turning on any lights, I did a quick circle through the kitchen and moved into a small formal living room, and then the master bedroom. The bed was made and all lights were out. I made my way up the contemporary stairwell in the middle of the home. I could hear the TV more clearly now. It was definitely *Ocean's 11*. I could hear George Clooney's character, Danny, say, "I'm not sure what four nines does, but the ace, I think, is pretty high." Man, I loved that movie back in the day, probably watched it more than twenty times, used to dream of being as smooth a con as Danny Ocean.

I reached the top of the stairs, peeked around the corner, and spotted three doors, all open. I figured two were bedrooms, the other an office. The sound from the TV was coming from the office. I had a bad feeling in the pit of my stomach. Men as OCD as Ted Bowerson don't walk out of their house and leave the TV on all day. I approached the office, took a slow glance inside the room.

A massive glass desk faced the window, away from me. The large flat-screen TV hung on the wall to the left. There were George and Brad Pitt and the rest of the gang. A desk lamp was aglow. The office had a balcony with an even more spectacular view of the city. But I paid it zero attention, as my eyes were locked in on the arm and hand I saw sticking out from behind the large black-leather executive chair with its back to me.

I took a few more slow steps into the room, peered around the chair. Ted Bowerson. Facedown on the desk, lying perfectly still in a stale pool of blood that I could now see had dripped down and collected onto the pristine hardwood floors around the wheels of the chair. He'd been shot through the back of the head, execution-style, as his hair was mangled and wet. I was tired of seeing blood. Smelling death. I wondered how long since they'd been there. Maybe right before they came to kill me.

I wasn't going to stick around to sort it out.

A few minutes later, I was hiding behind a large tree in the darkness of a neighbor's yard up the street.

My head was full of more questions.

Were they watching Ted's home? Did I leave any fingerprints inside? Could they somehow tether me to Ted's murder just like they did with Rick? Every step I took forward only brought more uncertainty and more confusion. And more death. That's what I was focused on more than anything else right now. I was frightened. And no longer just for my own life. It wasn't just about me anymore. In the past eighteen hours, I'd spoken with only three people about this thing, and two were already dead. Bullet holes through both of their heads.

The third person was my mom. I had to get back to DC and get to her before it was too late. She was the only real family I'd ever had, even if she'd been absent for most of my life.

SAM, AGE TWENTY-TWO

Boulder, Colorado

I finished the last exam of my last semester and then met my room-mate, Josh, at Farrand Field in the center of campus. It was a beautiful, sunny June day. We were in T-shirts, shorts, flip-flops. Our summer gear. I gazed around the expansive field, stared at the litter of pretty coeds. Farrand Field was packed with hundreds of students, as it was on most sunny days. They drank beer, studied, listened to loud music, sunbathed in bikinis, drank more beer, threw Frisbees and footballs around. Most of them would go home in a day or two and then come back for summer classes in two weeks. Some would head off to summer internships. Others, like me and Josh, would be graduating and leaving this place forever.

I was four years down at CU and near certain that my perfect GPA was still locked in place. My final government exam was a breeze. All my papers were in. No professors were threatening to drop me a grade. I had excelled at the top level, was graduating with the highest honors, and I'd already been accepted into Georgetown Law. For the first time in my life, I was starting to feel good about my future. My life before

Pastor Isaiah and Alisha was a distant memory. Except for one small piece. Something that had nagged at the back of my mind all this time. Something that had grown in the months leading up to my eventual departure from Colorado to Washington, DC.

Josh opened a small cooler and tossed me a beer. I popped open the can and took a long swig. It was cold and satisfying. I stared at the sunbathers.

"You sure you don't want to come with me?" Josh asked. "One last roommate hurrah?"

"To the coast? With your family? Nah."

"My family is cool with it, I swear."

Josh was headed to Hilton Head for two weeks before moving to DC, like me, where he was set to work in politics. It was his second ask. His family was wealthy and was always getting together. I think he felt bad that we had to move out of our apartment early, and I'd have to couch-surf for a week before driving to DC. Not that this would bother a guy like me with my past. He also hated that I had no other family. Other than Pastor Isaiah and Alisha, who now had new twin boys in their tiny home. I wasn't headed back there for break. Alisha already had her hands full. She didn't need a college student crashing on her living-room sofa. The lack-of-family thing had always really bothered Josh. I think for someone with two brothers and three sisters, whose parents were still together, and who had dozens of uncles and aunts and cousins around, he found my situation unfathomable. And unacceptable. *No family at all, Sam?* He'd asked me several times our first week as new roommates three years ago. I had assured him that was correct. Just me. There was no one else.

"I'm good, Josh. I got things to close out here, anyway."

"Like what?" Josh said, not buying it. "You don't even have a place to live. My parents will pay for everything. You don't have to worry about it. We have plenty of room."

"I appreciate it. But I'm good."

Josh shrugged, chugged his beer. "Suit yourself, Callahan."

I smiled. "I always do."

I wouldn't tell Josh, but the truth was, I had a meeting in two days with a private investigator. A guy I'd hired recently with the little extra cash I was making waiting tables. The investigator had finally found my mother. I was starting to think she was probably dead. Which would have been fine. Maybe easier. The investigator was traveling back into town now.

I didn't plan to ever tell a living soul about her. Not Josh. Not even Pastor Isaiah.

I guess I just privately wanted to see if she was still alive before I left Colorado and never looked back.

We met in his dusty office, a tiny cluttered square on the second floor of a crumbling building above a dingy pool hall. The place was a dump, but it was not like I could afford to hire an expensive investigative firm from the corporate district. Billy Dixon was a former Chicago cop, now semiretired. Moved to Denver to be near his two granddaughters. He had a thick mustache, glasses, bushy gray hair. He wore the same cheap light-blue suit every day. I really liked him. He was sympathetic to my plight and actually seemed pretty good at his job. But it still took us nearly six months to find her. I had engaged his services the day after I'd received my acceptance letter to Georgetown Law.

"Make yourself comfortable, Sammy," Billy said.

For some reason, he always called me Sammy. I didn't care. Billy moved in behind his old wooden desk, shoved around thick piles of paperwork. I sat in the same worn folding chair I always did when visiting him. You could hear the crack of billiard balls beneath us in the pool hall and smell the cigarette smoke seeping up through the floor.

Billy shoved a manila folder toward me.

"Where is she?" I asked.

"Houston."

I nodded.

"She goes by the name Nancy Weber now. I think she's changed her name several times over the years, as she's moved about. I found several different identities. And she's moved around a lot. All over the South. But she's been in Houston a few years now. She lives by herself in a tiny apartment in a crummy part of town. Saw different guys coming and going." Billy paused. "You sure you want to know all of this, Sam?"

"Yes, keep going."

"She's not in great shape, to be honest. Lots of drug use, that's pretty clear. A neighbor said she works a few night shifts a week at the twenty-four-hour deli when she's sober enough. I got lots of photos. They're all in the file."

I hadn't touched the file yet. Of course, my mom was a drug addict.

"She have any other family? Other kids? Anything?"

Billy shook his head, his neck jiggling. "Nothing that I could find."

I grabbed the file, didn't open it. I wasn't sure I wanted to open it. "You're certain it's her?"

Billy sighed, almost like he didn't want to confirm it. "Yes, it's her, Sammy. I got DNA evidence from her place, ran the proper tests. A match. It's all in the file. This is your mother."

I nodded. "How much do I still owe you?"

"Six hundred."

I pulled a white envelope from my back pocket, counted it out in cash.

"You want me to keep digging for more?" Billy asked.

I shook my head. "No, this is good. Thanks."

"Sure. Good luck, son."

A week later, I pulled my Ford Explorer over onto the side of the highway at dusk, the sun setting behind me, just inside the state line of Colorado. Kansas was only a hundred yards away. I could see the **WELCOME TO KANSAS** sign up ahead. I was on my way to Washington,

DC, to start a new life. Unlikely ever to return to my old life. Unlikely ever to walk the same streets that I'd lived on as a kid. I was never coming back. My Explorer was loaded down with all my earthly possessions, which included two large duffel bags of clothes and a half dozen banker boxes filled with my collection of schoolbooks and folders.

Staring at the state line up ahead of me, I felt the weight of the moment.

I had survived Colorado. I had survived my past.

I reached over to a pile of folders in my passenger seat. I found the manila folder that Billy had prepared for me with the photos of my mother. I had not yet opened it. I just couldn't do it. It had sat there untouched in the passenger seat for a week. I got out of my car, walked a hundred feet into the grassy plains along the Colorado-Kansas border, away from the noise and traffic of the highway. Then I took out a cigarette lighter and lit the corner of the manila folder on fire. I dropped the folder onto the dirt in front of me, watched it burn up. When it was nothing but ashes, I stomped it out with a shoe and returned to my car.

Then I drove across the state border.

FOURTEEN

Saturday, 10:00 p.m.
Austin, Texas
Two days, two hours till Election Day

The Hog had bushy red hair and thick red eyebrows. Tall, maybe six foot four, he must have weighed close to four hundred pounds. He was huge and covered nearly head to toe in designer tattoos. They were crawling up and down both robust arms and appearing again out of his massive brown cargo shorts all the way to his orange flip-flops. Even his giant toes had ink marks on them. Most of it looked like a battle scene right out of the Lord of the Rings trilogy, with dragons, warlocks, dwarfs, and many other fantastical creatures. The only skin not covered with ink was his face, where he sported a well-trimmed red beard. He looked like the world's largest leprechaun.

Affinity Tattoo and Piercing was located in the heart of Sixth Street, Austin's downtown party strip, with live music of every possible variety blaring out of the open doors of dozens of bars, pubs, and other hot spots for more than five blocks. There was also a music festival going on in the city. Crowds of students and young professionals were growing by the minute. It would be an all-out zoo by midnight. Police barricades already blocked off the entire street, which was fine with me. Easier to get lost in the circus of thousands of inebriated people. No one would be paying too much attention to me. I hoped.

As instructed, I asked the woman near the front counter of the tattoo joint to see the Hog. I felt stupid saying it. Who calls themselves that? But then, there didn't seem to be such a thing as "stupid" in this place, as the woman had two rainbow-colored unicorns frolicking around on her neck, three diamond studs in one nostril, and the word *chill* tattooed in bright pink and purple with lots of tiny hearts above her right eyebrow. She didn't flinch an inch when I said "The Hog." She led me through to the back, where I shook hands with the giant leprechaun. He seemed to be friendly, but his manner indicated that this was serious business.

He quickly led me through a door to a dark back hallway and into a private office. Three different giant computer screens were set up across a crowded metal desk. Several old posters of classic Atari games covered the walls. Asteroids. Centipede. Defender. Space Invaders. The Hog invited me to sit in a cheap metal folding chair. I got the feeling he didn't see too many guests. He then fell into a leather office chair on wheels that I thought would burst at the joints but somehow held together under his girth.

"So, you're friends with Maverick?" he asked, fiddling around on his cluttered desk. He had a surprisingly soft, effeminate voice for such a large man.

"Yeah, that's right," I said. The less said, the better. I wasn't surprised that the Hog referenced Tommy simply as Maverick. He probably didn't even know Tommy's real name. Just like Tommy didn't know the Hog was actually Eugene Bernard Fitzgerald, according to a subscription label I spotted on a copy of *Fantasy & Science Fiction* that sat in a pile on the floor beside my chair.

"I'd say a damn good friend," the Hog continued. "Maverick gave me over ten thousand action points for this. You believe that? Shot me right past levels five and six and straight to level seven. Incredible. You must have some seriously dirty pics of him." He laughed heartily.

I forced a fake chuckle, as if I understood, but I had no idea what he was talking about. Ten thousand points? Figured it was some kind of fantasy game they played online together. The Hog probably operated in a world where everyone knew what the term *action points* meant and just assumed that I did, too, since I was pals with Maverick. I would not burst his bubble. God bless Tommy. Sounded like he really pulled out all the stops for me.

The Hog found what he was looking for, handed me a thick, weighty manila envelope.

"Here you go, man. You're all set."

I looked down. "Everything's in here?"

The Hog shrugged. "Everything Maverick sent over for me to put together. Check it out. It's all there. New driver's license, a credit card, Social Security card, passport, cell phone, and tablet."

I undid the clasp, peeked into the envelope. I pulled out the stack of new cards, wrapped in a rubber band, grinned for a brief moment at the name listed on a newly issued Texas driver's license that shared a slightly altered photo with the one that was on my current Colorado license. Dobbs Howard. I knew immediately why Tommy had chosen that name. *The Treasure of the Sierra Madre*. Tommy's favorite Western movie of all time, starring Humphrey Bogart and Walter Huston. He insisted I watch it. Bogart's character was named Dobbs. Huston's character was named Howard. Dobbs Howard. It could be a whole lot worse, I guess. At least he knew better than to go back to John Wayne. I needed zero extra attention right now.

I flipped through the other cards, finding Dobbs Howard listed on each and every one, including my new passport, which was stamped. I had apparently been to Austria, Germany, Switzerland, and France in the past two years. I also found a new phone and new tablet. I turned both on. They were fully charged and already preprogrammed to an account that belonged to an individual named Dobbs Howard. I was in awe at the attention to detail. These guys were amazing. I was a brand-new man. If only it were that easy.

"You need a gun?" asked the Hog, eyeballing me.

I looked up, hadn't considered it.

The leprechaun shrugged. "Maverick didn't ask for it. But you're in the middle of a crapstorm. That's pretty clear. I've seen the news. Not that I care. But I know some people."

It was tempting. But I couldn't get a gun on an airplane to DC, which is where I was headed first thing in the morning. "Nah, I'm good. Thanks, man."

"Sure. Good luck, Dobbs."

FIFTEEN

Saturday, 10:27 p.m.
Austin, Texas
Two days, one hour, thirty-three minutes till Election Day

I was being followed. I was sure of it.

I felt a chill rush through me and settle in my chest.

I was right smack in the middle of the thick throng of partygoers, the envelope stuffed in the back of my jeans, when I spotted him. He was dressed in a black-leather jacket, jeans, black cowboy boots. He was fifteen feet ahead of me, standing next to a street pole on the corner, looking like he belonged. But he stood out because, for one, he wasn't moving along with the masses, and second, his eyes were already locked in on me, as if he'd been tracking me up the sidewalk. I jerked to a stop, causing two drunk college girls to bump into me. They yelled at me, gave me dirty looks, but I paid little attention. Square Jaw was already sizing up the situation. He glanced behind me, made a subtle motion of his head. I turned and found Elvis, in a brown jacket and jeans, twenty feet down the sidewalk. They'd found me. And they had me trapped. Did they know about Affinity Tattoo? No, I doubted that. Only Tommy knew about that. And there was no way Tommy would ever give up that info. I was sure of that. The Hog? I wasn't so sure. He'd shown his hand by offering a gun and telling me he'd seen me on the news. Which didn't make me too comfortable.

I stood still for a second on the sidewalk, a host of people brushing past me on both sides, bumping my shoulders, annoyed at me for causing a traffic jam and not moving along with the crowd. Live music from a hard-rock band was blaring out from the open door of a pub directly to my right. Surely they wouldn't shoot me in public. No, they would have to get me alone first. I had a chance. My mind was mapping it out. Time to go.

I ducked in quickly behind the crowd that was cramming into the pub. It was packed to the walls, as the partiers flooded the wooden bar, the booths, and every square inch in front of the band area. The lead singer was half singing, half yelling, and sweating profusely. The crowd loved it. It was a massive hard-rock jam session.

I pushed my way aggressively through the crowd. I glanced back. Square Jaw was already inside the joint with me, but I didn't spot Elvis. I shoved my way around a gang of frat boys toward the very back. One of the guys shoved me in return a little, shot me a look. A fight look. Then I had an idea. Nothing like a good old drunken frat-boy brawl to create a sudden and chaotic distraction. I spotted the back door in the hallway by the restrooms. My target. I had my path. Time to pick a fight. I had multiple opponents, but I could take them if I moved fast. I reared back my right fist and popped the frat boy in front of me, the guy who gave me the dirty look, solid in the jaw. Not so hard as to do any serious damage, but enough to shock him and piss him off. Then I elbowed the big guy behind me in the gut, and with a quick lunge from side to side, shoved two more guys to my left and right. The whole crowd kind of shifted and swayed with the ruckus, like a ship tilting on large waves, as the frat boy turned back and swung wildly, not hitting me but connecting with the ear of another guy right next to me. The big guy I elbowed was unsure who did it and just started shoving everyone within reach. Within seconds, more shoving ensued, and fists started flying. We were off and running. I got popped once in the neck. Then I ducked my head low, avoided a few punches, pushed my way through the wave of twisting bodies, and found the clearing to the back hallway.

I pressed through the rear exit door into the alleyway a few seconds later.

I could hear the fight growing wilder and more out of control behind me. It had completely drowned out the band. The cops would probably be in the pub within minutes.

The alley was dark with overflowing metal dumpsters that smelled like rotten food and vomit. I stepped into the clearing, peered both ways up and down the alley. Then I saw the silhouette of Elvis enter the opposite end. I knew it. They weren't stupid. He had circled the building strip, anticipated my escape. Forty feet away. Worse, he spotted me and began a dead sprint. I saw his hand reach under his coat. While they wouldn't shoot me in public on the main street in front of the bar, they sure as hell would shoot me in a dark alley.

I turned, leaped over some boxes, raced in the opposite direction. The alley poured out onto Brazos Street, where the sidewalks were busy but not as full as Sixth. We were a block off the party strip. I spotted the famous Driskill Hotel on the corner across the street. I raced across through oncoming traffic, causing a taxi to screech to a halt and several horns to blare.

I hit the glass doors and found the hotel plush and spacious. The Driskill was active even at this late hour. Lots of folks huddled everywhere. It was obviously a popular stay for the music-festival crowd. I took a peek behind me. Elvis had not yet followed. Had I lost him? I wondered if he'd gotten caught up in street traffic. I peered to my left to the main entrance of the Driskill off Sixth Street, the opposite side of the lobby. That's when I noticed Square Jaw suddenly walk in from the front sidewalk. His eyes again connected with mine. He'd somehow made it out of the pub unscathed. I spotted a man in a room-service uniform step out of a service hallway near the front desk. It was no longer time to be cool, to avoid attention, and blend into the crowd. It was time to run.

I exploded forward into the service hallway and burst through a swinging door to the hotel kitchen. I was greeted with the clanking of dishes, hissing, steam, and commotion, guys in room-service uniforms loading or unloading trays, men scrubbing dishes with hot-water sprayers, a few chefs whipping things on and off burners and barking orders like drill sergeants. I dissected a path around them, took off running again, but not without knocking a kid right over and sending a dinner plate sailing through the air and crashing to the floor. I zigzagged and found the back hallway on the opposite end of the kitchen. Racing past a service elevator, I turned a corner, spotted a big red EXIT sign above a metal door. A wave of relief hit me. Freedom. I hit the door with the full force of my shoulder, pushed it wide open, poured out into another dark alley behind the hotel, my lungs so on fire that I thought I might collapse.

Then I froze in place, stopped breathing altogether.

Elvis was standing right outside the door. Like he was waiting on me. A gun was in his hand. A small smile spread across his face. I had no time to rush him or take a swing or do anything as the long, skinny black barrel of his gun lifted up, pointing right at my forehead. I had come so far. I thought of my mom. And the girl I hadn't spoken with in five months. I heard two quick and powerful puffs of air. *Thump. Thump.*

I felt nothing. Instead, Elvis jerked. Then his eyes went glassy, and I saw blood starting to roll down his face. He fell to his knees on the concrete, dropped his gun, and collapsed awkwardly.

He was dead, and I was still alive.

Fifteen feet behind him, near the corner of the dark alley, I noticed him. It wasn't more than a half second before he slipped away, but I took a clear mental snapshot. Gray beard. Trimmed neat. Short white hair. Probably in his early sixties. Wearing all black: black turtleneck, black blazer, black slacks. He had quickly shoved a gun with a silencer barrel back under his blazer and pivoted around the corner. Gone. Just like that. He clearly was a professional. And though it was only a millisecond, and the security light in the alley was sketchy, I swear the man had the most crystal-blue eyes.

SIXTEEN

Sunday, 12:32 a.m.
Austin, Texas
One day, twenty-three hours, twenty-eight minutes till
Election Day

I stood bare-chested in my blue boxers in my motel bathroom.

My hair was now blond, almost white. This time around, I did a much better job with the hair-coloring kit I'd purchased at a twenty-four-hour drugstore. I had more time and space to get the color right. Maybe in my next life, I would just become a hairdresser. That sounded a helluva lot better than my current life.

My motel room was on the second floor of the Quality Inn & Suites, a half mile from the Austin–Bergstrom airport. Fifteen miles from the dead body of Elvis behind the Driskill Hotel. I was sure the hotel staff had discovered him within minutes of my rapid departure. The fourth dead body I'd witnessed in twenty-four hours. The blonde woman. Rick Jackson. Ted Bowerson. And now Elvis. I walked to my room window and gazed straight down at the parking lot. Still no sign of anything suspicious. Not yet, at least.

I'd disposed of yet another bloody shirt. I'd purchased a new blue hoodie to replace the gray pullover that was now in the dumpster behind the motel. I felt fortunate when the motel front-desk clerk swiped my new credit card and it went through without a hitch. *Thanks, Mr. Howard. Enjoy your stay with us.* Man, I owed Tommy.

I couldn't stop thinking about the gray-bearded man. His face and eyes were branded into my mind. He had swooped in and saved me. Two perfect bullets and then vanished. I couldn't help but believe he was the same man who'd been inside my mom's room earlier that morning, claiming to be an FBI agent. I mean, seriously, how many nice-looking sixty-something, gray-bearded men with the "prettiest blue eyes" could there be in this situation? I highly doubted more than one. Could he have been in DC that morning, then jumped on a plane and traveled to Austin the same day, just in time to rescue me?

To clear my name and get back to DC, I needed to figure things out. Who was he? And how did he find me?

More important, why did he want to keep me alive?

I thought about Lucas McCallister. Did someone set him up? Could this have been a final effort by the Mitchell campaign to stop its plummet in the polls and save the election? Was that why I'd received the text? Then I thought about Square Jaw, who was working security for Congressman Mitchell, and became even more confused. Why would they text me to witness the event and then want to kill me? And why would Lucas McCallister take the bait this close to Election Day? With a growing four-point lead? Even the weakest man I knew could keep his pants zipped for four days, especially when you considered what was at stake.

So many questions. My head hurt.

But each of these questions paled in comparison to the biggest in my mind right now.

Did someone want Lucas McCallister elected so badly this coming week that he would help cover up a murder and then send out a team of professional killers within hours to eliminate any and all possible connections to it? Because I highly doubted that McCallister's campaign manager could pick up the phone and make such calls. There was no twenty-four-hour assassin hotline. No, it would have had to be someone else. Someone close to the campaign. Someone much more powerful and capable. And someone with a whole lot at stake on Tuesday.

I needed to find out that answer. It might be my only way out.

A brown wallet was sitting on the bed, its contents spread out in a circle. The wallet belonged to my dead friend, Elvis, from the hotel alley. I'd made sure to snag it before bolting. Elvis was actually Greg Carson, twenty-eight, of Morgantown, West Virginia. There was an American Express card, a Visa card, and an Exxon gas card. Twenty-seven dollars in cash. A photo of a brunette of similar age. Nothing written on the back. Gas-card receipts. A former Marine Corps ID, an ID for Stable Security out of Dallas, an ID badge for a training facility with Redrock Security, and a Gold's Gym ID. Also business cards from a hunting company, a bail bondsman, and an auto shop.

Using my tablet, I wasn't able to find any mention of a Greg Carson from West Virginia who'd been in the Marine Corps. That search came up completely blank. And though there were several Greg Carsons listed on Facebook, none matched the profile of this guy. Not that I expected to find a guy like this on social media. I did find the website for Stable Security Services in Dallas. They claimed to offer the highest level of private security in Texas. I wondered if Congressman Mitchell's team had contracted Elvis and Square Jaw from Stable Security. I'd heard of Redrock Security. Redrock was a private military contractor that employed thousands of former military specialists for operations around the world. The Gold's Gym ID was for Roanoke, Virginia. The hunting company, Jackson Wing Hunting, was in North Carolina. The auto shop, Bert's Auto & Body, was in Blacksburg. I was at a dead end.

There was nothing obvious that gave me answers.

Who sent you to kill me, Greg Carson?

I'd also started reading up on the news of the manhunt for one Samuel Callahan, a current student at Georgetown Law School. A murder suspect. It was on the home page of *USA Today*. There were quotes in the article from some of my law professors and classmates. It was surreal. They were all in shock. No one saw it coming. I was thankful there was no mention of a mother in a health-care facility. It would be a very difficult relationship to track, which is why it was all the more confusing how the gray-bearded man had been there with her this morning.

I probably should have stopped reading, but I couldn't get myself to pull away. It was like an out-of-body experience, as if I were reading about someone else's life.

Not my life. Not me.

Then I read another stunner. The FBI was now officially involved in my case. They had entered the scene earlier that evening. It was no longer just some mysterious gray-bearded guy claiming to be an FBI agent while sitting with my mom. This was real. I watched a video clip from a news conference from a few hours earlier, with a serious man with hard eyes in the standard dark-blue FBI windbreaker, standing in front of cameras in San Antonio, promising to find me at all costs. They had reason to believe this was not an isolated matter, that I was on the run, and that I was very dangerous, which was why they'd seized control of the investigation. He was right. It was not isolated. For a moment, I thought of simply turning myself in, just walking straight into the downtown police station tonight, letting them slap on the cuffs and begging for some type of asylum. At least I'd stay alive. Tell the truth, the whole truth. Pray for the best. Even with Tommy Kucher's help, I was surely no match for the FBI. They would discover Dobbs Howard. They would track the credit cards. They probably already had.

They were probably on their way to my motel right now.

I inhaled deeply, let it out slowly. Returned to the window, studied the parking lot. There was something stopping me from turning myself in to the authorities. I was no dummy. It didn't take being in law school to figure this one out. Truth was like clay. Whoever had their hands on the clay could shape it however he wanted. My hands were nowhere near the clay. I had to change that first.

But I was working against the clock. I had hours, not days.

I turned from the window, fell back onto the bed. The TV was on FOX News, but the sound was muted. I was thankful for a hurricane in the Atlantic that was approaching the tip of Florida and promising to throw some houses around. There was at least some distraction going on that took a little attention away from me. I wanted to call my mom, make sure she was OK, but I resisted the urge. She would be asleep, anyway. And she could very well be under some type of surveillance. I didn't want to invite any more unwanted attention to her. No, I'd wait to see her in person. I wasn't entirely sure at this point how I was going to make that happen tomorrow. Not with my face suddenly on all the national FBI Most Wanted posters.

I would figure it out. I had plenty of time to think. I had all night. I was certain there wouldn't be much sleep coming my way. My mind was too frazzled. My United Airlines flight, a ticket I'd purchased with my new credit card under Dobbs Howard, was set to leave in only five hours, at 5:35 a.m., and would arrive in DC around nine fifteen. Right now, I desperately needed to see two people ASAP.

My mom, of course.

And Natalie Foster.

SAM, AGE TWENTY-THREE

Washington, DC

She was attractive, that was for sure. Not attractive in that drop-dead gorgeous, too-skinny model kind of way. She had something else going on that was like a magnet. I think it was her sexy confidence. I wanted to talk to her, but it seemed as if every guy who went up to her was shot down almost immediately, like she was playing a game of Whack-A-Mole.

I'd been watching her from across the bar. We were at a professional mixer in downtown DC. A bunch of soon-to-be-rich lawyers yukking it up with DC's professional elite. I wasn't really sure why I was there. I despised this kind of event. But Marty Watson, one of my classmates at Georgetown, had somehow dragged me along. I didn't really like him. He was an arrogant Harvard grad with a wise mouth and ridiculously wealthy parents, but I put up with him since he was on my mock-trial team. Marty was currently flirting with the confident brunette.

I asked one of the brunette's tipsy girlfriends, a girl who was dating another one of my classmates, about her. She gladly gave me the inside scoop. Natalie Foster, a reporter for a popular political-news blog called *PowerPlay*. A Midwest girl out of the University of Missouri, one of the best journalism programs in the country. Her dad apparently used to play pro baseball for the Saint Louis Cardinals back in the day. She had a bunch of brothers. No current boyfriend.

I couldn't tell if Marty was making any progress. Then I saw his hand move down the back of Natalie's black cocktail dress and rest below the waist where it didn't belong. Natalie's big eyes flashed. Marty was smiling wide. So brash and arrogant. Natalie reached down with both hands, grabbed my law-school classmate by the right wrist, twisted it violently in self-defense fashion, and then flipped him over onto the dirty hardwood floor. Marty landed with a thud and let out a gasp. He never saw it coming. Everyone turned to stare. Some were already laughing at the scene—a petite young woman in a cocktail dress and heels putting a martial-arts move on a big, obnoxious guy. Looking dizzy and disheveled, Marty lay sprawled for a moment on the floor in his dark suit. He'd clearly had too much to drink.

"What the hell?" Marty muttered.

"Might want to watch those hands, Harvard," Natalie replied.

There was more laughing. It was impressive. I smiled. Now I definitely had to meet her. Natalie walked ten feet away and joined a pack of girlfriends at the other end of the bar. Marty got himself up and limped off in defeat. I pulled at my gray suit jacket to straighten it out, worked out a plan in my mind. I was never good in bars. I let the dust from Marty's situation settle, then I took a deep breath, exhaled, and walked over to Natalie standing with her girlfriends.

The three girls stopped, stared at me. My eyes were only on Natalie.

"Can I help you?" she asked.

"Maybe. I have a proposition for you."

She gave me a suspicious head tilt. Waited for my best obnoxious bar line. "What kind of proposition is that?"

"A contest, really. If I win, you have dinner with me."

The other girls giggled. Natalie's eyes narrowed.

"And if I win?"

"If you win, I make a significant donation to your favorite charity."

She was understandably skeptical. "OK, so what's the contest? By the looks of you, let me guess. Beer drinking? Belching?"

The girls laughed again. I grinned. "Not exactly. Although those ideas are tempting, I had something else in mind. The batting cages. I was thinking something simple. Like ten pitches each at high speed. Winner takes all."

This caught her by surprise. "Batting cages?"

"Yeah, you know, as in baseball batting cages. Are you familiar with the game?"

She did not like that question. "You can't be serious?"

I shrugged. "What do you say, Ms. Foster? Are you up to the challenge?"

She was intrigued, I could tell. Her eyes softened, and she exchanged a quick smile with her two girlfriends. "OK, slugger, let's go!"

I had not anticipated an immediate response. But there we were, standing outside a batting cage five miles away only twenty minutes later. It seemed the whole bar was interested in watching, as word had spread fast. A bunch of half-drunk yuppies at the batting cages, still in their suits and party dresses, creating a late-night spectacle. Natalie didn't even want to change her clothes. She said it was unnecessary—she could beat me in a dress. I took off my suit jacket, loosened my tie, and rolled up the sleeves to my dress shirt. I was really nervous. I hadn't expected her acceptance; I only thought the offer would lead to more conversation. And now we had a big crowd watching. Natalie insisted I go first. My muscles felt tight. It had been five years since

I'd last swung a baseball bat. But I was athletic enough. It felt natural in my hands.

Someone hit a button, and the crowd grew silent. The first baseball flew out of the machine and barreled down at me at seventy-five miles an hour. I took a quick swing, knocked it right back up the middle. The guys cheered behind me. It had turned into a guys-versus-girls challenge.

Another pitch. Another knock into the far-off net. Cheers from my boys, who started chanting, "Sam! Sam! Sam!"

More pitches, more solid contact. The eighth pitch got me. I fouled it off at my feet. There were dramatic *ooh*s and *ahh*s behind me. I knocked pitches nine and ten back up the middle and then turned and raised the bat in celebration. Nine out of ten was pretty good. There were at least no humiliating swings and misses. I felt certain of victory.

Surprisingly, Natalie did not seem concerned. Or she had a great poker face. Either way, she kicked her heels off, put on a helmet, and grabbed the bat. She took a few practice swings, and for the first time, I wondered if I was in trouble. The bat came off her shoulder with such ease and precision. Like watching Derek Jeter swing. Natalie was a natural athlete. And she clearly knew what she was doing. I stood outside the cage and just marveled.

Someone hit the button, the pitches started racing toward her, and she cracked them right back up the middle. One. Two. Three. Four. The cheers from the girls grew louder with each swing. More people had gathered in behind us. I felt sweat on my brow. Seven. Eight. Nine. *Crack! Crack! Crack!* Chants now of "Natalie! Natalie! Natalie!"

Before pitch number ten, Natalie actually turned to me and gave me a quick wink. I couldn't believe it. Then she got back in her stance and nailed swing number ten. The ball sailed into the net. Ten out of ten. I'd been defeated. And the entire crowd was going absolutely nuts. Natalie stepped out of the cage and handed me the bat.

"I've had a soft spot for children living with HIV in Uganda ever since I took a mission trip there in high school. You can give through Cherish Uganda."

She grinned at me. All I could do was smile back. I was smitten.

Ten minutes later, as everyone was stumbling through the parking lot, Natalie sought me out in private. "How about a drink, slugger?"

We stole away to a popular rooftop bar at the W Hotel.

I learned that Natalie had turned down offers with the *New York Times* and the *Washington Post* straight out of college because as someone raised in the generation of Twitter, Facebook, and Instagram, she wanted to work in the fastest-paced environment possible. The news race was no longer measured in days or even hours but in mere minutes and seconds. She loved that. It was intense and exhilarating. She was very competitive, as I'd just discovered at the batting cages. *PowerPlay* had a small but dynamic young team of political journalists and editors. She had thrived there the past two years.

"What about you, Sam?" she asked. "What's your story?"

"Finishing up my first year at Georgetown Law."

"I see. Your dad a rich lawyer?"

"Why do you ask that?"

She shrugged. "Almost every guy I meet in this town has the same story. Swimming in their father's wake. Out to make their first million."

"I actually don't know my dad. Or my mom."

This caught her by surprise. I decided just to put it out there. I don't know why. There was just something so real and genuine about Natalie that I wanted to spill my story. So I did. Told her about the orphan boy who grew up in foster care, lived on the streets for many years, went to juvie for three months before being rescued by Pastor Isaiah. I felt so vulnerable but not insecure. She hung on every word. I did not feel judged with Natalie. I felt safe.

"You should be proud of yourself, Sam."

"I don't really stop to think about it too much. I've just been surviving."

"You're doing more than surviving. Georgetown is prestigious. You'll probably have your pick of top corporate firms, the opportunity to finally make a lot of money."

"I'm not going corporate."

She was again surprised. "What are you going to do?"

"Practice street law. Work at one of the clinics. Help the homeless, foster kids and parents, low-income families. People like me. Feels like a better fit."

She couldn't tell if I was serious. "Are you kidding?"

I shook my head. "I guess I've seen and experienced too much. The little man always gets screwed, Natalie. It's just wrong. I can't turn my back on it. Plus, to be honest, the thought of putting in a hundred hours a week at some fancy firm to help one huge corporation win a lawsuit over another huge corporation is not appealing."

"So, you really don't care about the money?"

I shrugged. "I don't know. I've never owned more than two pairs of shoes at one time in my whole life. This is my only suit. I've lived for months at a time in a crumbling office building, in alleys, and even in abandoned cars. I don't need much money. A fifty-thousand-dollar salary at a street clinic already seems like a gold rush to a guy like me. How many designer suits and gold watches does a man need? I don't know if that makes any sense."

She smiled wide. "It makes sense. In this town, it's refreshing."

"Well, I'm not trying to make a statement. Or impress you. It's just how I see it."

"I can tell. So, three months in prison, huh?"

I laughed. "Come on, not exactly prison. But yes, I was locked up in a juvenile correctional facility for three months. Not the best of times."

"For stealing cars?"

I nodded. "I won't bore you with details."

"Are you kidding, Sam? I want to hear *every* detail."

Her eyes danced. She was into me. I could tell. Which was good. I was into her.

We talked for four hours straight.

SAM, AGE TWENTY-FOUR

Washington, DC

We spent the day riding roller coasters at Kings Dominion amusement park in Virginia, an hour south of Washington, DC. I hated roller coasters, but Natalie couldn't get enough. So I grinned and bore it, and spent the day having my stomach tossed about on rides like the Intimidator 305, with its three-hundred-foot drop; the Hurler, which sent me twisting and turning at more than fifty miles an hour; and finally Drop Tower, which sent us plunging from twenty-seven stories up at more than seventy-two miles an hour. I nearly vomited my cheeseburger across her lap afterward. Nothing seemed to phase Natalie.

We were sitting at a table having ice cream when it happened.

A teenager snagged Natalie's purse from the table and ran.

I reacted on instinct. Took off after him. But he was a fast kid. Much faster than I was, which was why he was probably good at stealing purses. He split a crowd, and I could barely still see his shaggy head up ahead of me headed toward the carousel. But then, my mind started doing its thing, pulling up a mental map of the park, one I'd only looked at once but had somehow memorized.

Still running, I peeled off to my right, opposite of where the kid was seemingly headed. I heard Natalie yell behind me, "Where are you going, Sam?" But I just kept on running. I cut through more rides and crowds and found a long sidewalk ahead of me leading toward the Eiffel Tower ride in the middle of the park.

Within seconds, I spotted the kid headed my way. I slid in behind the Eiffel Tower crowd and then sprang out at the last minute to intercept him on the sidewalk. I tackled him with a shoulder, and the kid easily went down. He was half my size, and he seemed stunned that I'd somehow snagged him. I wrestled the purse away from him. He seemed afraid. He was only thirteen or fourteen. Reminded me of myself.

Holding him for just a second, I said, "This ain't worth juvie, kid. I promise you. Get better friends and make a better life for yourself."

Then I let him go. He peeled himself off the sidewalk and bolted through the crowd.

Natalie was beside me a few seconds later.

"He got away?" she asked, panting.

I nodded. "But not before I got this." I held up the purse.

"My hero. But how the hell did you do that, Sam?"

After speaking with park security, we were back sitting at a table under some shade. Natalie wouldn't let it go. She was fascinated by the turn of events.

"I don't get it," Natalie said. "It's like you knew exactly where he was going."

"Yeah, it's kind of hard to explain."

"Try," she said.

"It may freak you out."

"I already think you're weird."

I laughed. "OK. Have you ever had visions? Seen things before they happened?"

"Nope. You do?"

"Well, sort of. Ever since I was little, I've had this ability to see images like maps in my head. They just formulate in my mind, like mental jigsaw puzzles—from quick sights, sounds, smells from my surroundings. Not only do I see these, but I can also envision clear escape paths, either for myself or for others. I really don't know what happens, to be honest. But under duress, things usually slow way down for me. I often get this flush of focus and clarity that allows me to see things really clearly and get myself out of some tense situations. It used to help me on the streets. Not so much in my law classes."

"You *are* a freak."

"I tried to tell you."

"So, you're telling me when that kid took off today, you just saw a map in your mind and anticipated where he would go?"

I nodded. "I got lucky."

"It wasn't luck. I watched the whole thing. You're good. Are you sure you weren't created in a secret government lab somewhere? Because you're like no one I've ever dated before. You have this weird photographic memory, you get perfect test scores at Georgetown while barely studying, you're superathletic, and now this: your mind just creates maps out of nowhere in your head."

"You forgot to add that I'm incredibly handsome."

"Moderately handsome," she clarified.

"I'll take that."

She laughed. "You keep surprising me, Sam Callahan."

"Is that good or bad?"

"I haven't decided yet."

SAM, AGE TWENTY-FOUR

Glendale, Missouri

It was her father's sixtieth birthday celebration. The whole family would be there.

Although we'd only been dating two months, Natalie extended the invite to go home with her. I knew it was a big deal. She'd admitted that she hadn't taken anyone back to Glendale to meet the family since she'd moved to DC several years ago. All four older brothers, along with their wives and kids, would be there for the weekend festivities.

It was a big moment for us—if I was going to survive in this relationship. I knew how much her family meant to her. I didn't want to blow it. I'd already fallen for her.

We made the ten-hour drive. When we arrived, there were four large SUVs already parked in the long driveway and about a dozen kids running around the expansive front yard, a mix of boys and girls throwing around footballs, baseballs, and Frisbees. The Foster men and their wives had been a fruitful bunch. Natalie had grown up on fifty wooded acres called Foster Farms just outside of Glendale, where her father, Thomas Foster, had raised some crops and pigs and goats and other assorted farm animals when he wasn't playing pro baseball. The house was a large white plantation number with a porch that wrapped all the way around to the back. Natalie said her father had built the place by himself with the help of his older brother during two successive off-seasons early in his playing career. Natalie and her brothers had never lived anywhere else. One home for life.

I couldn't even fathom it. I'd counted at least thirty homes I'd lived in at one time or another, not to mention the abandoned buildings, churches, alleys, and under bridges. I'd actually never had a *real* home, unless I counted my year with Pastor Isaiah and Alisha. And I had only one family member I knew about, whom I'd never met. Natalie mentioned that twenty-one family members would be at Foster Farms for the weekend. We could not have had more polar-opposite childhoods.

Glendale was a picturesque small town just southwest of Saint Louis, where Natalie's father had been a utility player for the Cardinals for a dozen years, and then a hitting coach for another decade. When her brothers started high school, he retired from his big-league coaching gig to volunteer as a coach at their small high school. Two of the brothers had made it all the way up to Triple-A baseball. Both were baseball coaches now—one at a nearby high school and the other at a college in South Carolina. A third brother sidestepped the family sport and excelled in football instead, where he'd played three years as a reserve tight end for the Atlanta Falcons before banging up his shoulder and going into banking. The youngest brother, who was only a year older than Natalie, had become a sports physical therapist. He was the runt of the bunch at only six foot two and two hundred pounds. They were all large men like their father, who was six foot four with a thick mustache and looked like Tom Selleck. Even at sixty, he looked like he might still be able to play third base for the Cardinals. The farm life had kept him in good shape.

We got out of the car, and relatives immediately swarmed us. Mostly little kids racing up to hug their Aunt Natalie. We walked around the side of the house to the back, where there was a massive deck. I could smell food on a large grill and hear the sound of a football game on an outside TV. I began meeting brothers, youngest to oldest. Roger. Evan. Keith. Gary. Each handshake seemed to squeeze a little harder until my hand was throbbing. I didn't mind. I was dating their baby sister. Then I finally met the patriarch of the family, Thomas Foster. I swear his massive right hand nearly swallowed mine whole.

His eyes were firm. He had not smiled yet. Or let go of my hand.

"Thanks for having me to your home, Mr. Foster," I offered.

"My daughter didn't really give me a choice, son. She insisted that you come."

He stared even harder at me.

"Daddy," Natalie interjected. "Be nice."

Her father slowly smiled at me, let go of my hand.

"Just messing with you, Sam. Welcome to Foster Farms."

The first activity on the weekend agenda was a family football game. Nearly everyone played, except for two of the wives, including Natalie and the kids. I think the two oldest brothers, Gary and Keith, who were on the opposing team along with Natalie, found it an easy opportunity to indoctrinate me officially into the family. Or maybe run me off, because even though it was supposed to be flag football, and we were all wearing the yellow belts with yellow flags, the two brothers' full-on tackles on me were fierce, and I could feel my bones crunching and the bruises adding up. Natalie kept telling them to take it easy, but they just kept crushing me and smiling. I returned every smile—I would never let them know that I thought I might have a cracked rib already. Natalie's father was the QB on my team. The game had gone back and forth for the past hour. We were now down a score on what everyone had deemed the final play of the game. Dinner was ready.

In the huddle, Thomas Foster looked up at me over that thick mustache.

"OK, Callahan. Time to show me if you've really got what it takes to date my daughter."

"Sir?"

"She deserves a winner, son. And we're not winning right now."

"Let's change that."

He liked that answer, grinned. He gathered everyone more tightly together in the huddle, and then he drew out a play in the grass with his thick fingers. The two younger brothers, Roger and Evan, who were on my team, would run a crisscross pattern on the left side of the field. Thomas drew a line with a finger to show that I would come right underneath them. The pass would go to the youngest brother, Roger, who would immediately pitch it back to me as I headed in the opposite direction. We'd try to catch them napping. From there, Thomas said it was up to me to somehow get into the end zone and win the game. *Don't let me down* were his final words to me.

I went to the line of scrimmage, licked my bottom lip, tasted blood on it. One of the eight-year-old boys snapped the ball between his legs to his grandpa. I cut up the field ten yards, then dashed across the middle like Thomas had told me. Keith tried to give me a shoulder to knock me off balance, but I sidestepped him. I was focused. Hell, I wanted to win this game. Find some favor. Natalie's father avoided the rush from the two ten-year-old twin girls, then tossed the football downfield to Roger, who caught it in full stride. Right when Natalie was about to pull Roger's yellow flag off his belt and end the game, Roger flipped the football back to me. I zigzagged around two of the younger boys, spinning furiously so they couldn't grab my flags, and then found myself ten yards from the end zone. But between me and victory were two hulking men. Natalie's oldest brothers. I could hear Natalie's father yelling, "Get in the end zone, son!"

I wanted this so much. I sprinted upfield, juked right, then left, made Keith grasp at air and plant his face in the dirt, then darted around him and ran straight at Gary. I spun when I got to him, but he grabbed my T-shirt collar before I could get free. I drove my legs forward, dragging him, reached for the orange cone of the end zone. My shirt began to shred as Gary's massive hands tried to pull me down from behind. But he was too late. The ball crossed the line before I collapsed onto the grass. The nieces and nephews on my team shouted in joyful celebration and then decided to dog pile on top of me in the end zone. In between tiny arms and legs and laughter, I looked up and could see Natalie's father taunting the two oldest sons with a goofy celebration dance. They did not look happy.

Then I spotted Natalie, smiling at me from across the way.

After dinner, Natalie's father asked if I could help him in the barn. He needed to feed the pigs.

Natalie was leery, but I gave her a look that said everything was cool. No big deal.

I followed his instructions. We grabbed bags of pig feed, filled up some troughs, dragged the hose around to fill up the water, and watched as a half dozen pigs raced out of stables to eat for the night, pig slop and drink flying everywhere—it reminded me of how the large family inside the house had just licked their plates clean. The sun was setting. We quietly hung by the fence for a while, enjoying the breeze if not the pig smell. It was a really nice evening in Missouri. I had to admit I liked life on Foster Farms. And I liked this family.

Thomas was quiet for a long time before he decided to speak.

"My daughter says you haven't had the easiest life," he said.

I shrugged. "No, sir, but I suppose everyone has challenges growing up."

He nodded. "She really likes you, son. I can tell."

"The feeling is mutual. You have an incredible daughter, sir."

"I do. I feel fortunate. When I lost her mom, Natalie was only twelve, and I worried about what it would do to her with no woman in the house. I figured the boys would be OK. I understood them. They were boys like me. But I wasn't sure about Natalie. I mean, she'd always been able to hold her own with her brothers, but she was in a pretty volatile place."

"She turned out pretty tough herself."

He smiled. "You got that right. She's the toughest of them all. And so damn stubborn. She will not back down from anything. Just like her mother."

"I'm sorry for your loss, sir."

He turned to me. "You're the last one who should be saying sorry about someone else losing a family member."

"Well, I still am. From everything Natalie has said, Mrs. Foster was an amazing woman."

He nodded. "Yes, she was. Amazingly tolerant and patient, that's for sure. And she was so passionate with these kids. Especially Natalie."

He stared at me for a second, exhaled slowly. "Son, I want you to know something. I'm sure when I asked you to come out here with me to feed the pigs, that you maybe thought I wanted to warn you, like the stereotypical protective father, to place the fear of God in you about even thinking about hurting my baby girl. But that's not it at all. I want you to know that I see a lot of myself in you. I lost both of my parents when I was just a kid. It was just me and my older brother from early on. We lived with my uncle on the farm, but other than keeping a bed for us and some food in the pantry, he wasn't really around too much. We had to fend for ourselves and become men when we should have still been kids. Now, I'm not comparing it to what you went through, please understand me, but I just want you to know that I can relate in some way, and that I really respect you for what you've made of yourself out of those tough circumstances. It shows me something about your will and your character."

"Thank you, sir. I appreciate that."

"Listen, if you ever need someone to talk with, maybe an old man like me who's been around the block a few times, please don't hesitate to call me. Or, hell, just come stay the weekend. I could use the help. You've got an open bed here, if you need it."

"Thank you, Mr. Foster."

"Call me Tommy, OK?"

"OK."

"We'd better get back inside before those boys of mine eat all of my favorite pie."

He put his hand on my shoulder and held me firmly in place for a second longer. "Oh, and Sam, one more thing. If you do hurt her, I will kill you. You understand?"

He smiled, winked at me.

"Yes, sir."

Natalie flipped a switch in a gray electrical box by the concession stand, and the large overhead lights began to pop up slowly all around the small softball field. Glendale High. Natalie had been a two-time all-state second baseman. Her old bedroom at Foster Farms was still littered with hundreds of trophies and plaques and ribbons of every kind. She'd gotten a scholarship to the University of Missouri to play softball, where she tore her ACL in her right knee her freshman year while turning a double play. She'd rehabilitated well, but at that point had decided to shift her full focus to journalism, something that had clearly paid off. Just last weekend, I'd escorted her to a ceremony at the National Press Club where she received the Mollenhoff Award, given for excellence in investigative reporting. Natalie had won the award for a series of stories that uncovered a rogue crew of DC police officers who'd used their power to rob from several local store owners. Her stories had led to an official FBI investigation that resulted in four critical arrests. She was a rising star.

We crossed through a gate, walked to the middle of the ball field.

"So, this is where the magic happened?" I asked.

"Two straight state championships."

"You're a real badass, you know that?"

"Yes, I know."

"Of course you do. I never did stand a chance that night at the batting cages, did I?"

She grinned. "Never, which was what made it so fun for me."

We sat on the grass near the pitching mound. The night had cooled off some as gray clouds had moved in.

"I really like your family, Natalie."

"Even my brothers?"

I smiled. "Especially your brothers. Even though they almost put me in a full-body cast."

"They like you, too. I can tell. So does my dad, which says a lot."

"Your dad is a good man."

"I'm really glad you came with me."

"Me, too. This has been a good day. I feel like I know you a lot better."

She laughed. "Well, there are many things I wished my brothers wouldn't have shared."

"What? Like how you used to kiss the pigs?"

"Hey, not all the pigs. Only my special pig, Annabelle. I named her after my mother."

"Whatever. Just no pig kissing while we're here, OK?"

She grabbed a lump of dirt, threw it at me. "If you don't shut up, there'll be no kissing of any kind. I can promise you that."

I laughed, grabbed her around the waist, pulled her toward me. "I'll be your pig tonight, babe."

"That's not much of a stretch."

I smiled. We kissed. She pulled away. I could tell she was thinking about something serious.

"What?" I asked.

"I was just thinking about your mom, Sam. Have you ever tried to find her?"

I shook my head, lied. "No. And I don't really care to."

"OK, we just haven't talked much about it. I was just curious, that's all."

I quickly changed the subject. "I have you. That's all I need. And right now, I want to make out with the All-American second baseman on her championship home field."

"Oh, really?"

I pulled her down with me onto the grass. We began to kiss. Then it started to rain. And it gave us very little warning. The beads were heavy and intense from the first drop. We were getting pummeled within a few seconds.

"Are you kidding me?" I said, staring up into a suddenly stormy sky. "Talk about ruining a good moment."

I started to get up, but Natalie pulled me right back down to her on the grass. "Hey, a little water never hurt anyone, right?"

SEVENTEEN

Sunday, 5:02 a.m.
Austin, Texas
One day, eighteen hours, fifty-eight minutes till Election Day

The Austin airport was nearly empty at five in the morning.

I didn't like this, as it made me feel even more vulnerable, more exposed, more likely to be spotted. It felt like every set of eyes was on me, both travelers and airport employees, even though my hair was now a different color, my pair of round glasses was fake, and I wore a black-knit ski cap. I wished I were stuck in a thick pack of travelers, but I had to get on the first flight out to DC. I couldn't delay until midmorning when there would be thousands more people in the airport. Every minute mattered. I had to take risks, and this was one I was willing to take. Even if I felt like I had a target on my back.

There were airport-security guys every hundred feet. Every time one of the men lifted a walkie-talkie to his mouth as I walked past, I had to force myself to walk evenly, not stare or stop, and certainly not take off running. I decided I'd rather jack cars for future travel than skirt through airports, if I had the choice. Unfortunately, I didn't have time for a cross-country drive right now.

I had a black backpack with all my current worldly belongings hanging over my shoulder. Tablet, a change of clothes, all my toiletries. Even though there was a chill in the airport, I started to sweat heavily as I handed my new driver's license to the security guard behind his podium, along with the airline ticket. I tried to appear confident, casual, at ease. I was simply Dobbs Howard. I'd decided that Dobbs was a middle-school soccer coach, if anyone asked. Inside my chest, my heart was sprinting the hundred-meter dash.

The security man reminded me of Peter Falk from the old *Columbo* TV series. I used to watch episodes while studying in my dorm room at CU late at night. His small eyes bounced slowly back and forth behind his eyeglasses among my driver's license, my airline ticket, and my face. He was taking three times as long with me as the businessman in front of me who'd just passed through easily. *Come on, man.* I swallowed, then reminded myself not to swallow.

Finally, Columbo stamped my boarding pass and sent me through to the next step. I exhaled. My backpack made it through the conveyer-belt scanner. I stood in the tube with my arms above my head, and then I was finally released into the secure inner sanctum of the airport. I'd passed the first hurdle of my journey.

From there, I found my way to the very back of an empty gate, away from everyone else, and sat facing an opposite direction, waiting until the very last minute to board my United flight out of Austin. I hopped on during the final boarding call, head tucked low, eyes on my shoes. The plane was full, and I was near the back. An aisle seat. The only one I could get last minute. A plane stuffed with mostly businessmen and women, according to their travel garb, headed to the nation's capital. I was thankful to feel the airplane lift up off the runway and into the air without any feds suddenly rushing on board, yanking me off, and dragging me to a dark holding room. I tried to close my eyes, relax. I pretended to sleep for the first thirty minutes.

The airplane leveled off at thirty thousand feet, and the flight attendant began serving drinks. I had coffee, black. So did my travelmate, an older redheaded man in a dark suit, who tried to strike up a conversation about it. He couldn't stand the flavored coffees that everyone else had to have at Starbucks. Just give it to him black. Like a real man. Right? I did my best to be polite, nodded in agreement. I said very little. He seemed to catch the hint. I was not an airplane talker. So he took out his copy of the *Austin American-Statesman*, unfolded it. I cursed under my breath. Of course. A photo of me was on the bottom-right corner of the front page. A law-school yearbook photo, along with a story of the manhunt.

DC Law Student Suspected of Murder, FBI Involved

I wondered if the man would put it together. I was wearing glasses and the black-knit cap, but my face was the same. It wouldn't take more than a few seconds of close comparison to notice a strong resemblance. His eyes seemed to be on the top article, about the current conflict between Russia and Ukraine. The middle article was about the current state of pivotal national-election races, including a graph showing that McCallister's lead over Mitchell in Texas had grown to five points. We were now less than two days from Election Day. How long would these articles hold his attention before reaching my photo?

I had to act. The way I figured, I had several options. Walk to the front, pull the emergency-exit door, and take a dive out. Float off and really end this thing altogether. Or option B, pretend to puke in the airplane restroom for the next two hours, which would undoubtedly draw even more attention. Or the most viable option, get him talking. I'd learned early on that every man over sixty has a trigger point. A button you could push to get them going. Men at that age wanted to feel like their lives had meaning. That they'd invested in something worthwhile, something worth sharing with younger guys like me. My go-to triggers were usually military service, career, or family. I could usually find that button within a few seconds. My eyes did a quick scan. Dark suit. He was traveling on business, not vacation. No wedding ring. Divorced? Widowed? Black briefcase on the floor in front of him. Manila folder he'd stuck in the seat pocket with paperwork in it. I spotted the words *MBA Conference* scribbled at the top. Mortgage Bankers Association. Bingo. My entry point.

"You think the Fed is going to adjust the interest rates again?" I asked.

The man looked over from behind the newspaper. "Sorry?"

"I saw the folder in front of you. You work in banking?"

He peered around the paper at the folder. "Oh, yes, I do. Headed up to a conference right now. You asking about interest rates?"

"Yeah, I was curious if you thought the Fed was going to drop the rates again. I've been thinking of purchasing a condo, my first mortgage. Not sure about the timing."

And that's all it took, really. The newspaper was quickly folded, stuffed in the seat back, and away we went, as the banker began rattling off every bit of information and advice he'd stuffed up in his boring old brain. I kept him blabbing on for the next thirty minutes. It was painful, but I could do this for the next two hours, if necessary. Fortunately, he eventually needed to use the bathroom.

I let him out, watched him amble up the aisle, then quickly reached for the newspaper. I took a glance to my left at the two men sitting across from us. One man had his eyes closed. The other had on reading glasses and was lost in his Kindle. Rather than ditch the newspaper altogether, which could open myself up for questioning in some way, I simply took a little bit of my coffee, and let it drip across the photo of me on the *Stateman*'s front page. Within seconds, the picture blurred as the small puddle soaked into the thin newsprint. When I was certain there was no chance of recognition, I folded the paper and returned it to the seat back.

And then I exhaled deeply for the first time in thirty minutes.

How many other newspapers were currently on the airplane? How many pictures of me? I would have to avoid all eye contact and all conversations, basically any interaction with anyone for the next two hours. I pretended to be asleep again, thought about my mom. I felt the weight of our journey together in that moment—the ups, the downs, the cancer—and it only made me want to get to her quicker.

SAM, AGE TWENTY-FOUR

Washington, DC

The argument started at dinner and then carried over to her place afterward. Natalie had found an e-mail I'd printed out from Billy Dixon, the private investigator from back in Denver who'd found my mother two years ago. I'd carelessly left it out with my stack of schoolwork on top of her kitchen table. After burning the file and starting my new life in DC, I thought the desire to know my mom would fade and eventually die. I was wrong. The deep longing to connect with her in some way continued to haunt me. So I'd finally contacted Billy and simply asked him to keep me posted every few months or so about my mother's whereabouts and how she was doing. Natalie was pissed that I'd lied to her. She finally let it go after I apologized profusely, but she couldn't understand why I'd go through all the effort to find her and then not at least meet her. What was the point? Around and around we went on it. I tossed my jacket over the chair in the living room, dropped onto the sofa in frustration.

"You don't understand, Natalie," I said. "You can never understand."

"You're right. I can't, not fully. My parents didn't abandon me, but I understand loss, Sam. I understand the pain and anger. Don't forget that my mom died when I was twelve years old. Unlike you, I can never go see her again. So, don't lecture me, OK?"

I rubbed my face with both hands. "I know. I'm sorry."

She sat close to me, calmed down. "Look, I'm not saying you have to go build a relationship with your mom. Not at all. I understand that's really hard. But I just think it could do you a lot of good to meet her. Maybe hear what she has to say. It might put some things in better perspective for you. There are two sides to every story. Maybe you don't know everything."

"I don't care about her side. In my mind, there is nothing that she could say to me that would justify what she did. Don't you get that?"

Natalie grabbed my hand. I hated it when she touched me during an argument. It always dropped my defenses and left me powerless. "Yes, I get that's how you *feel*. That's how I felt for a long time after my mom died. Angry at her for leaving me, even if it was a car wreck. Angry at God for taking her away. Angry at my dad for letting her drive during an ice storm. Angry at everyone. But eventually, I had to deal with it to move on. I'm not saying it's easy. In fact, it may be the hardest thing you ever have to do in your life. I wasted a lot of teenage years being angry. It impacts everything. The hate will never go away on its own. It will stay there forever like a heavy anchor holding you back."

"Thanks, Dr. Phil."

"Don't make me slug you."

"I think I'm doing OK."

"Yeah, sure. Is that all you want for your life? To just do OK? I want more for you. I want more for us. I know you used that pain and hate for a lot of years to survive on the streets. It was the fuel you needed. I can't blame you for that. But you're not on the streets anymore. You're set to graduate from one of the most prestigious law schools in the country. You're doing really well, making a new life for yourself, and you've even got this superhot girlfriend."

She smiled. I shook my head at her.

She continued. "I'm just saying that you're not a survivor anymore. You've survived and moved on. Staying angry just seems pointless to me. And honestly, really stupid."

"I wish you'd tell me how you really feel. Stop holding back."

She gave me a small smile, shrugged. "I'm a straight shooter."

"Yes, one of many things I like about you." I stood, paced around the room. I hated that she was right. Finally, I stopped and turned to Natalie. "You're not going to let this go, are you?"

"Never." She smelled victory. "I'll go with you, Sam, OK?"

For some reason, that was all it took. "OK."

Billy said my mom was currently residing in a state-run rehab center. She was dealing with a variety of drug addictions, but she was actually twenty-nine days sober when we decided to fly down to Houston. I gave no warning to anyone at the rehab center, and I did not contact my mom in advance. I still didn't know if I would actually go through with it. Natalie had been convincing enough to get me to take this next monstrous step. She stayed back at the hotel while I took a cab over to the rehab center on a Saturday morning. It was a government-looking building in the middle of a seedy neighborhood.

I did not want to officially check in through front security, like everyone else, and establish any identification just yet. So, instead I followed a nurse in through a back entrance, just caught the automatic door with the toe of my shoe before it shut behind her. I cruised through a small kitchen like I belonged there and entered a sterile hallway with private rooms on both sides. At the first isolated nurses' station with a computer, I stopped and told the nurse that Dr. Scoggins was asking for nursing assistance around the corner. The nurse quickly jumped up and headed in that direction. I'd spotted the doctor's name on a marker board with the rotation schedule behind her station.

I slid into the chair behind the computer, quickly typed in the name Nancy Weber. According to the investigator, my mom had gone from Nancy Callahan to Nancy Pederson to Nancy Weber over the years. Her digital file filled the computer screen. I found the Print button and then snagged the pages from a printer beside the desk.

I hid with the paperwork inside a janitor's closet, with the lights off and the door wedged shut with a rolling cart. I sat on a chair and used my phone as a flashlight to read about my mom for the very first time. After so many years, it felt surreal. The front-facing photo of my mom on the first page matched the images the investigator had given me recently. Brunette with gray strands. Pale skin. No makeup. Hollow cheeks. Not much life in her face. She looked very sad. The file said she was forty-one, but she looked older than fifty. I did some quick math. That meant she'd been pregnant with me when she was fifteen. She was just a kid. She'd been in this same rehab center three times but had never lasted more than two weeks, so I gave her some credit for making it almost a month this time around. The file said she was addicted to a mix of prescription drugs that included painkillers, stimulants, and depressants. But according to the notes, they were very encouraged by her progress.

I turned a page, shifted to her counseling notes. Started to read with a lump in my throat. My mother was raised without a father by a drug-addicted mother who'd abandoned her in her early teens and moved to California. She never heard from her mother again. She'd never met her father. There were no siblings that she knew about. She'd lived on and off the streets in Sun Valley, the poorest neighborhood in Denver.

She hooked up with a drug dealer when she was fourteen, who took care of her for a little while, provided food and shelter in exchange for sex. When she got pregnant, he threatened her at gunpoint, demanding she have an abortion. She promised him she would and then changed her mind and hid from him for the rest of the pregnancy. While there was no likely way she could care for a baby by herself, she sure as hell was going to try. She felt this was her one chance to do something worthwhile in life. She wanted someone who would love her back unconditionally.

My name was finally mentioned in the file. Samuel Weldon Callahan. I was apparently named after my grandfather.

I shook my head, forced back my first tear.

The file said I was born in a bathtub at the home of a midwife who'd taken an interest in my mother at some point during her pregnancy. We lived with the midwife for the first nine months of my life, until the midwife got really sick and had to move to Chicago to live with one of her kids. At that point, we were on our own again. My mother found an abandoned dry cleaner's van on a lot near Mile High Stadium, and we slept there most nights. The file said she begged for work, begged for help, sold her body for money, but she was determined. With no family support, it was very difficult. We barely made it most days. I would get some baby formula while she starved herself nearly to death. Then winter hit again, and the bottom fell out. It got to minus ten at night for seven consecutive days. And with no heat in the van, blankets alone would not protect a baby who wasn't even a year old yet. My mom told the counselor she dropped me at the steps of Saint Luke's Medical Center on my birthday, begged for help for her child, whom she thought might die that night. When they took me away, she cried her eyes out. She decided it wasn't right for her to care for me anymore. I was better off without her. She'd almost killed me that night.

So, she walked away and never looked back.

I continued to skim the file. She had not had much opportunity to look back. She immediately hitchhiked to Fort Worth and tried to start her life over. She met a truck driver when she was seventeen, a man twenty years older, someone who seemed kind and said the right things. They got married. Then he began beating her regularly. She took it for three years before leaving in the middle of the night, changing her name, and settling in Baton Rouge. There had been more tumultuous relationships, more drugs, more abuse, more running. New Orleans. Biloxi. Birmingham. Pensacola. Tampa. Shreveport. Beaumont. Houston.

I was bawling like a child when I finished the file.

I folded the paperwork, stuffed it in my back pocket, and left the closet.

I found her in a rec room a few minutes later. She was watching TV by herself in the corner. Some old game show. I stared at her through a window for ten minutes, still wondering if I wanted to open up this wound. It was painful, as Natalie had said. She compared it to having to break my own arm again, after it had been shattered and healed incorrectly, so that a doctor could reset it properly and it could heal the right way. I knew Natalie was right. I had to break my own heart wide open if I ever wanted full use of it. The thought scared the hell out of me.

She wore pale-green scrubs like all the other patients, but she looked much better than the photo in her file. She'd put on some much-needed weight the past month, and there was more color in her cheeks.

I sucked it up, pushed through the rec-room door. I decided to walk right over before I lost my nerve and it all slipped away again. She looked up at me without any recognition. The first things I noticed up close were her eyes. They were my eyes. As blue as the sky. Then I noticed the simple small tattoo on the back of her left wrist. *SAMUEL*. The name facing up to her.

She didn't say anything. I didn't say anything. She seemed confused. "Ma'am, my name is Sam Callahan. I'm your son."

She cried for nearly ten minutes. In between breaths, she just kept quietly repeating, "My Samuel. I can't believe it." There were no hugs, but she took my hand in hers, just held it for a second. It took every fiber of my strength not to join her in crying. I wouldn't let her have that yet. Maybe ever. She asked if we could go for a walk, that she needed a cigarette. We went out the back to an enclosed garden area. Several other patients were out there smoking. She asked how I found her, so I told her, but I left out a lot of details. She recounted our story—the same story I'd read in the file. I gave her bits and pieces of my life up to that point. She kept saying how sorry she was at every lull in the conversation, of which there were many. I resisted the urge to ask her why she'd never come to look for me. I held a lot back. I didn't trust her. She promised she was done with the drugs. They had taken decades from her life. I knew every drug addict says that and usually falls back into that life eventually.

I drifted in and out of acting soft and then hard, depending on the moment. I just couldn't help myself. The emotions were overwhelming. One moment, I wanted to cry and wrap my arms around her. The next moment, I wanted to curse her out, run away, and never look back, like she had. She kept grabbing my hand, wanting to hold it. I kept politely pulling it away from her. A nurse came out looking for her, said it was time for her group session.

I wasn't sure what was next. I felt numb.

"Will you come see me again, Samuel?" she asked.

I shrugged. "I'm supposed to fly back to DC tomorrow."

She nodded. "Can we keep in touch?"

My moment of truth. I could say no, and it would be OK. I would have fulfilled what Natalie wanted me to do. I could bury this and not have to deal with it anymore. But my heart wouldn't let me.

"I'll leave my phone number and e-mail."

She grabbed my hand again. This time, I let her hold it for a few seconds.

Thirty minutes later, I was back in my hotel room with Natalie.

I didn't have to say much. The tears came quickly. I couldn't help it. I'd been holding them back. They were thick and filled with such deep and conflicting emotions. Natalie didn't say anything. She just let me cry, wrapped in her arms. She cried along with me. We held each other without a word for a really long time.

SAM, AGE TWENTY-FOUR

Washington, DC

The call came on a Tuesday, right before my Constitutional Law class.

Over the past two months, my mom exited the rehab program and managed to stay sober while finding some steady work as an administrative assistant at a small construction company. Natalie and I had visited her a second time while we were still in Houston. My mother even took the Greyhound up to see me the previous weekend—she was scared of flying. It was really rocky at different points. Natalie was a tremendous buffer to have around. She knew how to say the right things, keep conversation moving, and just play nice. I did not. I was still so angry, so I said some things at times that I shouldn't have. My mom always took it in stride. Like it or not, we were each other's only family. So we were desperately trying to persevere through these early days of our new relationship.

She called me several times a week. I returned most of the calls.

I don't know why I answered this one. I was already really late for class. My mom had not been feeling well the past month. She couldn't shake it, so she'd gotten some tests done. I think that thought had stuck in the back of my head and compelled me to answer.

"Hey, Mom," I said. I'd started calling her that this past weekend. It was a breakthrough for me. For us. "Listen, I'm already late for class. Can I call you back later?"

"It's cancer, Samuel."

Her words struck me like a strong fist to the gut.

"What . . . what do you mean?"

"The tests came back today. Just met with the doctor. He called it stage-three CLL, chronic lymphocytic leukemia."

I slowly sat on the sofa in my apartment, my legs weak. *Cancer?*

"You there?" she asked.

"Yeah, I'm here."

"Now, I don't want you to worry about me, OK?" she continued. "I'm going to be just fine. I can handle this. I just thought you should know, that's all."

"OK . . . thanks." It's all I could say. The wind had been sucked out of me.

"Get to your class now. I'll call you later."

She hung up. I didn't move. I was numb.

Three weeks later, I was packing up a small U-Haul right outside her apartment in Houston. After her diagnosis, I had wrestled with what to do for a week. I hadn't asked for this. I was so pissed at God again. Give me back my mom only to take her away again? Really? It felt like too much on top of everything else. I so desperately wanted to cut the cord, walk away, put the wall back up, and just move on with my life. But I couldn't do it. And Natalie wouldn't let me, either. So, I finally asked my mom to move to DC to get her treatment near me so I could better help care for her. She stubbornly refused for more than a week. She said she could take care of her own damn self, that she didn't need a handout, or for me or anyone else to feel sorry for her. I swear I could hear my own voice in hers. Both of us stubborn as hell.

When her health worsened suddenly, I told her I was coming down to drag her back to DC with me, and she finally relented.

I shut the back of the U-Haul, sealed the door tight.

"That everything?" I asked her.

She nodded. "That's it. Let's get on with this."

She wore a blue handkerchief over her head, coveralls, and she was sweating profusely. I kept telling her to take it easy, to rest, but she kept pushing back. It was a constant wrestling match. We'd given away most of her cheap old furniture to her neighbors. We were only taking a bed, a dresser, her favorite recliner, and boxes of her personal belongings. That's all that could fit into her room at the new medical facility. She said good-bye to an old neighbor lady, then we climbed into the U-Haul together. I started up the engine, my mom in the passenger seat next to me. I did not have Natalie in between us as my buffer. She was on a deadline for a big story, plus she thought it might do me some good to have one-on-one time with my mother.

We had a twenty-hour road trip ahead of us.

I shook my head, said a prayer, and put the truck into drive.

The conversation came in awkward spurts. Like me, my mother wasn't a talker. She was the strong, silent type and had no problem sitting quietly and staring out the window, so I did my best to make small talk. Within an hour, we'd already covered all the important topics. *Favorite food? Favorite movie? Favorite actor? Actress? Favorite book? Favorite sports?*

When I found out she liked Bruce Springsteen, like me, I plugged my phone into the stereo, and we listened to his *Wrecking Ball* album. That bought us an hour of comfortable silence as the U-Haul rumbled on through Louisiana, but it eventually played out.

More silence. More short, random conversations.

Somewhere near Lake Charles, she asked, "You going to marry Natalie?"

It caught me by surprise. "I don't know."

"You're a fool if you don't, Samuel."

"Thanks. Are you the expert on marriage?"

It was an unnecessary jab, I knew it, but I often found myself saying these things with her to keep a certain protective barrier between us. To let her know that while I was willing to do this whole mother-son deal, I was still pissed at her. She always rolled with it. I don't think there was anything I could say that would get a rise out of her. I'd tried to push her buttons and start fights, but she never really took the bait. Kind of pissed me off. I wanted to fight with her.

"No, I'm not," she admitted. "But I could give you a very long list of what not to look for in marriage, that's for sure. That girl comes nowhere close to that list. She's special."

"I agree."

"So, don't screw it up!"

"Can't make any promises. I think screwing up is in my family's genes."

Another jab. And down the road we went.

We ate dinner at Half Shell Oyster House in Biloxi. The gulf was a block away.

Mom said she loved fried oysters. I was happy to see her eating, as she hadn't touched much food at all since I'd been with her the past two days. She said the cancer was stealing her appetite. Nothing ever sounded good. I could tell she'd lost quite a bit of weight already. It pained me to think it would only get worse.

I ate a bowl of gumbo. The restaurant was half-full on a weeknight.

"When did you get the tattoo?" I asked her.

She looked down at her wrist, at my name, kept chewing.

"A week after I left Denver."

"Why?"

"What kind of stupid question is that?"

"A simple one. Great, you got that tattoo, but you never came back to look for me?"

"I thought about it every single day since the day I left you."

"So, why didn't you?"

She wiped her hands with a napkin, took a long moment. "I haven't been in a good place in more than twenty years. It's always been one step forward, two steps back. Or three or four steps back. Half-stoned most of the time. Going back never felt like the right thing to do. I always figured you were better off without a failure like me."

"I wasn't better off."

"I didn't know that, Samuel. I'm sorry. And I was too afraid to ever find out."

We were quiet for a moment.

Then she said, "I need a cigarette."

We slept in separate cheap motel rooms. Hit the road again before daybreak.

We passed through Alabama and then Tennessee. My mom told me a story about visiting Knoxville once, as a kid, during one of her mother's good spells. She said they went out to Dollywood—Dolly Parton's amusement park—and that she and her younger sister had a blast riding roller coasters and eating corn dogs and cotton candy all day. One of the few bright spots of her entire youth. She'd never forget it. She actually had a smile on her face.

"I didn't know you had a sister, Mom," I said.

The smile disappeared. "She drowned in the river when I was ten."

"I'm sorry."

A deep sigh. "I think that was the last straw for my mother. She gave up after that, gave in to the demons. She went completely off the deep end. Fell deeper into depression and drugs and never recovered. She took off forever when I was thirteen."

"At least you got thirteen years," I jabbed.

"That's true."

"You haven't seen her or spoken to her since?"

"Only once, on the phone. Very briefly."

"What happened?"

"I found her in Las Vegas about seven years ago. It wasn't too hard. She hadn't changed her name or anything. I got her on the phone. But when I told her who I was, she just sat there in silence. Never said a word. And then she hung up on me."

I actually felt bad for my mom. "There's still time, I guess."

My mother shook her head. "She died five years ago. Drug overdose."

"How do you know?"

"A friend of hers mailed me a package with a note. It had a photo of me, my mom, and my sister together when I was a kid. The friend said my mom always kept it on her mirror. She didn't talk a whole lot about it, but the friend thought I should have it, and thought I should know what happened to her."

I didn't know what to say, so I just kept my mouth shut. I decided right then and there that I needed to back off a little. Cut my mom just a little slack. Stop living in my own pity party. It wasn't doing anyone any good.

It was a pretty quiet ride the rest of the way to DC.

SAM, AGE TWENTY-FOUR

Washington, DC

I met with the director at Brookwood Cancer Center in his private, spacious office. He'd called me with high urgency an hour ago. My mom had been a resident at Brookwood for the past two weeks. It was our second facility during her first month in DC. We lasted only two weeks at the first one. My mom bit a nurse on the arm her first week and called her the vilest of names. She swore to me that the nurse was rude, disrespectful, and intentionally trying to hurt her. When it happened again a week later, and the same nurse threatened to file charges against the center, the director asked us to find another facility to receive our care. So we did. And now, I was being called into the principal's office because my mom had supposedly acted out again.

Director Fields was a nice middle-aged guy with a peaceful demeanor. He asked me to have a seat across the desk from him.

"We have an issue, Mr. Callahan," he began.

"I sort of figured that. What did she do? Was it biting?"

He looked at me funny. I had not mentioned anything about her biting or us getting kicked out of another facility before coming over to Brookwood.

"No, I'm afraid it's theft. Your mother stole a wallet in the cafeteria today."

I was stunned. "What? No way. Are you sure?"

"Yes, quite sure. This isn't the first time, I'm afraid. We didn't know it was your mother until we had a second occurrence this morning. That's when we went back to look at the security video."

He pointed toward a flat screen on his wall to my right, raised a remote control. The TV flashed on, and there was security footage of my mother eating in the cafeteria. Another lady of similar age sat a few feet down from her at one of the long tables and placed her wallet on the table next to her tray. My mom began making small talk with her and then scooted over to join her. I couldn't believe what I was watching. My mom was a con. Like me. In the middle of conversation, my mom did a shift of the hands, a distraction technique, and scooped the wallet off the tabletop in one smooth motion. Then she politely said good-bye to the lady and was out of the screenshot a second later. The wallet was no longer sitting there.

"Here's the other incident from three days ago," said Fields.

The screen went to more security footage. This time they were back in the cafeteria, but it looked like they were playing bingo. Fields paused the screen, pointed.

"Watch this man right here. He's wearing a gold-and-diamond watch on his left wrist."

The man refilled his cup from a water fountain, took a swig, and then he began to walk back to one of the tables. Fields paused the TV again.

"This is your mother."

I scooted to the edge of my seat. Fields hit Play. I watched as my mom walked past the man with the watch, gave a slight accidental bump, a quick one-hand-on-shoulder apology, the other hand down low, and then they separated. The watch was clearly gone from the man's wrist. I sighed, shook my head.

"Needless to say, Mr. Callahan, we frown on theft here."

"I understand."

In that moment, I had conflicting thoughts. I was so pissed at my mom. I knew we were goners from this place. She was going to die from the cancer while living in my efficiency apartment.

But I have to say, I was also very impressed with her skill set.

She was smooth as silk. Now I knew where I got it.

I found her in her private room, folding stacks of her clothes on her bed. Obviously anticipating moving out of this place. The small TV in the corner was on *Family Feud*.

She looked up at me, frowned. "They kicking me out?"

I nodded, crossed my arms. "Yes. We're no longer welcome here."

She cursed, kept folding. "This place was lame, anyway. We can do better."

"Why, Mom? Why did you do it? Do you need extra money for something?"

"No, I guess I was just bored."

"You're kidding."

She seemed defensive. "All anyone does in this place is sit around and wait to die. The staff acts like we're already dead. It's depressing as hell. Well, you know what? I'm not going to do that. I'm not going to stop living while this cancer tries to eat up my body. I want to feel alive for as long as possible."

I sighed. "I really appreciate that, Mom. But you think perhaps we can find another way to feel alive?"

"Like what? Skydiving? Drag racing?" She smiled.

I shook my head. "We'll figure something out."

I found her suitcase in the closet, started helping her stuff her clothes into it. We had to be out by the end of the day.

She finally said, "I really am sorry, Samuel. I know I screwed up. I know I'm making this hard on you. I'm a mess. I wouldn't blame you for sending me back to Houston."

"I'm not sending you back anywhere."

"Well, I'll behave, I swear. The third time's a charm, right?"

We exchanged a quick smile.

"Natalie said you can stay at her place tonight while we work on securing another facility tomorrow. But I'm going to hide her purse."

"She is so sweet. Have I told you to marry her yet?"

"Only two hundred times."

"Well, then, you know I mean it."

"Yes, ma'am."

We finished packing her suitcase. I looked around. I'd have to hire yet another moving crew to come get her furniture by tomorrow. I needed a fourth or fifth part-time job.

"Mom, I have to ask you something. Where did you learn to steal like that?"

"What do you mean?"

"You know what I mean. That was professional."

She laughed. "My Uncle Judd. He was an incredible pickpocket. Taught me some cool tricks the one summer he was around. I think I was six or seven. He used to tell my mom he was taking me to the park, but we'd always go down to the dog track instead. He'd send me into the crowds, and I'd come back with pockets full of cash. It was fun."

"Nice. Where is Uncle Judd now?"

"Oh, he died in prison a long time ago."

"Of course."

EIGHTEEN

Sunday, 10:17 a.m.
Washington, DC
One day, thirteen hours, forty-three minutes till Election Day

I'd never been more grateful to walk off an airplane. I practically sprinted.

Dulles International Airport was buzzing, as usual. I kept my head tucked low, focused on the airport carpet in front of me, navigated the terminal, and finally found the outside exit, where I grabbed a waiting cab. I hopped in the back, gave my driver the address for Angel Cancer Care in Bethesda, a thirty-mile ride, and sank deeper into the cracked vinyl seat as the cab pulled away. I had made it to DC. Considering the circumstances, it was quite the feat, even for me.

But I still had a long way to go.

I'd developed a plan to see my mom. There was a young custodian, a friendly black kid named Cedric, a freshman at Howard University. He took really good care of my mom's space. He was a hard worker, polite, and we'd bonded because he was a foster-care survivor who'd done well, like me—well, before I was a murder suspect on the run from the FBI. Through one of my law professors at Georgetown, I had connected Cedric with the vice principal at Walt Whitman High in Bethesda in a mentoring-type role. Cedric was grateful and learning a lot.

I could leverage that now. But he was such a good kid. Could I trust him not to call the police immediately?

Angel Cancer Care was a cluster of three redbrick buildings with about fifteen private rooms in each, nothing fancy. The one-story buildings were old, built in the fifties. The grounds were drab with little landscaping, the decor was dreary, and the carpets were tattered. The staff, though, was friendly and caring, and most important, it was the only care facility left as an option for us. We had to make it work.

The cab dropped me off on the corner. I studied the surroundings for several minutes and wondered who else was out there monitoring the property. I noticed no obvious police cars out front, no black government sedans with tinted windows, no random men in sunglasses and trench coats. Who had found my mom so quickly? My mom had a different last name from me. I didn't talk about her with my friends. There was very little to connect us from my past. Although I did pay the facility bills out of my personal bank account.

I tugged the hood from my long-sleeved blue sweatshirt up over my head and covered my new short blond hair. DC was a crisp forty-five degrees with some rain mist. Miserable weather, really. The leaves were starting to fall. The city was quickly headed toward the harsh bite of winter that everyone around these parts complained about so much. Being from Denver, the cold didn't really bother me, but I could do without the rain.

To be cautious, I took a stroll around the block. The center was at the edge of a nice neighborhood. Most of the block was old, two-story, Federal-style homes. My mom and I liked to walk the neighborhood when she felt strong enough, especially the past few months as the leaves had turned, showcasing their beautiful fall colors. It was a Norman

Rockwell painting down every street. She had not felt strong enough the week before I left on my tracker assignment. I was concerned about her heading downhill really fast. Cancer can be so brutal, giving you hope one moment, then cruelly ripping it away the next. But my mom was a fighter. She never felt sorry for herself in spite of her difficult life.

When I could find no sign of anyone monitoring the facility, I approached the property from the back, where a small parking lot held a half dozen employee cars. I was thankful to find Cedric's old maroon Pontiac Sunfire in one of the spots, the Howard University sticker on the front windshield. He was on duty, as expected. Cedric normally worked the morning shift on weekends, from five to noon. I didn't need him to be out sick today. As custodian, Cedric was frequently taking the trash out back to the only large metal dumpster located near the employee parking lot. I hovered around it for about twenty minutes before Cedric made an appearance. He had a shiny shaved head, an athletic build at about my height with a thousand-watt smile, and wore the standard dark-gray medical scrubs. The kid always seemed to be in a good mood. He opened the back door of the middle building and pushed his yellow custodial cart out. His headphones were in his ears, and his head was bopping up and down. He rolled the cart over to the metal dumpster and began tossing in trash bags.

I stepped out from behind the dumpster. It did not startle him. He was a tough kid from the streets. I doubted much startled him. He did pause, though, and stare at me for a moment. I pulled the hood down off my head. Now he recognized me, and he popped out his headphones. I wondered if Cedric paid attention to the news. Would he recognize that he was standing five feet from a Most Wanted man? If he did, he sure didn't seem to be overly concerned about it.

"Nice hair, Sam."

"Thanks. I need to talk to you."

He tossed another bag in the dumpster. "We're talking, aren't we?"

"I need some help."

"Yes, you do. Your mom is worried about you."

"You talked to my mom?"

"Sure, first thing this morning."

"I'm innocent."

"OK, cool. I'm down with that. Unlike most people in this country, I still believe in innocent until proven guilty."

"That's good to hear."

Another bag tossed into the dumpster. "What do you need?"

"I need to see her, my mom. But I obviously can't walk straight into her room. I'm not sure who to trust right now."

"And you want me to go get her? Bring her out here to you?"

"Yes."

He pressed his lips together, considered it. Cedric shrugged. "Sure, I can do that. No harm there."

"And, Cedric, you can't tell anyone I'm out here."

"No worries, Sam the man."

I waited fifteen long, excruciating minutes. I began to wonder if I was wrong about Cedric, that he couldn't be trusted. Would the police be pulling up at any moment? The feds? What was taking so long? My mom moved a lot slower these days, but not that slow. Especially if she heard I was waiting for her outside the building.

He finally reappeared from the same back door. My mom wasn't with him. There were serious lines in the kid's forehead, which of course made me concerned. I stepped out from behind the dumpster again.

"What's wrong?" I asked.

He shook his head. "She's not here."

"What do you mean? Where is she?"

"I don't know. She was checked out."

My heart started pounding. My mind began to spin through dramatic scenarios. "Wait . . . checked out by whom?" Only family was allowed to check out a resident of the facility.

"I knew you'd ask, man, so I checked with Claudette, at the front desk. The paperwork has the name Larry Manor. Under family relationship, it states 'uncle.' Your mom signed the release form herself. It all seems very legit."

"When?"

"This morning."

I was in a near panic, barely able to breathe. My mom did not have an Uncle Larry. I was the only living family member I knew about— unless she'd kept something from me. I'd never heard the name. So, who was this man? And why would my mom sign out to go with him? Did she go voluntarily? Had someone stuck a gun in her back and forced her out the front door? Cedric could read the fear in my face. He tried to reassure me.

"I asked around, Sam. I think it's cool. Janice met him, too, said he was a real nice older man, very polite, very pleasant. She said your mom seemed totally comfortable with him. Nothing strange about any of it. The man had all the proper identification and paperwork. It seems solid."

My eyes flashed open. "This man . . . he have a gray beard?"

Cedric's eyes narrowed. "Yes. That's how Janice described him. Gray beard, dark suit."

My throat tightened. I sank down to my knees. The world was spinning. I couldn't even respond. My mind was reeling. I didn't understand. I'd taken the first flight out of Austin. There were no other earlier departures, not even in neighboring cities like San Antonio, Dallas, or Houston. I checked them all. I would have flown out from anywhere. The gray-bearded man had been in Texas with me last night before midnight. Ten hours ago. How did he get back to DC before me? He couldn't have driven. Impossible. The only explanation was a private plane. He must have access to some serious financial resources, or at least someone did. Someone who had kept me alive last night but who had now taken my mom. The same man who'd killed a guy right in front of me last night probably had a gun pointed at my mom right now. A professional who knew how to kill. They'd taken her because of me. Because I'd accepted this job and responded to that damn text.

For all I knew, my mom could already be dead right now. Because of me.

Cedric was asking if I was OK, his hand on my shoulder, but I couldn't respond.

I was numb. I couldn't breathe. I couldn't think.

They had my mom, which meant they had me.

I had to find Natalie.

NINETEEN

Sunday, 11:02 a.m.
Washington, DC
One day, twelve hours, fifty-eight minutes till Election Day

Natalie Foster's daily routine never changed. She was always working. The news didn't pause for the weekend. She was up early and at the office before sunrise, writing, researching, making calls, then breakfast meetings with sources, leads, and players in the game. She'd head back to the office to write some more, then quickly change before lunch into a jogging outfit for a four-mile loop around the National Mall. After showering and changing at the gym, she would stop at the smoothie shop for lunch, then make her way back to *PowerPlay*'s offices four blocks from the White House. I'd run with her several times. It always turned into some kind of competition, of course. Everything did with her. Usually a dead sprint up the massive steps of the Lincoln Memorial, Rocky Balboa–style, and into the lap of Abraham Lincoln, where we collapsed and rested.

It was a depressing gray day in DC. The mist had not let up. There was a numb panic inside me. I had no idea where my mom was or if she was even still alive. I would find her, no matter what it took, even if it meant giving up my own life to do it. I desperately hoped Natalie would be willing to help.

I was standing behind a thick column next to the massive monument to the sixteenth president of the United States. Even with the nasty weather, there were still packs of tourists out, all in their raincoats, holding umbrellas, phones, cameras snapping. Only the committed runners were still out on the lawn in this weather and on the sidewalks around the Reflecting Pool. Natalie was a committed runner. A few sprinkles and some puddles wouldn't stop her from her routine.

She arrived on schedule, bounding up the massive steps, under the protective covering of the giant building in front of Abraham Lincoln. She looked fantastic. I expected nothing less. She wore black running pants, pink Nikes, and a black Windbreaker. Her brown hair was in a tight ponytail. Earbuds were in her ears. I watched her from the column for a minute or two as she checked her pulse, bobbed her head up and down some to her music, began to stretch. I wondered if she was listening to Pink Floyd, Led Zeppelin, or the Stones. She grew up with those classic bands, her dad's favorites.

I hadn't spoken to Natalie in more than five months. Not since we ran into each other at a coffeehouse, did the awkward side-hug thing, and sidestepped any serious conversation. She avoided eye contact altogether and quickly excused herself. There was a lot of pain there. I could feel it pinch in my gut. But I needed her right now, in more ways than one.

I took a deep breath, exhaled, stepped out. The blue hood was covering my new blond hair. My gray running shoes were the same ones I used to wear while jogging with her more than a year ago. I waited until a small pack of tourists cleared the area in front of Abe, then made my way over to where she was pulling a leg up behind her. My heart was pounding the same way it did when I was back in that batting cage, trying to win her over for the first time.

When I was within five feet, close enough to break a comfortable level of personal space, she looked up and locked eyes with me. Her head stopped bobbing, mouth parted. Her eyes met mine. It was only five seconds, us standing there, staring, but it felt like five minutes of silence. She noticeably swallowed, put her leg down slowly, plucked out the earbuds. She stepped closer and hugged me, really tight. This time, it wasn't awkward at all. She was holding me close to her. I held her back and almost lost it. I could feel her breath on my neck and the puddles forming in my eyes. Of course, she knew all about my current situation. Natalie was plugged-in minute-by-minute with every single news story going on in the world, a news junkie. Used to drive me crazy, her phone buzzing every two minutes with a new breaking-news alert.

She took a step back, spoke quietly. "Sam, are you OK?"

I shook my head. "No, I'm not."

She seemed to be examining my new hair under the hoodie.

She nodded. "I've been trying to call you, texting, e-mailing. I've left like a hundred voice mails. What's going on?"

"None of it is true. I promise. I got pulled into something very dangerous."

We paused as a large pack of Asian tourists made their way up to old Abe, sitting presidentially in the big chair. I peered behind me, noticed a security guard hovering near the front steps. He wasn't watching us, but it still made me nervous. Any Barney Fife with a badge and a gun made me twitch right now.

"I need your help," I whispered.

She nodded again. I could see that she was thinking, brainstorming. When her brain was processing through critical new information, she always looked down, a far-off stare, her forehead creased, biting gently on her lip. She looked up, resolved.

"OK, meet me at my place in one hour," she said. "Use the back door, from my parking spot. Code is still the same. I'll be waiting."

I felt a tidal wave of relief push through me. "Thank you."

She grabbed my hand in hers, a quick squeeze. Then she put the earbuds back in, brushed past me, trotted down the steps, and continued on her run through the Mall.

Standing there, I couldn't help but relive it all over again in my mind.

SAM, AGE TWENTY-FOUR

Washington, DC

Komi is an exquisite, high-end Mediterranean restaurant near Dupont Circle.

Fancy and expensive isn't exactly my style. I'm perfectly content with my usual six-dollar cheeseburgers from Five Guys on Friday nights. Natalie, on the other hand, had mentioned more than once in the few months that we'd been dating that it was one of her favorite dinner spots in the city. She began to insist over the past few weeks that we should dress up and show some class every so often. I wasn't sure I agreed with her on that, but she finally wore me down. We would eat at her dear Komi. The dinner tab would run us up over three hundred bucks tonight. That made me want to choke on my own tongue. When Natalie saw the look on my face at the mention of the daunting price tag earlier that same week, she tried to insist we should each pay our own way. No big deal. She wasn't some precious princess that needed the guy to pay for everything. She had her own career. She didn't expect me to carry the full weight of our social life together. I refused her offer. I might have been near broke, but I would not let chivalry die.

So, we dined on braised goat, salmon, scallops, all appropriately paired with the most excellent wine choices, according to the waiter. He spoke with an accent. I couldn't understand him half the time, but Natalie interpreted for me. She seemed perfectly at ease in this environment. Which made me wonder what she was doing with a poor street kid like me. She'd grown up with affluence. Her father was very successful. She knew life in the big city and life on the farm. She was just as comfortable in this high-dollar establishment as she was at the cheap BBQ joint we liked to frequent up the street. I, on the other hand, was completely out of my element. I wasn't sure which fork to use or how to pronounce most of the menu. I wasn't used to wearing my only suit out to dinner. After all, I had eaten out of dumpsters behind places just like this one at one point in my life.

I did not want to let these internal feelings of tension ruin my evening. So I tried to focus on Natalie in her short cocktail dress and heels, but this just made me wish we were on our way back to her place. Admittedly, the food tasted much better served warm and fresh and on perfectly clean plates. It was indeed exquisite. Every bite was bliss. I finished off my salmon, sipped my wine, took in the quaint dining room. The restaurant, with its crisp, formal white linens and perfect mood lighting, was filled with other couples also dressed to the nines who seemed perfectly fine dropping down a few hundred dollars on tiny plates of food. There were a lot of easygoing smiles and empty wineglasses.

"What are you thinking?" Natalie asked.

"Trying to pick out the one guy in here who makes less money than me. Other than our waiter, perhaps."

"Our waiter probably makes twice as much as you."

I smiled. "You're right."

"I told you I would pay for myself, Sam," Natalie said, looking guilty.

"I'm just teasing, Natalie. If this makes you happy, it makes me happy."

"It does, thank you. You should be OK with treating yourself every once in a while."

"I guess." I shrugged. "Besides, I'm overdue at the cash-for-fluids medical clinic, anyway. That should help pay for tonight."

"Right." She laughed. "How's your mom today?"

I had come straight to dinner after seeing my mom. "Oh, she's her usual firecracker self. But she seems to really like the people there, which is good. She's actually made a few friends. And she likes the neighborhood. Some of the ladies at the center invited her to the church up the street. And so far, no reports of biting or stealing. I'm hoping this will last."

Natalie grinned. "She's funny. I really like her."

"Well, that's good, because she adores you. She won't shut up about it."

"Good. Please tell her I feel the same."

"She asked me to invite you to come with me tomorrow. We're walking over to the park to feed the birds. And smoke about two packs while doing it. She can't understand why the birds won't come closer, even though there's a haze of smoke all around her. But it gets her outdoors for at least an hour, which seems to be good for her."

"Yes, I would love to come with you."

"OK." I took a sip of wine. "Hey, you mentioned earlier in your text that you had some exciting news to share with me."

She nodded. "Yes, right. I'm going to be an aunt again. Gary and Amy are pregnant."

"They have the twins, right?"

"Yes. But they had a lot of trouble getting pregnant. They had to do fertility treatments to get here. So it's a huge blessing that they are finally expecting again. My dad wants us all to come to Foster Farms two weekends from now for the whole family to celebrate."

"Your dad is always looking to throw a party, isn't he?"

"Yes. But family is everything to him. Do you want to come?"

"Sure. If I haven't already worn out my welcome."

"My dad specifically asked me to bring you along."

"Really? He must need help bathing the pigs."

She smiled. "I'm sure that's it."

The waiter brought out a small plate of assorted specialty chocolates for dessert. Natalie picked at one. I devoured the rest of them like they were cheap peanut-butter cups. Probably not the appropriate way to eat them—I'm sure each chocolate had its own matching wine—but they were ridiculously good. Like little drops of chocolate heaven that melted immediately in my mouth. Everything about Komi was ridiculously good. Especially my company.

Then the bill showed up. I paid through gritted teeth and tried to hide the fact that I wanted to punch the waiter who made more money than I did in the mouth.

Afterward, we decided to take a walk around the fountain at Dupont Circle. It was a cool evening. We held hands. Natalie snuggled in really close to me. She was being extra affectionate after dinner. I wasn't sure if she felt guilty about the bill or if it was a positive response to my taking her to her favorite restaurant, the good food and drink, or what, but I was no longer thinking about the money. I just wanted to hold her close to me. We stopped and stared at the water flowing over the sides of the fountain and splashing into the pool below. It felt like a perfect evening. Until it took a dramatic turn.

Natalie suddenly pivoted to face me full-on, both my hands interlocked in hers, and looked me square in the eyes. Something important was coming.

"You know that I love you, don't you, Sam?" she said.

And there it was. Three heavy words. My stomach immediately tightened up like a clenched fist. My tongue felt thick. I wasn't prepared to respond. I understood the weight of this moment. The weight of those words. It was the first time those three critical words had been spoken by either one of us. They had been on my lips many times before tonight, but I'd been unable to say them to her for some reason. They stuck in my throat. Just like tonight.

"I had a feeling," I managed to say in reply, forcing a smile.

She waited, but it was all I could say. I just froze. *What a jerk.* I leaned in to kiss her, and although she kissed me back, I could feel the reservation in her lips. No one says those words unless she hopes to hear them immediately back. I had failed her. Fortunately, a street musician began strumming a guitar and singing a few feet away from us, and a small crowd began to gather around. We turned to listen as well. Although we continued to hold hands, her grip had loosened in mine, and I could sense a cloud starting to hover over us.

My heart beat twice as fast the rest of the evening.

I dropped her at her apartment later with a quick kiss and left.

I didn't sleep at all that night. Why couldn't I say it back?

She hit me with the follow-up question at dinner a week later.

"Are you ever going to tell me you love me, Sam?"

I obviously knew it was coming. That's why I'd avoided her for almost a week. I was dreading it. The words she'd said to me at Dupont Circle were not something that could hang out there for very long without some kind of eventual reciprocation or explanation. I was struggling like crazy with my emotions. I had bailed on several possible dates in the interim, citing study groups or tough law exams or general busyness with my part-time jobs. I was doing everything I could to avoid what I knew was a relationship-defining moment. Maybe *the* relationship-defining moment. Something Natalie was apparently ready and willing to embrace.

I could avoid it no longer. Natalie deserved a response.

We were sitting at a table in the corner of Chef Geoff's restaurant. We had just finished a screening of the classic film *Casablanca* at the National Theatre nearby. Natalie was always dragging me to watch classic movies. She loved the old Hollywood glamour. Another favorite pastime she shared with her father growing up. I could see her lips moving during *Casablanca* as she silently quoted the lines. I had a lot of catching up to do. There had not been much movie watching in my youth. A movie was great because we didn't have to talk about the elephant in the room. But the elephant was still on the loose.

"What if I'm incapable of it?" I replied. It was an honest response. If I could give nothing else, I would at least be honest with Natalie.

She scrunched up her face. "Incapable of saying it? Or incapable of loving someone?"

"Both."

"I believe love is defined in actions, not words. Your actions already say you love me."

"Then why do I need to say it?"

She did not like this reply. "A girl likes to hear it, Sam. A girl needs to hear it eventually."

A waiter delivered our food and spared me from the sword in that moment. I understood what Natalie meant. I had obviously thought about little else the past week, since she'd first said it to me. I felt caught in some type of emotional trap. Things had been going so well between us. Almost too well. It really scared me. Natalie had become a part of me somehow on the inside. Like no one ever had before. After almost seven months together, I didn't feel like I even knew myself or my life without her anymore.

I was more than scared. I was frightened out of my mind.

The truth was that I'd grown to love her more than anything in life. More than I thought possible. I'd never let someone inside the walls like I had with Natalie. She had pulled the layers back so masterfully, like a heart surgeon, poking, prodding, and healing. Add the role she'd played with my new relationship with my mother, and it all felt a bit overwhelming at the moment. I'd been having a hard time sleeping the past week. The voices in my head were getting louder and angrier. I'd started to become so afraid of losing her that I'd been having nightmares about it, waking up in cold sweats. I'd learned early on in life that if you don't want to be hurt by someone leaving, you become proactive—you leave first before that person ever gets the chance to leave you. It was like hitting first in a school-yard fight. It's just the smart thing to do. Get the first lick in before the other person ever gets the chance to shatter your nose. Or your heart.

That had been the pattern of my life up to this point. The way of survival. I was battling those emotions now. I didn't know what to do with them. Unable to commit fully but unwilling to walk away. It was true that I could not imagine my life without Natalie. But over the past week, since she'd openly expressed her love to me, I had become even more afraid of the pain I'd experience when she finally walked away from me. I was certain she would eventually walk away when she finally got so far inside that she knew the real me. Not the image I still managed to portray, but the real Sam Callahan. The scared, broken, and angry kid who was still hiding behind it all. She was way too good for that guy. I knew it. She knew it. Everyone knew it. She wouldn't stay.

Everyone always leaves. Always.

Natalie finally broke the awkward silence. "Look, Sam, I'm not going to force you to say it. Good grief, I have my pride. I just don't get it. We've been together long enough. I mean, honestly, I could have told you that I was in love with you after just two months together, but I didn't. I held back. I wanted to wait on you. I just wonder how long you're going to make me wait."

"I don't know, Natalie."

She did not like this answer, either. Neither did I, but I couldn't think of anything else to say. I didn't have another answer. It was the truth. I couldn't joke or charm my way out of this tonight. I saw tears begin to form in the back of her eyes, but she quickly pushed them away. She was much too tough for that.

"Then I don't think I can do this anymore," she said. "I'm not in this to get hurt."

I began to panic. She was hitting the Eject button. The wall was going up.

"I'm not trying to hurt you, I promise."

"But you are, Sam. Whether you want to or not."

More awkward silence filled the air. She was having a hard time holding the tears at bay. I could feel them in my own eyes. She folded her napkin, stood suddenly. She was bailing. Making a run for it. And I couldn't blame her.

"I'm going to go," she said. "I need to go."

"Natalie, wait."

"I have been waiting. Very patiently."

"Wait a little longer."

She shook her head. "I can't. It's too hard. I think it's best if we spend some time apart. Until you figure out what you really want. Because I can't keep going deeper and deeper into this with you if you're not willing to come along with me."

I reached for her, but she pulled her hand away, headed for the door.

I turned, wanted to rush after her, but I just sat there.

She was right. I had to figure this out soon, or it was over.

Pastor Isaiah was in town a few days later for a pastors' conference.

It was perfect timing. I desperately needed wise counsel.

We met at a local basketball park near his hotel to shoot some hoops. Although we spoke on the phone every few weeks and e-mailed often, I had not seen him in more than a year. We only saw each other when he came to DC on church business, which he fortunately did at least once a year. He gave me the biggest bear hug when I walked up to the basketball court.

Pastor Isaiah looked as fit as ever, as if he could be a point guard for the Wizards. We used to play hoops four or five times a week at the church court when I lived with him back in Denver. They were great battles, where we traded off victories and talked about life in between games.

I missed those days. I missed him.

"Good to see you, Sam."

"You, too. How was the flight?"

"Just fine, thanks."

"How long are you in town?"

"Only two days. Conference is over on Thursday, then back home to Alisha and the kids."

"How are they?"

He pulled his phone out of his gym-shorts pocket, showed me some pictures of the twins and Grace. They were all growing up so fast. Grace was already in second grade. I couldn't believe it. And the two boys, who were already three, looked just like their daddy.

"Kevin is clearly the athlete," Pastor Isaiah said. "Myles has already taken to the piano. He has an ear for music. I can see him leading worship at Zion one day. He loves the stage."

"Just like his daddy."

We shared a laugh.

"They miss seeing their Uncle Sam," Isaiah added.

"I miss them, too."

Pastor Isaiah nodded. "How is your mom doing, Sam?"

"She's doing OK. Some days are worse than others."

"I'd like to go see her with you while I'm here, if that's OK."

"Sure. She'd love to see you."

Pastor Isaiah kicked the basketball up with the toe of his sneaker. "OK, enough talk. Let's play ball."

We played one-on-one, like usual, and Pastor Isaiah ran circles around me. He was like the Energizer Bunny, so full of energy and bounce. It seemed like every shot he took split the rim and landed in the chain-link net, whether inside or beyond the three-point line. I was dragging like I had a load of bricks in my shorts. We played to twenty-one, like we always did, and he clobbered me 21–7.

We took a quick break and drank some Gatorade I'd brought with me. I sat on a metal bench while Pastor Isaiah stretched out his hamstrings.

"What's the deal?" he asked me. "I'm used to kicking your butt, but that was just embarrassing. You OK?"

"I guess I'm a little distracted."

"By what? My biceps?" He flexed his right arm and smiled.

I forced a smile but looked at the ground and didn't say anything.

He stopped smiling. "Uh-oh. What? Is it Natalie?"

The look on my face gave away my answer. Pastor Isaiah sat next to me.

"What happened?" he asked.

"I blew it."

"Tell me."

I explained to him what had transpired in the past ten days, including our devastating dinner a few nights ago where Natalie had walked out. I had not spoken with her since. There had been nothing but sleepless nights as the demons inside me choked my ability to work myself out of this mess on my own.

"I don't know what to do," I finished. "I feel stuck. Lost. Hopeless."

He put a strong hand on my shoulder. "That's because you can't heal yourself, Sam. You have to let God do that."

"Well, that's just great," I replied, annoyed. "I wish He would stop taking his sweet time. Because it's, like, I have all of these sinister voices in my head telling me, 'Run, Sam, Run. Save yourself.' I can't even think clearly. They're just yelling at me all the time right now."

"These voices have faces?"

I nodded. They did. Faces that I still hated.

"Abusive foster parents?" he asked.

"Something like that."

Pastor Isaiah exhaled slowly. "You love her, Sam?"

"Of course I do. Madly."

"Then maybe this isn't such a bad thing. A little time apart can be a good thing. Before you're farther down the road. Alisha and I went through six months of counseling before Pastor Gregory would marry us. He saw the signs in me. He, of course, knew about my past, the abuse, the demons, and he recognized that I still had my own abandonment issues that needed to be addressed fully before I could commit to marriage. You need to let God deal with these voices inside you, Sam. I'll help however I can. You're not a lost cause, I promise. But it could take some time. Natalie deserves that, don't you think?"

"What if I lose her?"

"Then you never really had her."

I didn't call, text, or e-mail for a month, and neither did she. It was painful.

But I had a thick chain of fear around my neck that I couldn't pry off. Every time I reached for the phone and pulled up her number, I just froze. I couldn't press Call. I couldn't hit Send. I couldn't do a damn thing but sit there like I was stuck in quicksand, slowly dying. Unable to rescue myself from this hole in the ground. I was so afraid of openly loving her back. I was trying to deal with it, following Pastor Isaiah's counsel. I'd even started meeting with one of his mentors in DC once a week. A good man of sixty who'd counseled a lot of abandoned kids who'd become dysfunctional adults over the years. It was going to take time to extinguish the wicked voices in my mind.

Time felt like the enemy right now.

Natalie broke our communication stalemate and texted me twenty-seven days later. It was the simplest of messages, but it hit me with the weight of an earthquake and shook me to the core.

Good-bye, Sam.

I already had tears in my eyes when I knocked on her apartment door. I pounded the wood repeatedly with a fist. I didn't know if she would answer.

I pounded the door again. "Please, Natalie, answer the door."

She finally did. Just cracked it open. I could tell she'd been crying. Her eyes were puffy and red. But she was not crying at the moment. There was a defined resolve there. Natalie was so much braver and tougher than I was. She deserved better.

"Why are you here, Sam?" she asked.

I shook my head. "I don't know. I had to see you."

"I meant what I said. It's over. I'm strong, but I'm not strong enough to sit around and not hear *anything* from you for a month. That's just cruel."

"I'm sorry, Natalie. I've been trying to sort this out."

She opened the door more fully, stepped into the doorway close to me. She had her white robe on over pajamas. It was eleven thirty at night. She put her right hand on my face, caressed my cheek with her soft fingers. Then she leaned in, and we kissed. It was deep and full of such raw emotion. She pulled away.

"I love you, Sam. But I can't help you figure it out anymore."

"Natalie . . . wait."

"Please don't come back here again."

Then she turned and shut the door behind her. I heard the lock turn with a final click.

TWENTY

Sunday, 12:16 p.m.
Washington, DC
One day, eleven hours, forty-four minutes till Election Day

Natalie lived on the third floor of a red brownstone near Dupont Circle, a building tucked in with a cluster of others of various vibrant colors, like a box of crayons. There was some parking in the back in the alley. I was glad to see her silver Jeep Cherokee with the faded Saint Louis Cardinals sticker sitting under the metal carport cover in her designated spot. She had not had a change of heart and skipped out on me. I walked up the cracked concrete steps to the back door of her building, typed a code I'd once used often into the security keypad beside the door. The door lock clicked open. I was inside. Each floor of the brownstone had its own separate apartment. I took the stairs up three flights to the top apartment, which belonged to Natalie. A hundred vivid memories suddenly flooded my mind as I stood outside that familiar door. The last time I was here, she'd embraced me with passion, and then asked me never to come back.

The pain in my stomach had grown to the size of Alaska. Where was my damn time machine? I wanted to go back and push Decline on that phone call from Josh, inviting me into this ordeal, and I wanted one more chance with Natalie.

I swallowed, knocked twice. She cracked open the door. Finding me, she led me inside. She had cleaned herself up, showered, her hair still a little wet, and changed into a pair of snug jeans and a gray Missouri Tigers hoodie. She was barefoot, as she always was inside her apartment. Her toenails were bright red. I experienced a rush of familiar smells. Hazelnut coffee brewing. Her perfume lingering.

Natalie had a gorgeous apartment. A simple one-bedroom with a separate living room, small kitchen, full bath, but unlike my despicable bachelor pad, she had it decorated in warm colors—browns, reds, yellows, candles everywhere, rugs that matched, actual artwork on the walls, everything tied nicely together. There used to be a framed photo of the two of us at a Cardinals game on the entry table. It was no longer there.

She sat in a maroon chair next to the sofa. She had a large mug of coffee in front of her. I put my backpack down, sat on the sofa with my elbows on my knees, feeling awkward. I'd wished for months to be in this position, back in her apartment, begging for forgiveness and another chance, and now I was finally sitting here again. Seeing how her brown hair curled up around her shoulders, watching her pick at her cuticles nervously, I felt the trade-off to get back here was almost worth it.

"Are you sure about this, Natalie?" I said, breaking the ice. "It's risky, me being here."

"I can take care of myself, Sam."

"Yes, I know. Did you tell anyone else I was going to be here?"

She gave me a familiar look, one I'd seen almost daily when we dated, her head tilted to the right, her eyes narrow, her lips pursed. I called it the "Don't be a dumbass" look.

"Sorry," I said. "I'm not in my right mind. I've been living a nightmare the past two days."

"Tell me everything."

I told her the whole story and left out no details.

Somewhere in the middle of it all, Natalie had switched into journalist mode and grabbed a notepad, and she started scribbling down notes.

"I've seen four dead bodies in the past thirty-six hours, Natalie."

She bit her bottom lip, shook her head.

"You called me back the other night," I mentioned. "Right when the guy was coming after me in my motel room. Why?"

She shrugged. "I don't know. I woke up, saw a missed call from you. And I just had this really weird feeling that something was wrong."

We always had that type of connection. "I don't know what to do," I said, moving on. "Where do I go from here? How do I find my mom?"

"You think that this gray-bearded man has your mom?"

"Yes, but I don't know where or why. It doesn't make any sense to me."

"Yeah, if this man wanted you, he could have had you in Austin. And he could have taken your mom yesterday when he visited her."

"Exactly."

"She's alive, Sam. You have to believe that. It doesn't make sense otherwise."

"I keep repeating that in my mind."

"We will find her."

I liked that Natalie was using *we* and was already in it with me.

She stood, started to pace the small living room while processing. "We need the video, Sam. That's your ultimate protection in this thing."

I exhaled. "I know. There's probably some kid out there in Boerne who found my phone and has no idea what he has on it."

"But the video still exists. Rick sent it somewhere."

"Right. But not to our group server. He uploaded it somewhere else. Tommy is trying to find it, but he says it's a needle in a haystack."

"Rick lived here in DC?"

"Yes. He has an apartment here. He was living out of a hotel room in Austin for the campaign."

"Wife? Family?"

"No wife. He wasn't married. I don't really know much about him. We didn't spend that much time together. I think his mom lives in Canada. I believe he has a sister in California. Or Oregon. That's about all I know, really."

"I'll look into it. And I'll check on your mom. Maybe there is security video."

"You have to be careful, Natalie. I've only told three people anything about this. Rick and Ted were dead within hours. Now my mother is missing."

"Sam, this is what I do for a living. Let it go."

"OK, I know, which is why I came to you, but I'd rather catch a bullet to the head than have something happen to you, too."

"I'll be fine. Focus. OK?"

"OK."

"You bring the wallet belonging to this Carson guy with you?"

"Yes, in my backpack."

"I want to see it. Tell me more about the other one, the security guy for Congressman Mitchell. Don't leave out anything."

I told her everything I could think of about him, including the fact that I hadn't been able to find him in any other video or pictures when searching the Internet, which wasn't surprising considering security guys are trained to stay in the shadows. However, I was certain he was standing there directly behind Mitchell for that news conference. Natalie scribbled away.

I walked to the kitchen, filled up a mug of coffee, stared out the window. The rain was coming down harder now. Natalie was already on the phone, making some initial calls. I pulled out my tablet, logged in to Leia's Lounge to see if Tommy had anything new for me. I perked up. He had left a message for me to ping him. I did. Tommy was online twenty seconds later.

Maverick: Glad to see you're still alive.

The Duke: Glad to confirm it. What do you got?

Maverick: Found your license plate on the Escalade. Rental car. Hertz dealership, San Antonio International Airport. Jill Renee Becker. 124 DeKalb Avenue, Brooklyn, New York. Shooting over a copy of the signed contract to you now.

The Escalade from the motel parking lot with the blonde woman driver. I opened the new message in my mailbox, found the relevant information on a signed-and-scanned document. There was also a copy of Jill Becker's driver's license. I studied the photo. It was definitely the same woman from the motel. I would never forget that face.

Maverick: I also believe I found your mystery server. This look familiar?

A logo showed up beneath his message. It was a cartoon pig skull and crossbones. I recognized it immediately.

The Duke: Bingo!

Maverick: It's a server called AZA Golden Pig. Very small, very obscure. Out of Sweden.

The Duke: Do you know if Rick Jackson had an account?

Maverick: Not yet. Too hard to tell with aliases and whatnot, but I was able to hack all messages that were sent through this server exchange at the exact time stamp you gave me. And I found this one that looked interesting: Download this immediately, hide it, don't view it. Wait to hear from me. —RJ

RJ. Rick Jackson? It had to be him. Rick had sent the video to someone specific. Who?

Maverick: Best I can do without more time. They've got some serious security walls up at that place. Some of the best I've ever seen. Rivals anything the government or military has thrown up. It's Fort Knox. Don't get me wrong, I think I can get around it, but it might take me several more days. Might have to pull in some help. I'll keep at it and let you know.

The Duke: Thank you.

Maverick: Adios, amigo.

I waited until Natalie was off the phone.

"Tommy found the blonde. And more. Check it out."

She sat on the sofa with me, her elbow touching mine, and stared at the tablet and read my exchange with Tommy Kucher. She jotted all of the information down on her notepad. I did a quick search for the woman online. I found a few random mentions of Jill Becker in some fashion productions in and around New York City over the past few years. There was a picture on one fashion designer's website, where Jill Becker had been an assistant director for a show a year ago, and it definitely looked like the same woman. There was absolutely no mention of the death of Jill Becker on any news website anywhere. They had simply made her disappear.

Natalie was back on the phone, calling a contact in New York City. She was a machine. I did more research, she worked the phone, made notes, and we both spun our investigative wheels for the next hour. Being in the same room with her was a comfort, just like old times. I needed the comfort right now. She dropped her phone on the coffee table, sat down next to me again on the sofa. We were shoulder to shoulder. I said it without even thinking.

"I miss you, Natalie."

She closed her eyes, sighed. "Sam, please. Now is definitely not the time."

But I couldn't stop. "Are you still with the doctor?"

During our last encounter at the coffee shop, she made it a point to say that she was happy in her new relationship with some ER doctor at Sibley Memorial.

She shook her head. "Don't ask. There was a big hole in his story." She paused. "A wife."

"Ouch. Sorry." I wasn't really sorry, of course. Inside, I was doing a happy dance.

"No, you're not, jerk, so don't even pretend."

I smiled. I wouldn't push it any further. For now. Staring down at her notepad, I said, "Do you think Congressman Mitchell or someone from his team could really be behind Jill Becker? That it was all a setup to get McCallister?"

"Absolutely. It's a tight race. They are down five points with only a few days to go. They needed a game changer. McCallister has all the momentum. It would take something dramatic to tilt the election back into their favor. You were in a perfect position as a legitimate tracker. And someone wanted you there."

"But why would McCallister take the bait so close to victory?"

"I'm thinking there is more to this Jill Becker. Maybe she was not a random choice."

"Maybe. The question I keep asking myself is, who would actually kill to cover this up? Who would hire trained professionals to kill Rick and Ted? And me?"

"I don't know. Desperate people do desperate things. I've worked in this city long enough to have seen some really bad stuff. Dark and despicable things. One thing I do know for sure: nothing, absolutely nothing, is beyond some people when they are seeking positions of true power or wealth. Or if they are trying to keep from losing them. There's more to the story, clearly, and we have to go find it."

"Well, I hope we can do it quickly. I don't think I can keep running and hiding for too much longer. I'm almost out of hair colors."

She took a peek over, smiled. "Yeah, the blond has got to go. It's not doing it for me."

"That makes two of us."

Natalie's phone buzzed on the coffee table. She reached over, read a message, cursed out loud, which startled me.

"What is it?" I asked.

"It's not good."

She flipped on the TV. It was already tuned to CNN. A live FBI press conference in Austin. An FBI special agent was reporting that one Samuel Callahan, twenty-five, of Washington, DC, was also now the main suspect in a second death, that of Ted Bowerson. They had secured incriminating security video footage of Callahan inside Bowerson's home, where they found Bowerson shot and killed. The screen cut away to news footage outside Bowerson's home in Austin. FBI agents were moving about in the background. Callahan should be considered very dangerous, the agent explained. Several photos of me at various law-school functions flashed on the screen, along with an FBI hotline for tips and information. The FBI agent urged the public to be on the lookout and to take precautions.

The screen cut back to the news anchor. Natalie and I exchanged a heavy look.

I closed my eyes, dropped my head back into the cushions.

The hits just kept on coming. I needed an attorney.

SAM, AGE TWENTY-FOUR

Washington, DC

David Benoltz taught my Federal Courts class. He was an acclaimed criminal-defense attorney with his own firm in the heart of the nation's capital. David had earned a hard-nosed reputation defending clients against serious criminal charges. He'd been a regular legal analyst on CNN and had tried some very public cases against the federal government. David was an engaging teacher with a lot of energy and passion. He'd taken a serious liking to me because I refused to kiss ass like the rest of my classmates. I asked real questions that were open and honest and often made me look stupid. He appreciated that. Everyone else was too busy posturing and trying to appear like they knew it all. I was there for the right reason: to learn how to be a damn good lawyer.

David invited me out for a drink after a month of sitting in on his lectures. We sat in a wooden booth in the back of a bar. Four empty bottles of Guinness were already in front of us. David was in his early fifties with a dark goatee and round spectacles. He'd been divorced twice and had two grown kids my age. His boy was an actor out in LA. The girl was an assistant district attorney in Chicago. Both had inherited his legal genes—one with courtroom theatrics, the other with passion for the law. David made no apologies that he lived and breathed the law and slept on the pullout leather sofa in his spacious office most nights of the week, even though he owned an expensive town house nearby.

"What about you, Sam?" David asked. "Where are you from originally?"

"Denver."

"Is that where your family is? How'd you end up in DC?"

I thought about it for a second. "I don't have family. I grew up in foster care and on the streets. I got into a little trouble in my teens, and after that, I decided I wanted to make something of my life. Maybe help other kids growing up in the system. I went to undergrad in Colorado, did well enough, and then moved here for law school. That's me in a nutshell. Nothing too exciting."

"I beg to differ," David countered, a small smile crossing his face. "A car thief, huh?"

I tilted my head. He'd checked me out. "Something like that."

"We'll get to that later. I'd say you did more than well at CU. A perfect four-point-oh all four years in a difficult major. Then you scored a near-perfect one seventy-six on the LSAT."

I shrugged. "I got lucky."

"No one gets that lucky, Sam. I studied like a madman and squeezed out only a one sixty-two. And I'm sharp as a whip. You obviously have the brains for this stuff."

I didn't know what to say, so I just sipped my beer.

David continued. "So tell me, how'd you survive all of those years? Your file says you skipped out on the foster system when you were only thirteen. That's a long time to be on the streets as a teenager."

"What file?"

"I may have dug around. One of my investigators even talked with one of your former street buddies. A guy I think you all called Casper?"

I was surprised at the mention of that name. It was all surprising. Why was David investigating me?

"Yeah, I know Casper. Been a lot of years. Where did you find him?"

"Colorado State Penitentiary."

I wasn't surprised. Casper wasn't smart enough to stay out of jail.

"Casper had some interesting things to say about you," David said.

"That kid always talked too much. Don't believe half of it."

"Well, they were good things. He said you had a mind that worked differently from the rest of them. That you are wicked smart. He said that you could see things the others couldn't and could get in and out of situations like some kind of ghost."

"A ghost wouldn't have gotten caught stealing cars and spent three months in juvie."

"He said you got caught only because they squealed on you. Otherwise, you were untouchable."

"Well, not really something to brag about, you know? Those days are behind me." My eyes narrowed. "Why are you creating a file on me?"

"I want you to come work for me, Sam."

I was shocked at the offer. "Criminal law?"

David shrugged. "All kinds of law. Look, I need a guy like you. Someone incredibly street-smart, who can better understand the minds and actions of our clients. And who can handle himself in more threatening situations. I have enough guys who are good behind their desks, good at research, good at filing motions and pleas for me. What I need is a true fixer."

"What's a fixer?"

"Someone who knows the law really well, but who can handle himself out in the field. A guy who's not intimidated by anyone or any situation. A guy who can make arrangements with people and get the job done no matter what it takes."

"Are you talking about bending the law?"

David shook his head. "No, of course not. But I am talking about butting right up against those boundaries." David sipped his beer, studied me. "Sam, look, I know you've set yourself on this noble path to practice street law, helping the underprivileged. And I commend you on that. I'm not asking you to consider abandoning that pursuit. There's plenty of room for that with my firm. There is no question we could stand to do a lot more pro bono work. But you're clearly capable of so much more. You can do things other people can't. And you don't have to work at a street clinic and be a broke lawyer your whole life to do it."

"Money doesn't motivate me."

He smiled. "I know. I think I like that the most about you. The fact that money doesn't drive you makes you even more lethal. But it does take a lot of money to pay expensive medical bills, you know?"

My mom's situation was obviously in my file as well.

"OK, tell me more," I said.

"You'd work directly with me. I'd be the only one giving you your assignments. Your office would be right next to mine. We'd be joined at the hip."

"How much are we talking here, David? What's the salary?"

"I thought you didn't care about money?"

"I don't."

He smiled, took a pen from inside his suit jacket, wrote some figures on a napkin, and slid it across to me. I didn't touch it but glanced down. It was three times as much as the street clinic where I was interning.

"That's not my final offer," David added. "Just a starting point for our discussion. We have clients all over the world, Sam. Fortunately for us, crime happens everywhere. You could travel the planet and see some cool places. All while still helping the people that matter the most to you."

I had to admit, I was intrigued. I really liked David. I didn't know what to say. The offer had come out of nowhere.

"No pressure," David reassured me. "Just be thinking about it, OK?"

"OK."

TWENTY-ONE

Sunday, 2:46 p.m.
Washington, DC
One day, nine hours, fourteen minutes till Election Day

Natalie headed back to her office to better work her sources, so I took a moment to slip away. I needed to speak with David Benoltz. With the hurricane near Florida fizzling, the national-media focus was squarely back on me and my impending capture. After all, it had now become a nationwide manhunt, and I was apparently on an all-out killing spree. This was a nightmare. I needed to start planning my escape route.

Which was why I was now standing in the parking garage beside his shiny black Lexus sedan, waiting for him to come down from the Benoltz & Associates high-rise offices near Union Station. I had the fake round glasses and the black-knit cap on my head. I'd checked the schedule and knew that David was set to guest-speak at a law-school ceremony at 3:00 p.m. I fidgeted in the shadows, waiting, hoping David wouldn't walk it today. Georgetown Law was only five blocks from his office, where he spent nearly every day and night of the week.

Across the walkway, the elevator dinged. It had been dinging regularly every few minutes. Each time, I perked up, only to be disappointed. This time, two women in business suits exited together, heading in the opposite direction. Finally, I spotted whom I hoped was going to be my criminal-defense attorney. David wore a dark-blue pin-striped suit and carried a black briefcase in his palm. He moved with steady focus across the parking garage to his designated spot.

David was reaching down to his car door when I popped into view on the opposite side of the vehicle. He looked over, startled. I knew that he carried a handgun at times, even though that was illegal in DC. David had represented some shady characters over the years. There were men in jail who despised David. Men with angry brothers and uncles and nephews. He'd had various threats on his life. He'd even been shot at once outside of his home two years ago and wounded in the thigh. That story was not part of his perfectly crafted recruiting pitch to me. It was shared only after he'd had a few too many bottles of his favorite Guinness after taking me to a Georgetown Hoyas basketball game last spring. He said it came with the territory, and he seemed proud of it.

It took him a couple of seconds to recognize me beneath my ridiculous guise.

"Sam?" he said, incredulous. "What the hell?"

"I need an attorney, David."

He nodded. "Yes, you do, son. Get in the car."

David made a call, canceled his speaking engagement, told me to keep my mouth shut for the duration of the car ride. I rode in silence for nearly fifteen awkward minutes as he drove north of the city before finally pulling off down a series of long gravel roads in a heavily industrialized area. We eventually entered the dirty gates of a massive auto-salvage junkyard. A huge machine nearby was crushing old vehicles like metal pancakes as black smoke puffed into the air. A huge forklift was moving smashed-up cars around the property. David parked the Lexus behind a pile of metal and steel in the back of the property, indicated with a nod of the head for me to get out. We circled around to the rear of the car. It was no longer raining, but a mist still hung in the air. There were puddles of mud everywhere. It smelled like burned rubber and oil. I wondered how many client meetings David had here. He knew exactly where he wanted to go to have this talk with me.

"Sorry for that car ride, Sam. We need a safe place to talk. I'm on a big case right now, a lot of shady players, both government and corporate, a whole helluva lot of heat," David explained. "There are espionage charges involved. My security guy is certain my car is bugged. But we're not sure by which side just yet, the feds or my own client. So, I'm being extra cautious. Hope I didn't freak you out."

"No, I actually appreciate the extra caution."

"Yeah, I bet you do, son. It looks like you got your nuts caught in a serious vise right now."

"You could say that."

"Not exactly the way I wanted my future star associate to start out his budding career. You want to tell me what happened?"

I did. From start to finish, in between the crushing of metal and glass nearby.

"You really think they took your mom, Sam?" David asked.

"Yes."

"Damn." David shook his head. "I gotta say, that's one helluva story."

"I'm not trying to impress you, believe me. Every word is true."

"Yeah, I believe you."

"How could the FBI possibly have anything on me, David?" I asked.

"That's a very good question. I'll have to do some checking."

"What do you think I should do?"

"That's easy. I think you should turn yourself in, with me at your side. Let me protect you. I'm the best, you know that."

"I can't do that. Not yet."

"Sam, listen to me. These guys are hunting you down, trying to put bullets in your head. Even the feds will shoot you in broad daylight at this point."

"I'm very well aware of that. I'm just not ready."

He looked at me for a moment. "Your mother?"

"What would you do? Leave her hanging out there?"

He shrugged. "I can't say for sure. Not to sound like a jerk, but she did abandon you once before. Are you really willing to stick your neck out there for her?"

"It's not the same. I have to find her. I have to protect her."

David sighed. "Noble. But a huge risk."

"I've survived this far."

"True. And that's impressive." David stroked his goatee with his right hand, considered his thoughts. "Natalie is investigating Rick's contacts?"

I nodded. "And the blonde woman."

"We need that video," David concurred. "That's the deal breaker, whether you're in custody or not."

"Do you see any serious harm to my legal case whether I turn myself in now or later?"

"Your legal case? No, not really. I mean, the more you run, the guiltier you look. But I can probably undo all of that in one or two days with the media. Unless, of course, another murder is somehow pinned on you. Any other dead bodies out there I should be worried about, Sam?"

"I don't think so. But who knows at this point?"

"Well, other than the serious risk on your life every moment you're not in custody, and this bad initial public perception, your case doesn't really change a whole lot, as far as I see it. Assuming no new trumped-up charges come up while you're still running loose out there. Especially if we have that video. You've got to find it, Sam."

"I'm working on it."

TWENTY-TWO

Sunday, 4:07 p.m.
Washington, DC
One day, seven hours, fifty-three minutes till Election Day

I waited for Natalie in the grandiose rotunda on the first floor of the Smithsonian National Museum of Natural History, near the massive elephant display. The museum was crowded, as usual, and as we'd planned. Dozens of foreign tourist groups of every tongue moved slowly through the vast and impressive maze of artifacts. Families with unruly preschoolers were being watched tightly by security guards, who made sure they wouldn't tip over the precious and priceless works of art and science.

We'd exchanged texts earlier, as our initial plan to meet back at her apartment had changed abruptly. Natalie thought she was being followed. She wasn't sure, but she'd noticed the same set of eyes on her as she went about her business the past few hours. Coffee shop. Dry cleaners. In and out of the office a few times along the sidewalks. She did not want to go back to her apartment. We needed to play it extra safe.

I had on the knit cap and glasses. My feigned focus was on a bronze plaque in front of me describing the world of elephants, but I wasn't reading a single word of it. Behind the glasses, I surveyed the scene in the three-story rotunda, looking for signs of Natalie and watching every other figure that came into my sight very closely.

I wondered how long a man could survive under the scrutiny of a massive nationwide manhunt. How much could the nerves take? I'd been running on maximum sensory overload for more than thirty-six hours straight, a near-constant state of panic and paranoia, always short of breath, always on edge, always fighting the urge to flee.

Natalie arrived five minutes late, right when I was about to worry she wouldn't show.

She found me in the corner. We connected eyes. She gave me a subtle nod, walked right past me into the popular dinosaur section of the museum.

I followed her, ten feet behind.

We walked slowly through the dinosaur displays. Natalie paused, read plaques, examined models, artifacts, did the serious museum thing. Several times, I noticed Natalie glance back. I did the same, just casual looks around while peering at the museum map in my hand, as if I wasn't sure which way I wanted to go next. I didn't see anyone I felt was overly suspicious. No one seemed to be watching me intently, either. We did this song and dance for about ten minutes until we found ourselves all the way in the very back corner of the first floor inside the Fossil Café. We sat at a table tucked away, side by side, so both of us could watch the entrance to the café.

"We good?" I asked.

She nodded. "I think so. I haven't seen him."

"What does he look like?"

"Blond hair. Tall. He's wearing a blue blazer and brown slacks. Aviator shades."

"Fed?"

She shrugged. "Not sure."

I wasn't convinced yet. "Well, I wouldn't be surprised if a random guy followed you around, Natalie. Looking for an opportunity to strike up a conversation and ask you out. You sure someone's following you because of me?"

"Let's just be discreet."

"OK. Discreet is my middle name at the moment."

"What did David say?"

She was all business.

"He said I should probably let him walk me straight in to the authorities if I wanted to live through this. Let him take over from there."

"He's probably right."

"You think I should turn myself in?"

She twirled a strand of hair in a finger, considered it. "Well, as a reporter on the hunt for a big story, no, by all means, stay on the run. Let's go find the truth, I'll write about it and expose it to the world. As someone who still deeply cares about you and doesn't want you to get killed, turning yourself in is probably the smartest thing."

"Deeply?"

"Of course. Don't be stupid."

"I do love you, Natalie. I'm sorry I couldn't say it before."

She cocked her head, her eyes softening, then hardening. "Don't you think this situation is complicated enough?"

"Sorry. I think I've lost the ability to filter my thoughts the past two days." I shrugged, gave a curt grin. "I guess I've learned the hard way that life is short. Better say what you want to say while you've still got the chance."

"You sound like a fortune cookie."

"I'm not turning myself in to the FBI until I have the video and my mom. So put that out of your mind."

She didn't argue with me. The reporter won out. "OK, well, I can't find anything on your mom. There are no security cameras at the facility. No one seems to know anything other than what Cedric already told you. I'll keep working on it. I've also checked on Rick Jackson. I got in touch with his mother in Toronto. She's brokenhearted, of course. Unfortunately, neither his mother nor his sister know anything about his work or what he was up to this past week. I've checked with neighbors, other coworkers. Everyone is shocked. Especially the coworkers, who have to deal with both Rick's and Ted's deaths at the same time. The only potential thread I've found so far is with a second cousin named Jeremy Lynch, who also lives here in the city. Rick's sister, Janice, said they were close. Jeremy just moved to DC six months ago from California. He got his master's degree in computer science from Stanford. Get this: Jeremy got recruited out of Stanford to become a computer analyst for the CIA."

"CIA?"

"Yes. But I haven't been able to get in touch with him."

"Why do you think there's a potential thread there?"

"Well, I tracked down a new girlfriend of his through social media. They'd been dating for about six weeks. She said that she was really worried about Jeremy. He's been missing since yesterday. Neither she nor any of their friends has spoken with him in the past twenty-four hours. Jeremy hasn't been answering texts, Facebook messages, nothing, which is really unlike him. She thought about calling the police but hasn't yet. She keeps expecting him to pop up somewhere, and she doesn't want to seem like the psycho-stalker girlfriend."

"You think Jeremy could be the recipient of Rick's server message?"

She shrugged. "He's the best candidate we've got right now."

"You have an address for him?"

"Yes. I plan to stop by after this."

"I'll go with you."

"I think you should stay underground."

203

"Why? As far as we know, I don't have a tail at the moment. But you do."

She frowned. "OK, fine."

"What about Jill Becker?"

"Not much yet. I'm digging. From what I can tell, she worked off and on as a fashion consultant in New York City. She had two short marriages, one for two years, and the other for fourteen months. She was fired from her last job at a small fashion publication in Brooklyn. One of the women who worked there told me she had gotten into some heavy drugs. Kind of fell off the deep end after her last divorce, became really undependable. So, they had to let her go, even though they really liked her. No one at the magazine was sure where she ended up."

"Probably at the bottom of a lake somewhere in Texas."

"We still have a lot more work to do there."

"And my buddy, Elvis?"

She nodded, kept ticking off facts from memory. I knew she had everything scribbled down in detail on her notepad. "Greg Carson served a six-year term in the marines. Spent time in Iraq and Afghanistan. Recon. Special Forces. The highest level. Got out about eighteen months ago. He was definitely a highly trained military operative. Trained to kill. You're very lucky to be alive, Sam."

"Maybe. I don't feel so lucky."

"My military contact says his file has some questionable marks, that Carson had some trouble staying in line. Caused some problems. Bad attitude. Not enough to get discharged, but he was right there at the edge. Not much family. An aunt in West Virginia said Carson had a difficult time after getting out. Came home for three months, but then left again after getting into several bar fights. Seemed to be doing better lately. She said he got recruited to do special private-security work, both overseas and in the States. She wasn't sure by whom. No one has called me back yet with Stable Security in Dallas. But I was able to confirm that Congressman Mitchell's campaign has contracted work with Stable Security in the past."

"What about Square Jaw?"

"Nothing yet. But he can't hide from me forever."

"I don't doubt it. You're pretty impressive."

"It's true. I can't deny it."

We shared a quick grin. It felt good.

"Let's go check out Jeremy's place," she said. "See if he's home."

I was about to get up when Natalie put a hand on my shoulder, abruptly leaned in, and planted a kiss on my lips. She pulled away, just an inch. I was damn near seeing stars. But it was odd; her eyes were not on me. Her head was turned slightly, eyes toward the front door of the café and hallway back into the museum.

I started to say something, but she shushed me.

"Don't move. I just saw him."

"The blond guy?" I whispered.

"Yes, he just walked past the door. Same guy."

I shifted my view, peered around her toward the door myself.

"Right there!" Natalie said, laying another one on me.

I managed to spot him through the strands of her brown hair. His short blond hair was combed over neatly. He looked like a banker, or maybe a stockbroker, in his blue blazer and slacks. The man, who appeared to be in his midforties, was clearly searching for someone. He wasn't there casually checking out museum exhibits. He stepped away from the entrance to the café and disappeared.

I can't lie. I wanted him to walk past again. And again.

"We've got to go," Natalie whispered, grabbing my hand, yanking. "Right now."

I sighed, carefully slipping out of the café behind her.

TWENTY-THREE

Sunday, 4:38 p.m.
Washington, DC
One day, seven hours, twenty-two minutes till Election Day

Jeremy Lynch lived in a simple one-bedroom apartment in north Georgetown in an old gray box of a building near Montrose Park. People were coming and going from the apartment building, so it was easy to get inside. We hit the old stairwell like we lived there, or at least like we knew exactly where we were going. We found his door on the second floor at the end of a drab hallway. The walls were a dull gray; the ceiling held cheap florescent lighting.

The plan was for me to hang back and let Natalie do the early talking, just in case the full-on sight of me freaked Jeremy out. I probably didn't need to be approaching any of Rick Jackson's family members right now.

Our plans changed quickly when Natalie found the door to his apartment already cracked open. We could hear some banging and bustling coming from inside. We shared an anxious glance. Someone was home, but something told me it wasn't Jeremy. Before I could say anything, Natalie knocked on the door twice, pushed it slightly open.

"Hello?" she said. "Jeremy?"

We had a three-inch view inside, enough for me to see that something wasn't right. I immediately noticed papers spread all over the floor right inside the doorway, a small entry table overturned. Natalie pushed the door open another few inches, and we could see the place was flat-out ransacked, like a tornado had hit it. I could see the cushions of the sofa removed, two wooden shelves pulled down to the carpet, their contents of pictures, mementos, knickknacks spread across the tiny living-room floor. Boxes tossed about and torn open.

"Hello?" Natalie said a little louder.

Sudden noise came from the back hallway. Then a guy wearing a gray jacket, jeans, and a scowl came rushing around the corner. He hurried up to the door, pushed it nearly closed, leaving a six-inch gap, enough space to converse with Natalie. I took a step back, so as to remain as inconspicuous as possible. The guy was clean-shaven with a military-style haircut. A small jagged scar above his left eyebrow. I noticed a tattoo poking out of his collar near the back of his neck.

"What do you want?" he demanded, not the least bit friendly.

"Sorry to bother you," Natalie said. "Is Jeremy home?"

"No."

"You know where I can find him?"

"I think he's at work."

"On a Sunday?"

"Yes."

The guy was clearly not interested in their conversation and agitated at the sudden interruption. The six-inch part in the door was already slowly closing on us. Then I saw it poking out from inside his opened gray jacket. A gun stuck in a black shoulder holster. My heart started racing. This was not good. I fought the urge to grab Natalie, bolt on the spot.

"Are you his roommate or something?" Natalie asked, pressing forward, putting a palm out toward the door.

"Building management."

He shut the door in her face without another word. We exchanged a quick look. Then I grabbed Natalie by the hand; we made our way toward the stairwell, stopped, huddled.

"No way that guy was building management," Natalie insisted.

"No," I agreed. "That place was destroyed. And he had a gun."

"What?"

I nodded. "Saw it inside his jacket."

She bit her lip, stared off. "He was looking for something, Sam."

"The same thing as us, I suspect. We should get out of here."

"No, let's wait for him," she countered.

"Wait for what? To get shot at?"

"No, wait to see where he goes. And to follow him."

I looked at her like she was crazy.

"You want to get to the truth or not?" she asked.

I reluctantly agreed. I was perfectly fine with getting shot at—well, not exactly fine, but more OK with it than with the thought of Natalie dodging bullets. Still, she was right. We needed to know more about this guy. We took the stairs down, waited in the lobby, near the mailbox corridor, out of view of the stairwell. We did not have to wait long.

Our new friend in the gray jacket bounded down the stairwell fifteen minutes later and hit the glass doors to the sidewalk with a burst of speed. We followed, doing our best to stay just far enough back so as not to lose him. He spun to his right on the sidewalk, where he flagged down a cab from up the street. He slid into the back. The cab eased forward.

We waited a moment, then sprinted up to the same curb, spotted a cab on the opposite side of the street. We had no time to lose. I stepped out into traffic to wave it down and nearly got sideswiped by a speeding van, which blared its horn at me and buzzed me within inches. The taxi did a quick U-turn, and we jumped inside. We gave quick instructions to follow the taxi. It was waiting at the red light a block ahead of us. I promised a big tip if our driver stayed close. He seemed fine with these instructions, weaved in and out of traffic, slowly making up space. Fortunately, the other taxi was not in a rush. We caught up quickly.

"He was a marine," I said to Natalie.

"How do you know?"

"Tattoo on his neck. *Semper Fidelis*. Wonder if he's connected to Elvis?"

She shrugged. "This is DC. Former military everywhere."

"Maybe so."

Six minutes later, the other taxi dropped the gray-jacketed man on the corner of Twentieth and P Street in front of an ornate cream-colored office building. The man bolted out of the taxi and straight inside the glass doors. We tossed some cash over the seat and did the same, trying to keep up. Natalie was clearly up for the chase. I could barely keep up with her. The mention of a hidden gun had seemed to inspire her. We stepped carefully into the lobby just in time to see the man enter an elevator before the doors shut. We rushed across the lobby and watched the numbers above the elevator door gradually light up as the carriage ascended. Two. Three. Four. Five. It stopped on the fifth floor.

We searched the directory. There were three business suites listed for the fifth floor of the building. Jacklow & Smithson, Attorneys at Law; Northwest Media Consultants; and Roots. Natalie wrote them all down in her notepad. We found the stairwell, thinking it might be safer than the elevator. We hustled up the stairs, Natalie again beating me to the top, where she slowly poked the door open on five. The hallway was quiet. I suspected most offices were closed on Sunday.

Right in front of us were clear glass doors for the law firm. The lights were all out in the lobby inside. No movement. No signs of life. Down the hallway to our left was another set of glass doors for Northwest Media Consultants. Again, the lights were all out and no sign of anyone inside. But on the opposite end of the hallway, we found a final set of glass doors for the third office suite. Although the light was out in the main lobby, we spotted lights and shadows of movement down a hallway. We could hear the murmur of distant conversations. I looked at the name on the door again.

Roots?

TWENTY-FOUR

Sunday, 5:41 p.m.
Washington, DC
One day, six hours, nineteen minutes till Election Day

Natalie and I agreed to meet again in a few hours. She wanted to get back to her office at *PowerPlay* to dig deeper into Roots. At this point, it was still safer for us to be apart than to be together. Especially if the blond banker had given up at the museum and headed back to wait for her outside her office building. I had a few places to go, anyway.

I took a cab to E Street, home to my tiny studio apartment on the fourth floor of Capitol Plaza Apartments. I strolled in the light rain, hands in my pockets, hood over my head, eyes on the concrete in front of me. There was nothing fancy about my apartment building. It was a boring yellow building stuck in the middle of DC among other boring concrete-and-steel structures. It was a block from Georgetown Law School. I imagined the FBI had made a visit, and perhaps Square Jaw's colleagues.

It wouldn't take them long to cover the 425 square feet.

I watched from the opposite sidewalk for a few minutes, making sure nothing strange was going on around the front of my building. Then I waited until two guys in suits entered and followed them through the glass doors. They headed up the steps to the elevators. I skipped past them, found the stairwell, bounded up the steps two at a time.

I cracked open the door on the fourth floor. I could peer all the way down my hallway. There was nothing going on right outside my doorway. I wasn't sure what to expect. I eased into the hallway, not wanting to bump into a neighbor right now. There had no doubt been a lot of activity going on around my apartment the past thirty-six hours. I'm sure they'd all been questioned yesterday about their neighbor who had gone psycho down in Texas with a handgun. I could even imagine Mrs. Worley, the curious old lady with the beehive of red hair down the hallway, standing at her door answering questions about me from the police.

I hustled down the hallway, feeling exposed. When I got to the door of my apartment, sure enough, they'd been here. I found it sealed off with yellow tape that read POLICE. DO NOT CROSS. I knelt down to the floor, reached around behind the edge of the doorframe. I found an apartment key I had hidden in a crack, wedged between the doorframe and the wall. I stood, put the key in the door, turned the knob. There was no noise coming from inside the apartment.

I scooted under the police tape, careful not to disturb it, shut the door behind me, took a moment to look around. The place was a mess, partly because I rarely cleaned it, but it was obvious other parties had been inside and had a very rough look around. I didn't have much. The worn brown-leather sofa made out into a bed that I slept on at night, when I found the energy to unfold it. Most nights I just slept right on the sofa cushions. A short cabinet held a small thirty-inch flat-screen TV with rabbit ears. There was a cheap two-person kitchen table against the wall. The studio kitchen and living area were all together in one room—you could practically stand in the middle and touch everything.

My law-school books and notepads were spread out all over the sofa table. An old pizza box was still on the kitchen counter. My dirty dishes were in the sink. I had not done a great cleaning job before bolting town on my tracker assignment. Natalie had been in my apartment only one time, very early in our relationship, before she decided it was best for us to hang out at her place most nights. I couldn't have agreed more. This place was for sleep and study and little else. The stack of white file boxes in the corner, mostly filled with undergrad books from CU, folders, notebooks, and law-school materials, had all been dumped out and spread across the floor.

I stood there for a moment. A few weeks ago, I was just a law student. My biggest challenge was juggling three odd jobs, a full load of classes, a broken heart, and a cancer-stricken mom who liked to steal from her neighbors and bite her nurses. It was a hustle and a hassle and exhausting most of the time, but it was nothing compared to the past couple of days.

At any rate, I wasn't here to reminisce or whine. I didn't need to linger. I had a purpose for being there. I moved to the closet. Several of the boxes had been pulled off shelves, littering the floor, some clothes still on hangers, others strewn about and in wrinkled piles.

In the back corner of the closet, I found the small white shoe box that my mom had given me, filled with my most cherished items. There was a stack of photos of us together when she was a teenager and I was a baby, a piece of paper on which she'd written a song for me right before dropping me at Saint Luke's, some drawings she'd done, a few of her other childhood knickknacks, and pieces of jewelry. I also found the silver cross necklace hanging on a simple leather string that she'd given me after our reunion in Houston. Although it was nothing fancy, I never wanted to lose it.

I put on the necklace, tucked it inside my sweatshirt, dumped the contents of the shoe box inside my black backpack along with some extra clothes from the closet. I wasn't sure I'd ever return to this place again.

When I was back in the hallway, locking the door, I heard a familiar high-pitched whiny voice from the other end.

"Sam? That you?"

I took a peek over. Old Lady Worley was thirty feet away, squinting, adjusting her thick glasses.

With a deep voice, I said, "Police, lady. Go back inside."

Then I turned away, backpack over my shoulder, and hit the stair-well, hoping I could somehow get out of the building before that old lady got back to her phone and called the front desk to tell them that Sam Callahan, the murderer, was in the building.

TWENTY-FIVE

Sunday, 6:37 p.m.
Washington, DC
One day, five hours, twenty-three minutes till Election Day

I met Tommy Kucher at Big Planet Comics in Georgetown. He was in the back corner of the comic-book store, away from the street, away from the windows. It was a big deal for us to meet in person, especially when Tommy initiated it. He did not like to leave his private computer lair. Tommy wore his usual black skinny jeans, white T-shirt, and blue-jean jacket with holes everywhere. His black hair was spiked up on top and shaved on the sides. It had two shades of purple streaks in it. He looked even skinnier than normal, like he was barely a pound over one hundred twenty. He'd added a couple of rings to the left ear.

"Dude, nice hair," Tommy said, examining my bleached-blond look.

"Just trying to keep up with you."

I could smell the cigarettes on his breath. Wrapped around his skinny neck was a blue-and-gray tattoo that said *TOMMY COOL*.

"I'd say you've blown way past me," Tommy said. "It's not my face on CNN with the feds after me."

"I'd rather it be you."

We grinned. I peeked over my shoulder, toward the front. A clerk Tommy's age, around twenty, sat behind the counter, reading. There was another pudgy young wanderer in the store looking at comics, but no one else.

"What's going on, Tommy? Why are we here?"

He nodded. "I've been going hard at that server of yours in Sweden. Thought I was making progress, but then the whole thing just got buzz-sawed."

"What do you mean?"

"It got shut down, disabled. Completely jacked."

"Like a cyber attack?"

"Not just any attack, bro. This was the real deal. This was, like, the friggin' nuclear war of attacks. They wanted to make sure no one got back inside. I'm not sure they'll ever have it up and running again. It's been obliterated."

"By whom?"

"I don't know yet. But it's not some kid on a desktop in Romania or something, I can tell you that. This was elite. Like a CIA or Chinese military operation. Not too many I know of in the world who are capable of it."

I felt my heart sink. Had the video of McCallister gone down with the attack?

"That's not all," Tommy continued. "They started chasing after me."

"Chasing you?"

"Yeah, online. They began to track me in reverse. These guys knew I was hunting for something, and they began to hunt me right back. So I got out of there. Texted you."

"Can they find you? I mean, in real life?"

Tommy shook his head. "Nah, I was looped in through so many redirects from all over the world, it would be impossible. I'm not really too worried about me. But I am worried about you. Who did you piss off, Sam? Because this is not just the work of some IT guy working on a congressman's staff. You've messed with the wrong people."

"That's what I'm trying to find out."

"Well, the pig server is dead."

"We think that Rick Jackson might have sent that message to his second cousin, a guy named Jeremy Lynch, who's a computer analyst for the CIA. He's been missing since at least yesterday. We went by his place an hour ago and found it ransacked. Someone was there looking for something."

"You think he's dead?"

"I sure hope not."

"Jeremy Lynch?"

"Yes."

"Cool." Tommy nodded. "I'll be on the lookout. If he drops in somewhere online, I'll find him and let you know immediately."

"Watch your back, Maverick."

Tommy grinned again. "I ain't scared. You watch yours."

TWENTY-SIX

Sunday, 7:57 p.m.
Washington, DC
One day, four hours, three minutes till Election Day

We met at the Thomas Jefferson Memorial.

The sun had set, and the memorial was aglow in brilliant bright lights. At nearly eight, the crowds had thinned. I hid behind a massive column. I knew Natalie was zigzagging the city, in and out of subways and cabs, making sure she wasn't followed. She planned to do this for more than an hour, just to take the highest measure of precaution. She'd spotted the blond banker guy one more time on the sidewalk outside her office building. It made both of us very uneasy. Why was he targeting Natalie? Did they know we'd connected and were now working together? I had also cleared my tracks after meeting with Tommy Kucher, making sure I couldn't be followed. Acting completely erratic, to make it near impossible to trail me. I mean, if I didn't know where I was going from one step to the next, how could an assassin?

It was exhausting. I couldn't keep going much longer.

I thought about the nature of the cyber attack. Tommy called it the most sophisticated attack he'd ever seen. Was the military connected to this?

My mind drifted to thoughts of my mom. Something I'd been trying to resist. Why had they taken her but left no sign of any demands? No ransom request? No her-life-for-my-life exchange? They just made her disappear for no apparent reason. It didn't make any sense. I was sick about it. I'd touched base by phone with Cedric several times throughout the day. There was no sign of her return to the facility.

I sighed, leaned against the column, stared at the massive statue of Thomas Jefferson in the middle of the memorial. I spotted a man in a black trench coat across the way. He gazed in my direction a moment too long. I slipped back behind the column, scooted down the outside steps, slowly circled the monument, and then entered from a different corridor. Again, I peered inside, near the statue, from around a new column. The man was now huddled with a dark-haired woman of similar age, and they had two teenage boys with them. If he was a killer or FBI, it was a great cover. The family walked out of the monument together a few minutes later. I exhaled.

Natalie arrived right on time. She slowly circled the statue in the middle twice. Twice meant she was clean. Three times meant she was not clean and abort. She trotted down the outside steps, toward the shadows by the Tidal Basin. I watched for two minutes, then joined her. A chilly breeze was blowing in off the Potomac River. It was the first day of November. The election was barely a day away. I wondered if I'd live to watch Lucas McCallister claim victory. The thought of that was simply inconceivable and made me nauseated. Actually, the thought of Congressman Mitchell winning wasn't much better. I really didn't know what to think. Both men could have innocent blood on their hands. The good citizens of Texas could unwittingly be electing a cold-blooded killer to Congress either way.

"You OK?" I asked.

"Yes. You?"

"Now that you're here."

She didn't roll her eyes at me this time.

"What did you find?" I asked.

"Roots is a super PAC. Formed only six months ago."

"Political action committee?"

"Yes."

"Formed by whom?"

"The attorney on the paperwork is a partner for Hilman & Nesbit. So, it could be for anyone. The firm represents hundreds of corporate and government clients."

"So, a dead end?"

She gave me that "Don't be a dumbass" look again.

"Forgive me. What else?"

"Roots has spent ten million dollars in the past three months on six different congressional races going on in the country right now."

"All backing the same party?"

"No, different party candidates. Split down the middle."

"That's confusing."

"I think it's a smoke screen. Eight of the ten million was spent in Texas."

"District Twenty-One?"

"Yes. On TV ads slamming Congressman Mitchell."

"Wait. *Against* Mitchell?"

"Yes, that's right. I'm not sure what the connecting thread is. We've got one assassin hunting you down that apparently works for Mitchell. And another possible assassin, or at least a guy with a gun, breaking into Jeremy Lynch's apartment, and then heading back to the offices of a super PAC whose main goal seems to be winning the election *for* McCallister. There is a long list of names of individual givers, but most of the funding is coming from an obscure new lobbyist firm called

Tolstoy & Peters. Nearly ninety percent of the money. I can't seem to find much info on them; they are that brand-new. The website is very generic. No real names or faces. The whole operation feels a little suspicious to me."

"They have a physical address?"

"Yes."

"Let's pay them a visit."

"It's eight o'clock on Sunday night. No one will be there."

"Exactly."

She tilted her head. "What did you have in mind?"

I shrugged, smiled. "Maybe there's a key under the mat."

TWENTY-SEVEN

Sunday, 8:19 p.m.
Washington, DC
One day, three hours, forty-one minutes till Election Day

Tolstoy & Peters's offices were listed on the fourth floor in Watergate 600. It was near the Potomac, adjacent to the Kennedy Center, the massive old complex the President Nixon debacle made famous roughly forty years ago, coining the term *Watergate Scandal*. Since this was likely another political scandal, it felt somewhat appropriate. The spacious round lobby had several people crossing through and a security guard at a booth. We took the stairs up. No reason to step in and out of an elevator with anyone. The hallway was quiet. Most of the office suites were dark. We found a simple frosted-glass door with Tolstoy & Peters engraved on the outside. There were no signs of an alarm system, but the door was no simple lock and key. It was accessed only through a security key card. No magical paper-clip tricks with this one.

"Now what?" she said, like it was a challenge. "Can't pick that bad boy, can you?"

"Wait here," I instructed.

"Where are you going, Sam?"

"Just sit tight. I'll be back in three minutes."

I found the stairwell again, bounded down the steps, reentered the lobby. I paused, scanning the room for the security guard. Bingo. I noticed the white key card in a clear plastic holder clipped to a black belt. Right next to a black holster and revolver. I inhaled and let it out very slowly. It had been a few years, but there was no better time to shake off the dust. I waited as two men exited the elevator heading for the lobby doors, moved in behind them. We were walking in a small pack directly toward the guard. He stood behind the booth, studying a piece of paper in his hand. We were within ten feet. I veered to my right, toward the guard. His face was still planted in the paperwork. I held my phone in front of my eyes, still walking, like I was reading an e-mail. I bumped the guard, just a soft, easy nudge into him, and then pulled the key-card clip with my right hand. My fingers pushed it up under my shirtsleeve in one practiced motion. Like riding a bike.

"Geez, sorry, boss," I said, stepping away, not making direct eye contact. "Shouldn't walk and text, I guess."

The old guard gave a quick chuckle. "No problem. Have a good one."

His eyes went back to his papers. I did a quick circle back to the stairwell.

I was standing in front of Natalie thirty seconds later.

I smiled wide, held up the key card. "You were saying, Ms. Foster?"

She shook her head. "I don't even want to know."

"No, you don't. You can honestly deny it later."

I held the key card in front of the small security box. The light went from red to green, and the door clicked. Money. I turned the knob, pushed the door open. We stepped inside a small lobby with two brown-leather chairs, a coffee table, a small receptionist desk. No noise or signs of life inside the office suite. A hallway peeled off to the right from the lobby. The lights were off. I turned on the flashlight on my phone. The hallway looped around into a large open space with about a half dozen cubicles in the middle, private offices along the outside. There was enough space for about twenty workers.

I shined the flashlight into the cubicles. Natalie and I exchanged an odd look. They were all empty. One had a clean desk and an office chair. Nothing else. No phones. No computers. No paperwork. No office supplies. No trash cans. No sign of anyone using them at all. We checked the exterior private offices. Not a single one even had a desk. They were all completely empty, just carpet and bare walls. Other than the name on the door, there was no sign of this being a legitimate office.

"They move offices?" I asked.

She shook her head. "I don't think so. My info says they've been right here since they formed back in April."

"So, where is everyone? This place looks like they haven't even moved in yet."

"I think it's a front," Natalie said.

"You mean this firm isn't real?"

"Oh, it's real. But on paper only."

"Can you do that?"

"Sure. If no one asks any questions."

"So, someone created a fake PAC, and then also created a fake lobbyist firm to launder money through to it?"

"And I doubt it stops there. Every name on the donor list, for both the Roots super PAC and Tolstoy & Peters, both individual and corporate, could be fake. Layers deep. I'm thinking to hide who is really funding Roots. There are thousands of firms and tens of thousands of lobbyists in this city. It's a ten-billion-dollar industry. The only reason

I even connected Tolstoy so directly to Roots is because I asked some direct questions to inside sources. Otherwise, operations like this one could carry on with no one the wiser for years."

"Who would do that? It would take an incredible amount of time, money, and effort."

"Someone who has a lot riding on this election."

"Right," I agreed. "Someone who would kill to cover it up."

TWENTY-EIGHT

Sunday, 8:51 p.m.
Washington, DC
One day, three hours, nine minutes till Election Day

We stood on the sidewalk outside the Watergate complex in the night shadows.

"I think Jill Becker texted you two nights ago," Natalie said.

I turned. "Why?"

"Jill's maiden name was Jill Clayton. And it turns out, Jill Clayton attended SMU twelve years ago."

I tilted my head. "I'm not following."

"Lucas McCallister attended SMU twelve years ago. Before going to Harvard Law."

"Right. You think they knew each other at SMU?"

"Yes." She reached into her purse, pulled out a folded piece of paper, handed it to me. "It's a photograph I printed from an SMU digital-yearbook page."

It was a photo from some type of campus rally. A younger version of the blonde was in the picture, with the arm of a college-age Lucas

McCallister wrapped around her. Both were smiling. The yearbook photo caption read, *Lucas McCallister and Jill Clayton march against racial discrimination up Bishop Boulevard.*

Natalie continued. "I called a friend of Jill's in New York. They were roommates a few years ago, before Jill's second failed marriage. She admitted that Jill had been acting a little weird the last few weeks. Jill told her she had to go to San Antonio for something that would hopefully put an end to all of her financial troubles. I tried to get more, but the lady got really tight-lipped on me. It was clear that she knew a lot more; she just wouldn't talk about it. She hung up on me and hasn't called me back. I'm going to keep trying. But I'm not sure I can get more out of her."

"The end of all of her financial troubles? You think someone paid Jill and planted her in Boerne that night?"

"Yes, I think it's a strong possibility."

"Mitchell?"

"Still my first guess. Can't prove it. We really need to talk more with this friend."

"What if I go see her, get her to talk to me?"

"To New York?"

"Yes, I can take the train and be there by midnight."

"Why would she talk to you?"

I gave her a grin. "I can be very persuasive. You know that."

"That's true. But what if she recognizes you?"

I shrugged. "A risk I'm willing to take."

She didn't like that answer. "OK, you go. But I'm going to help you."

TWENTY-NINE

Sunday, 9:47 p.m.
Washington, DC
One day, two hours, thirteen minutes till Election Day

I just barely caught the last train to New York City out of Union Station. I snagged a coach seat by the window. No one was sitting beside me, thank God. I had no desire to fake small-talk again. I just wanted to be left alone for a few hours. The train was scheduled to arrive at Penn Station five after midnight. The Amtrak train wasn't crowded. This was both good and bad, depending on how you looked at it. Natalie dressed me up in a new disguise this time. She chose a black baseball cap with a white Yankees logo that we'd picked up at Union Station. Gray Windbreaker, zipped to the top, collar flipped up. Fake square-shaped black glasses that hid my eyes. She'd even taken one of her makeup pencils and darkened some of the hair around my chin into a more prominent goatee. I had to admit, I looked a lot different from the pictures floating around on TV screens and the Internet.

I'd also purchased big black headphones that fully covered both ears, which I now had plugged into Dobbs Howard's phone. I'd downloaded

Bruce Springsteen's *Devils & Dust* album. Bruce had helped get me through that very difficult season living on the streets of Denver as a teenager. While most of my boys had their ears filled with rap and hard-core metal, I had always been drawn to Springsteen. There was just something soulful and spiritual in his music that connected with me. I needed that right now.

When the train left the station and the lights finally dimmed, and no FBI agent or contract assassin popped out of a compartment somewhere with a gun aimed directly at me, I pressed Play on my favorite song on the album. "The Hitter" was about a kid whose mother had kicked him out at a young age. Violence was his way of life. The song recognizes that no matter our character or how many poor choices we make or wrong turns we take, we are still drawn back home. Even when we feel abandoned, we can't escape the innate desire for the comfort of our mother's embrace. My heart desperately longed to be near my mom right now.

I scooted way down deep into my very uncomfortable seat.

I closed my eyes, turned up the volume.

THIRTY

Monday, 12:32 a.m.
New York City
Twenty-three hours, twenty-eight minutes till Election Day

The ex-roommate was named Maggie Medina. She was a CPA at one of the big firms. Natalie said that she and Jill Becker had been roommates three years prior, before Jill had remarried. They'd kept their close friendship, according to multiple sources, which had been confirmed by the quick phone call with Natalie earlier that evening. Maggie lived in a red brownstone on the Upper West Side. I caught a cab from Penn Station, somehow feeling safer. Now I was in a vast new city in the middle of the night without any sign that someone had come along with me. I had slept in tiny spurts on the train, listening to the rhythmic hymns from The Boss, and the shake, hum, and rattle of the train.

The cab dropped me in front of Maggie Medina's brownstone. I needed to speak with her. It could not wait until morning. Hopefully, my gutsy plan would work. I took a deep breath, trotted up the steps, knocked firmly on the front door. According to Natalie, Maggie was not married. She had divorced five years ago. There was no immediate answer. I waited a few seconds and then knocked firmly again. Finally, I heard the rattle of chains inside. The door was cracked open a few seconds later by a black-haired woman wearing a white cotton robe. Her brown eyes were weary, like I had stirred her from bed. She didn't say anything, just stared, confused.

"Ms. Medina?" I asked, with authority in my voice.

She nodded.

I flipped open the black wallet, showing a gold badge. "Detective Aitchison, NYPD, ma'am. I need to speak with you for a brief moment."

I closed the black wallet quickly. The badge was a fake, of course. We'd picked it up in DC before I left. I knew from history that if you speak with enough confidence and authority in your voice, show some semblance of proper identification, people will believe just about anything. I'd cased many homes as a teenager wearing a fake cable-TV uniform with a name badge. If Maggie asked to examine the police badge more carefully, or to make a phone call to headquarters, which she probably should have done, I would've done my best Usain Bolt impression down Ninety-Fourth Street.

"Is something wrong?" Maggie managed. She seemed to be struggling to shake off the deep fog of sleep.

"It's about Jill Becker. I just need to ask you a few questions. It's urgent. Can I come in for a moment?"

"Jill? Yes, of course." She pulled the door open, led me inside to a small formal living room where she turned on two lamps. There was a small white sofa and two red sitting chairs opposite it. She sat in one of the chairs, invited me to sit on the sofa, which I did. I pulled out a small notepad, like I wanted to take official notes.

"Something bad has happened to Jill, hasn't it?" said Maggie.

"When was the last time you spoke to her, Ms. Medina?" I asked. Again, with authority.

"I think on Monday. The day before she left for her trip."

"To San Antonio?"

Maggie nodded.

"Were you aware of the nature of her travel plans?" I asked.

She considered her reply for a moment. "I'm not sure. Jill said there was some type of fashion convention going on there. Is Jill OK? You haven't answered me. She was my friend. Please tell me what happened."

She was fishing. I needed to push her further along.

"She's missing. That's why we're investigating."

Maggie lifted a hand to her mouth, stunned. "Missing?"

"Yes. If you care about your friend, I need you to be forthright with me, Ms. Medina. Do you understand?"

She nodded, her eyes suddenly welling up.

"Why was she really in San Antonio?"

Maggie exhaled deeply, swallowed. "I honestly don't know, Detective. Jill had been acting very strange the past two weeks. She said someone, a man, had come to see her privately and made her an unusual business proposition. She mentioned fifty thousand dollars up front, and then another fifty thousand dollars if all went well. A hundred thousand dollars. It was crazy. But she wouldn't give me any details. She'd borrowed ten thousand dollars from me earlier this year, when she was really struggling, and she's been unable to pay me back. She wanted me to know that it was coming soon. That's the only reason she'd even mentioned this man and the trip to San Antonio."

"She say anything more about this man? A name? What he looked like?"

Maggie shook her head. "No, nothing. She was actually very uneasy about telling me anything. I've never seen her so uptight. She said she hadn't had a single drink in a week, so she could be absolutely clear-minded and focused for the trip, which was a really big deal for Jill. Jill struggled with alcohol *a lot*, especially recently, since her divorce from Roger last year."

"And nothing at all about the nature of the business?"

"No, not a word. But it was something serious. She mentioned signing some very strict confidentiality agreement."

"And you haven't heard from her since?"

Another shake of the head. "She was supposed to come back yesterday. A reporter actually called me earlier today to ask about her, too. So I've been trying to reach her all day with no success. Now, of course, I'm thinking something really bad has happened to her."

"And no one else has come by asking questions?"

"No, just you and this reporter."

"Ms. Medina, how much do you know about Jill's past relationships?"

"Which ones? Her marriages?"

"Or boyfriends."

She paused. "That's a really long list, Detective. Jill has never had any trouble attracting guys. She's just had trouble attracting the right guys." She shrugged. "But that makes two of us, I guess."

"Does she have a history with anyone well known?"

Maggie's eyes narrowed. "Well known? Like an actor or something?"

"Or a politician."

Maggie shook her head. "No, nothing like that. I mean, she did once, back in college. But that was a really long time ago. And before he was any big deal."

"Who did she date in college?"

"Lucas McCallister."

Bingo. "The congressional candidate?"

Maggie nodded. "Although I wouldn't really call it dating. Jill called it a fling. I don't think they were ever an official item. Not boyfriend-girlfriend or anything like that."

"When did she tell you this?"

Maggie shrugged. "When we were first roommates. She didn't want to talk about it too much. She said that when Lucas's father,

Senator McCallister, was first forming a presidential exploratory team several years ago, some campaign guys visited her and offered her a few thousand dollars to keep her mouth shut about any relationship she'd ever had with the senator's son. I think they were trying to cover any skeletons in the old man's closet, even among his family. Jill took the money and had never said a word, as far as I know. Until that night with me, anyway."

"Had she mentioned anything about Lucas McCallister since?"

"No." Her eyes narrowed. "Is he involved?"

"No, ma'am. Just don't want to leave any stone unturned. Jill ever mention the name Tolstoy & Peters? Or a political action committee named Roots? Both out of DC?"

"No, I don't believe so."

I shut my notepad, stood. "I apologize for waking you tonight, Ms. Medina. But I appreciate your help."

"Of course. Will you please let me know if you find out anything?"

"Certainly, we'll be in touch."

THIRTY-ONE

Monday, 1:10 a.m.
New York City
Twenty-one hours, fifty minutes till Election Day

The cab took me over the East River on the Brooklyn Bridge.

Jill Becker lived in a small apartment in East Flatbush, Brooklyn. Natalie had spoken to the landlord. Jill was three months behind on rent. They had threatened eviction several times in the last year, and each time Jill somehow came up with just enough to hang around a little while longer. From all accounts, she was a desperate woman, and a perfect candidate for the assignment of taking down Lucas McCallister in Texas. Someone had done his homework. They had dug deep into McCallister's distant past, looking for bait. The type of bait they knew he would have a very difficult time resisting. Someone beautiful, of course, but it had to be more than that. There had to be a deeper connection for McCallister to roll the dice and risk the election.

I was dropped in front of a four-story yellowed building. There was no doorman, but the front door was connected to an intercom system.

To gain access to the building, a resident had to buzz you in from his or her apartment. The front door was well lit. I could not spend too much time examining the lock system to see if I could overcome it. There were still cars moving about along the street, and some stray walkers. I spent a minute or two studying the engineering, seeing if there was a quick point of leverage. I couldn't see one.

I chose a random button, pressed. No answer.

Another random button. It was late.

"Yeah?" answered a gruff male voice.

"Hey, this is Don in 2C, forgot my key. Can you please let me in?"

"Who?"

"Don, 2C. Come on, man, it's cold out."

"Don't know you." The line went dead.

I gave it another shot. Two more nonresponses. Then, finally, another answer. An irritated female.

"Hello?"

"Hey, this is Geno with Pizza King. Got an order for your neighbor, but they aren't answering. Can you let me in? The pizza is getting cold."

"Which neighbor?"

"Jill Becker."

"Jill lives above me. And I can see you from the window, pal. You don't have any pizzas. You want me to call the cops?"

I looked up, saw a fiftysomething hefty blonde woman peering down from behind the curtain on the second-floor corner unit. Busted. "OK, you got me, ma'am. I'm staying over at Jill's place. Can you let me inside?"

"Jill hasn't been home for a week."

"Yes, I know. I've been taking care of her things. Just forgot the key."

"I'm home all the time. I haven't heard a single footstep up there. I'm calling the cops."

This was a tough nut to crack. I sensed not to push.

"No need. I'm out. Have a good night."

I walked down the steps and disappeared around the building and out of sight. So, that was two swings and two misses. Moving on to Plan C, I looked up at the building. Now, I at least had a frame of reference of where Jill's apartment was located. She lived directly above the lady with a corner unit. I had to get inside. I had not come all the way to New York City to lose this lead. Unfortunately, it was going to take something more creative to get into her apartment.

I spotted a white repair van parked on the curb. I looked back to the building, toward the alley, where I noted the metal fire escape winding all the way up to the top of the building. OK, I was getting somewhere now. I walked quickly up the street, next to the repair van. Peered in the passenger window. *Bingo.* A toolbox was sitting on the floorboard. After confirming there was no one on the sidewalk in either direction, I pulled the twisted paper clips out of my pocket and stuck them in the lock. Worked a jiggle motion, like I had more than a hundred times in my life, and lifted the handle to pull the door open. I grabbed a socket wrench and some duct tape from the toolbox. After shutting the door, I circled to the front of the van and popped the hood. I had the caps off within seconds, wires pulled, and was working the socket wrench until I'd freed a spark plug.

I shut the hood gently, wrapped the spark plug in a shirt from my backpack. Then I laid the shirt and spark plug on the concrete and smashed the white ceramic component into sharp little pieces with the socket wrench.

I found the dark alley behind Jill's building again.

The corner units had windows to the front street and more windows to the side alley. The metal fire escape was attached to the building, but it did not extend all the way to the ground unless the stairs were released from above. I would have to find a way to get to the first set of stairs.

I climbed up onto a filthy metal dumpster and almost passed out from the smell inside. Among random trash bags and boxes, it looked like a bag of dirty diapers had burst wide open. I balanced on the edge of the dumpster, peered up. I would have to make a flying leap to catch the bottom of the stairs and pull my way up. Which also meant I'd have to chance missing, and dropping twelve feet to the hard pavement.

I had to move fast, before the smell made me pass out.

One. Two. Three. Leap.

My right hand caught the metal railing; my left hand missed. I dangled by one arm for just a moment, then swung my body to get my other hand up and onto the stairs. With both hands secure, I quickly tugged my body weight up to the first landing. I was right outside the irritated lady's apartment window. The curtains were slightly parted. I was very careful not to make a sound. I could see the flicker of the TV set in a dark room. I kept moving. Quiet with every soft step, up the stairs to the third level, where I squatted right outside a dark window to what I suspected was Jill's apartment unit. There was a light on inside, near the front door.

I quickly pulled my backpack off my shoulders. I used the flashlight on my phone and searched every corner of the windowpane. I spotted no tiny security boxes or wires anywhere. If the unit had an alarm, it was not on the window. I began peeling off strips of duct tape. First, I made a big *X* on the window with strips, then placed a big plus sign on top of the *X*, followed by a thick duct-tape border around the outside. I had one shot at this. I couldn't break the glass with multiple loud blows, like with a hammer, and chance having large shards fall everywhere. I needed a quick explosion.

I unwrapped the small pieces of white ceramic from the broken spark plug. *Ninja rocks* was what we called them on the streets. A tiny handful of these bad boys could break a car window in a split second, shatter it into a million pieces with a simple toss. We used them to do snatch-and-grab jobs with purses, laptops, cash—anything that was left on the front seats of cars in the parking lot at the mall. We could be in and out within three seconds. The ceramic material was a harder material than the glass. If the cops caught you with Ninja rocks in your pocket, they knew exactly what you were doing.

I took a step back, found the right angle, and threw the Ninja rocks at the window. Bam! Like magic. The window shattered. A billion tiny pebbles of glass. But because of the duct tape, it mostly held together, so there was no loud noise, no shattering. I simply had to peel off the tape and the shattered glass together, carefully, which I was doing now, all the way to the edges until it was gone. I climbed inside.

The apartment was small but neat and well decorated. A tiny kitchen, tiny living room, tiny bedroom. By flipping through the mail on the kitchen counter, I confirmed that it was indeed Jill Becker's place.

It did not look like anyone had been inside the apartment. Nothing seemed out of place. I assumed it was exactly as Jill had left it when she caught a plane to Texas earlier in the week. I found pictures on the shelves of Jill with girlfriends. One with folks that looked like her parents. I made my way to the bedroom, as lightly as possible, as I knew irritated lady was right below. I turned on the light to her tidy bedroom and found a queen-size bed neatly made. I searched her dresser and nightstand drawers, finding nothing unusual. Then I made my way over to a small rolltop desk shoved into the corner by the window and pulled open to the top. Jill was neat and organized. There was mail, magazines, books, notepads, and cards. The things you'd expect to find in a desk in a bedroom. I sifted through everything but found nothing suspicious until I spotted a yellow notepad by the base of the white desk lamp. It was the name and phone number at the bottom-right corner of the page that caught my attention.

Devin Nicks.

Our suspicions were correct. Congressman Mitchell's chief of staff had hired Jill. I plucked the page from the notepad, examined it more closely. It was hard to believe. Congressman Mitchell's team had thrown a wild, last-second Hail Mary to try to win the election.

I folded the paper, put it in my pocket, and turned out all the lights. Then I carefully exited the apartment along the same fire escape.

THIRTY-TWO

Monday, 1:36 a.m.
New York City
Twenty-one hours, twenty-four minutes till Election Day

My head was reeling when I stepped onto the cold sidewalk outside the apartment building. That's when I spotted him, dressed in a dark trench coat. The gray-bearded man was standing across the street, in the reflection of a café light, but in the shadows. For a moment, I wasn't sure what to do. Walk straight up and introduce myself? Run from him? But then I reminded myself that he'd likely taken my mom, so the decision suddenly became very easy.

We needed to talk. Right now.

I stepped off the curb, into the street, walking toward him with purpose.

He quickly turned the corner, slipped behind the building, and was gone.

So, I took off sprinting, bounded up the sidewalk, turned that same corner at full speed.

I stopped and quickly scanned every direction. No sign of him. I ran forward, peered into shop windows, car windshields, listening for engines starting up, the sound of footsteps on concrete. Nothing. I spun around in a slow circle, staring up at the windows of all the commercial and residential buildings on the block around me. He'd just vanished. Impossible. Or did he? Had I really seen him? Or was I now seeing visions? Sleep deprivation was known to make the mind do crazy things. But this seemed so real.

I screamed in frustration. Just let it loose at the top of my lungs.

"Who the hell are you?"

My yell echoed in the streets. I got a quick "Shut the hell up!" in reply from a friendly Brooklyn neighbor with an open window nearby.

But no answer from the gray-bearded man.

THIRTY-THREE

Monday, 2:11 a.m.
New York City
Twenty-one hours, forty-nine minutes till Election Day

I spent the night inside the historic Trinity Church on Broadway near Wall Street. I had only five hours to kill before I needed to be somewhere close by, so I didn't even want to bother with a hotel or motel. Why risk possibly being identified by a front-desk clerk when I wouldn't be sleeping, anyway? Of course, Trinity Church wasn't open to the public at two in the morning, but it wasn't on lockdown, either. I managed to find my way inside through a side door and now sat on a third-row wooden pew inside the enormous sanctuary. It was dark, but there was enough peripheral light to marvel at the massive stained-glass windows that stretched nearly to the sky. People had been worshipping in this building for hundreds of years. I figured with my mom's fate in the hands of a mysterious stranger, deadly assassins on the prowl, and the FBI intent on hunting me down, there was probably no better place for me to spend a few hours right now than on my knees inside a church.

It was dead quiet. Almost too quiet, after two straight days with so much noise in my head.

I pulled out my collection of photos from my backpack, began flipping through them. Some were when she was just a kid, holding me as a baby. A baby having a baby. There were many others, much more recent, including a photo of the two of us sitting on a red-checkered blanket at a Fourth of July festival this past summer. My mom looked so frail in the photo but still happy. My mom said she had no reason to frown. The cancer could have her. God had already answered her prayers. We were together again.

My eyes grew moist. I wondered where she was right now, at this very moment. Was she OK? Had they threatened her? Hurt her?

My breathing grew heavy.

I swallowed. But I couldn't stop it.

Before I knew it, the tears started trickling down.

She was the only family I had. I could not lose her.

THIRTY-FOUR

Monday, 6:55 a.m.
New York City
Seventeen hours, five minutes till Election Day

I waited in Battery Park, at the southern tip of Manhattan, with a view of the Statue of Liberty. It was the eve of Election Day. The sun was just up, and the city was rolling out of bed—yawning, stretching, and getting its day started. A few folks were out, taking early-morning walks, some with dogs, others with coffee and newspapers. I avoided those with newspapers. The tours of Lady Liberty nearby wouldn't begin for another hour. I was busy working the crick out of my neck from a night on a hard wooden pew. I'd managed to slip out unnoticed before dawn, before the clergy arrived.

Ten minutes ago, I'd texted Josh, my old roommate at CU, the friend who'd recruited me onto this disastrous tracker assignment in the first place. I saw on Josh's Twitter feed that he was in New York City with his team today, working a big political function for a New York senatorial candidate. He was staying downtown at the W Hotel just a few blocks away. I'd called the hotel first thing, but they could not or would not tell me his room number. Since I couldn't just sit around in the hotel lobby all day hoping for a chance encounter with my old roommate, I decided to take the risk and text Josh.

Need to see you. ASAP. Battery Park, Bosque Fountain. —Clyde

Josh wouldn't recognize my phone number, but he would know the text was from me. Clyde was a nickname we'd called each other regularly back in our campus days. It came from the name of the funny orangutan in the old Clint Eastwood comedy *Every Which Way But Loose* and the famous Eastwood line, "Right turn, Clyde." We must have watched that movie two dozen times our freshman year while playing poker and drinking too much cheap beer.

Thankfully, Josh replied almost immediately. Showing he knew it was me.

I'll be there in ten minutes.

I sat nervously on a cool bench in the park. It was a very crisp forty-five degrees. I had my black Yankees cap on, bill pulled down tight, headphones on, head bopping slowly up and down, even though I didn't currently have any music playing. Just an act. I spotted Josh walking up the sidewalk. I'd recognize that awkward, lanky gait anywhere. He was tall, about six foot five, and always walked with his shoulders slumped forward. He wore a black Colorado Rockies sweatshirt. Josh loved baseball but was one of the most uncoordinated human beings I'd ever been around. He practically pulled a muscle every time he did routine tasks like unloading the dishwasher. He was my age but looked ten years older because he was already prematurely balding on top.

He slowed near the fountain, began looking around.

I was sitting on a park bench twenty feet in front of him. Right under his nose. He didn't recognize me. If one of my best friends couldn't spot me right out in the open, hopefully neither could anyone else.

I slipped the headphones down.

"Josh," I said, loud enough to be heard over the water fountain.

His head whipped back around. He looked over at me for a second, puzzled, then seemed to put it together. He stepped over. I stood. We exchanged an awkward hug.

"I can't believe it," Josh said quietly, shaking his head. "I wasn't sure I'd ever see you again."

"Well, here I am," I said, with an edge. I couldn't tell if he was happy or sad to see me. I didn't really trust Josh right now. I needed answers.

"Sam, what happened out there?"

"You tell me."

His forehead wrinkled. "What do you mean?"

"Josh, don't play dumb with me. You got me mixed up in this!"

For a second, he looked defiant. But then he swallowed, his face drooping. "I didn't mean to. I swear. I had no idea any of this would happen. I promise you that."

"I don't care about your promises. Tell me why. Why did you call me for this job?"

He shifted his weight. "Ted called me up, said he had a new client. That he needed someone new for a special assignment. Said it could mean a lot of money, that he'd share if I could help him find the right guy. This client was not OK with whom Ted currently had tracking on the campaign trail. He wanted someone brand-new. Someone he could vet and handpick. Someone who wasn't so interconnected with the rest of the team. Someone who was really resourceful. A risk taker, a loner. He had all these specific requirements. Ted said it would pay really well. I thought of you. I knew you needed the money, Sam. For school, for your mom. So I turned in a file I'd put together on you, your background, your skill set, my recommendation. A few weeks later, Ted called me back and said the client wanted you. That I should set it up, whatever it took."

"And you didn't think this was information I needed to know?"

"I'm sorry. I couldn't say anything. It was part of the deal."

"So, you just took the money and put me out there in the war zone?"

"I didn't know there was more to it. I swear, Sam. I would have never done it had I known."

"Who was the client, Josh?"

"I don't know. Ted said I couldn't know."

"Come on, man. You have to have some idea. Was it someone from Congressman Mitchell's team?"

"I swear, I don't know. When all of this hit the fan, I panicked and called Ted. But I never talked to him to get any answers. And the next thing I know, he's . . . well, he's dead."

I could see the leery look in his eye. "And you think I actually killed him?"

He paused, unsure. I was flabbergasted. He actually thought I'd killed him. I didn't even know this guy anymore. The Josh I knew was long gone. DC had already changed him.

"Come on, Josh! Get serious. I didn't kill anyone. But I've got plenty of people out there right now trying to kill me. I've got the feds on CNN telling the whole world I'm a killer. Someone has even kidnapped my mom. I'm living a nightmare right now because of you."

Josh seemed shocked. "You really didn't have anything to do with Rick or Ted?"

"Hell, no! I mean, I was with them. But someone else put the bullets in them. And then they tried to kill me."

"Who has your mom?"

I wanted to punch him. "I don't know! Are you listening to me? I need your help."

Josh's eyes suddenly widened. He took a peek to his right. He turned back to me, lowered his voice even more. "You've got to get out of here, Sam. Right now."

I felt a flash of panic. "Why?"

Josh's face went pale. "The FBI will be here any minute."

I cursed. "How do you know?"

His face dropped even further. "I called them. Right after you texted. I'm sorry. They met with me one-on-one yesterday. They have a pretty clear case against you, Sam. Security photos. Prints. The works. I didn't want to believe it, but they had even me convinced. I'm sorry. I realize now I was wrong. You've got to go. Now. They asked me to stall you as long as possible."

I peered over his shoulder, spotted the first two agents. They were already here, only thirty yards away. They were walking quickly up the sidewalk, wearing trench coats and sunglasses. It wasn't bright enough yet for sunglasses. They had already honed in on us standing near the water fountain.

Josh followed my glare. "I'm sorry, man. I really am."

I ignored him, even though I wanted to take a swing at him. I glanced to my left. Two more agents. Twenty yards. Circling in from behind. Were more coming? I wasn't going to wait around to count them. I turned, leaped over a curb, and sprinted through moist grass toward the water. Racing away from both sets of agents, I did not spot any agents directly in front of me. I hit the sidewalk next to the water, raced past a female jogger. I took my first peek back. I spotted all four agents at a dead sprint in pursuit. I hit the edge of Battery Park, cut through a parking lot near the Staten Island Ferry dock. A NYPD police car suddenly appeared right in front of me, screeching to a halt, its lights flashing.

I was twenty feet out, trapped. The cop climbed out of the driver's seat.

I jumped, slid across the hood of the police car, landed on the other side, and continued my sprint. I wondered if bullets would begin flying. In a stroke of luck, a huge crowd was forming up ahead of me. Hundreds of tourists were waiting to get on the first Staten Island Ferry tour of the day.

I raced straight toward them. The feds and the police would have to shoot into a crowd, which I doubted they would do. I hit the crowd at full speed, trying not to knock anyone over. I pushed my way through, shoving people out of the way. I heard the sirens of more police cars off to my left. They were coming in full force. I wondered if it was about to all be over. I broke through the crowd into an opening, circled the ferry building, found my way next to FDR Drive on the other side. Another peek behind me. I'd created some additional space. But where was I going, exactly? I was literally on an island.

I was sprinting up the sidewalk along the FDR when a silver Honda Civic suddenly swerved right in front of me and skidded to a stop. I had no choice but to leave my feet, slide across the hood on my stomach, spill over onto the other side, and roll. My head hit the pavement hard. I saw stars.

A strong hand grabbed my arm. I looked up, shocked to see the blond banker guy from DC. The man following Natalie yesterday. His hand on my arm, pulling me toward his car. Oddly, it felt like he was trying to help me get away.

"Get in the car, Sam, hurry!" he said, lifting me up, looking behind us. "They're close!"

Without thinking, I did what he said, mostly because I spotted the mass of agents gaining ground. He had the back door open. I stumbled to my feet, dove into the car. He slammed my door shut, jumped into the driver's seat, and pressed the gas pedal to the floorboard. We kicked off the curb, back into the flow of traffic.

"Stay down!" the blond guy yelled at me when my head peeked up.

I slid back down. My heart was beating a thousand times a minute. I could hear multiple sirens pass by us from the opposite direction. But it didn't sound like any were turning around and following. We were losing them.

"Who are you?" I asked.

He didn't respond. The car turned at an intersection. He was driving swiftly through downtown traffic, headed north. I saw buildings whipping past.

"Where are we going?" I demanded.

Again, he didn't respond. I looked around the backseat, trying to find something that told me anything about my driver. There was nothing. It was clearly a rental. It smelled brand-new. Suddenly, the driver pulled the car over to the curb, stopping abruptly and slamming my face against the front seat.

He turned to me. "Get out."

"No. Tell me who you are first."

"I'm not at liberty to discuss that with you."

"OK, then, who do you work for?"

He gave me a stern look. "Sam, you've got only seconds."

I looked around. We were at the corner of East Forty-third and Park Avenue. Grand Central Terminal. A major subway hub. I had a chance to get lost again. I had a million questions, but it was clear that my new travel companion wasn't going to answer any of them. I climbed out. Before I could even shut the back door, the driver peeled back out into traffic. He was gone.

I frantically tried to process what had just happened. I glanced at the uniformed cop ahead of me, who didn't seem to notice me, and knew I had to keep moving.

I ducked quickly inside Grand Central.

THIRTY-FIVE

Monday, 9:46 a.m.
Bordentown, New Jersey
Fourteen hours, fourteen minutes till Election Day

I took a series of trains to New Jersey to get out of New York City.

Then I decided I was no longer comfortable on public transit. So, I borrowed a new white Ford Explorer from the parking lot of Jersey Gardens in Elizabeth and began my trek down I-95, back to Washington, DC. I threw my new phone, tablet, and IDs into the Elizabeth River. I would no longer be using anything that could be traced. They would surely connect me with Dobbs Howard since I'd texted Josh from that phone. Dobbs was dead. I would go nameless the rest of the way.

I drove the speed limit. I didn't need to get pulled over right now.

I was so confused. Who was the blond guy? How did he know how to find me?

That was twice I'd done a Houdini disappearing act with the help of strangers.

I thought about my conversation with Josh. I was indeed hand-picked. Someone had paid a lot of money and chosen me specifically to be out there on that campaign trail on that fateful night. I thought of the scribbled name I'd found on the yellow notepad inside Jill Becker's apartment. Devin Nicks, chief of staff for Congressman Mitchell. Had Nicks been the one to reach out to Ted Bowerson? Had he hired Jill Becker? Had he set this all up?

I was on the road to Philadelphia when I first spotted it in my rearview mirror.

Silver Honda Civic. Fifty yards back. At first, I thought there was no way it could be the same guy, the blond banker. I slowed my stolen Explorer to fifty miles an hour anyway. Traffic on I-95 began zipping around me. But not the Civic. The driver just hung back, keeping its distance.

I pulled off the interstate near Bordentown. And, sure enough, the Civic followed me. I zigzagged through several streets in the small township before parking in the lot right outside a ShopRite grocery. I left the Explorer and quickly made my way inside the store, but not without confirming the Civic was still with me, parking in a spot several rows behind me. The blond banker climbed out of his car to go grocery shopping with me.

The thought of walking straight out there and confronting him in the parking lot crossed my mind. But he'd made it clear that he wasn't going to volunteer information. So, I quickly made other plans.

I grabbed a hand basket, hit an aisle with other shoppers, then paused to make sure the banker was inside the store with me. When he stepped through the glass doors, I turned and headed quickly to the back of the store. I passed through a cold-meats section and found a dirty swivel door to the warehouse. I found a set of concrete stairs to the loading dock and bound down them two at a time. Within seconds, I was back outside, circling the building, making my way around to the front again.

I took a moment to peer into the parking lot.

There was no sign of the blond. He was still inside the store. I probably had two minutes to make this happen. I made my way up a row of cars and found his Civic. The door was locked. I dropped to one knee. I had never picked a car door lock so fast in my life. Inside the driver's seat there was nothing, and nothing in the cup holders. I opened the middle console, looking for rental paperwork. Nothing. Flipped down the visors. Nothing. Popped open the glove box. Generic rental paperwork but nothing that identified him. His blue blazer was folded in the passenger seat. I grabbed it, reached into all the pockets, and found it. An ID badge.

WILLIAM ALEXANDER, SPECIAL AGENT, CENTRAL INTELLIGENCE AGENCY

The CIA? Seriously?

I didn't have time to think. I slipped the ID in my back pocket, fell to the floorboard. I pulled out wires and quickly dismantled the car's starter.

I was back inside my stolen Explorer seconds later. The engine revved.

I quickly found the New Jersey Turnpike. This time I would push the speed limit. I had to get back to Natalie, and fast.

THIRTY-SIX

Monday, 12:14 p.m.
Washington, DC
Eleven hours, forty-six minutes till Election Day

Back in DC, I met Natalie on the plush grounds of Arlington National Cemetery, the vast burial plot for hundreds of thousands of honored military veterans. The sky was gray and hinting at more rain, but no drops had fallen just yet. Tumultuous clouds appeared on the horizon. The rest of my drive down I-95 had been thankfully uneventful. Although the blond banker had proven to be very resourceful, he would've needed a helicopter to catch up to me, as I chose to screw playing it safe and had my foot near the floorboard the entire rest of the way back to DC.

There was no further sign of CIA Agent William Alexander. At this point, I wasn't sure if that was a good thing or a bad thing. The guy had rescued me. I didn't know why. Regardless, I didn't like having a shadow.

I'd peeled off the highway near Baltimore, made a quick trip to Walgreens, then locked myself in a bathroom stall with a razor and shaving cream. My last hurrah. My head was now completely shaved.

Not a stray hair anywhere other than the slight brown shag on my chin and cheeks. After being chased through Battery Park, I needed another drastic change. For the first time, I could count the dimples and bumps on my scalp. I examined the scar on the left side above my ear. A dealer had smashed me good with a beer bottle when I was fourteen; he felt I hadn't moved my inventory quickly enough for his liking. I spent a night in the hospital after that one. Now the Yankees cap was gone, along with the Windbreaker. Instead, I wore a new black hoodie, which currently covered my bald scalp.

I walked for fifteen minutes through the rolling hills of the cemetery to the back of the expansive property, passing two different military funeral services going on at that very moment. Natalie had instructed me to meet her by the Battle of the Bulge memorial. I used the map and found her exactly where she said she would be, standing to the left of the memorial. I wondered if she even had a tail anymore, after the blond banker had ditched her and followed me to New York City. I still didn't know how that was even possible. I fought the urge to wrap my arms around her and pull her in close.

I stepped up next to her, my eyes on the small memorial.

"Hey," I said.

"How're you holding up?" she asked me.

"I've had better weeks."

I saw her studying my bald head peeking out from under the hoodie.

"Yes, it's all gone," I said.

She gave a small grin. "I like it. It's better than the blond look."

"Good to know. Maybe this will be my new look. Did you check him out?"

She nodded. We'd spoken by pay phone when I was in Baltimore.

"He's legit, Sam. He works for the CIA. Sixteen-year veteran. Terrorism Analysis Division. Lots of overseas experience."

"Wonderful. So, I'm a terrorist now. Any idea why he would rescue me from the FBI? Aren't the FBI and CIA supposed to play nice together?"

"I still don't know. There is nothing about his background that connects. At least, nothing that I've found just yet. And my contact at the CIA says that Alexander is on a paid monthlong leave of absence right now. But I do have something else for you."

She pulled out her phone, brought up a digital color photograph. It was a picture of several men in military fatigues standing in a huddle, smiling at the camera. I immediately spotted the now-familiar face of Elvis in front. Then my eyes moved two guys left and froze. There he was, my friend Square Jaw.

"Is that him?" Natalie asked.

I nodded. "That's the guy. Where is this?"

"Military training center in Virginia. Headquarters for Redrock Security."

I remembered seeing Elvis's Redrock Security ID. "How did you find him?"

"I got someone on Congressman Mitchell's team to ID him in some photographs. According to the aide, Congressman Mitchell recently had some domestic threats that they were taking seriously, so they'd contracted out additional private security. From Stable Security in Dallas. Your boy, Square Jaw, was one of those men. His real name is Tom Brickman. Former marine special ops from Oklahoma."

"So, both of these men worked for Mitchell?"

"Yes."

"You think Devin Nicks, his chief of staff, coordinated the encounter with Jill Becker to get McCallister, then it backfired when he accidentally killed her instead of simply messing around with her? And then they decided to cover their tracks on the whole thing by sending out these contract killers?"

"Not necessarily."

"What do you mean?"

"I spoke with Devin Nicks just twenty minutes ago."

I turned to her fully. "Seriously?"

"Yes. I got word to him that I was working a major story that could have serious implications for the campaign. Asked him to call me back right away. He did within ten minutes. I asked him directly about his relationship with Jill Becker. He flat-out said he'd never heard the name. So, I asked him a second time, very clearly. He again denied knowing anyone named Jill Becker."

"No surprise there, right?"

"Yes and no. I've spent a lot of time with these guys, getting quotes, and I've learned to read between the lines. Guys like Devin Nicks are usually more measured in their responses. Much more careful with their choice of words. They usually never directly confirm or deny anything, so they can always find an out to cover their asses, if needed. Nicks didn't do that with me today."

"So, what, you believe him?"

"I'm not sure, Sam. When he denied knowing her, he went on major offensive and then began grilling me for more info about her. Who was she? What kind of angle was I working? He was clearly desperate. They're down five points with only one day to go. The polls open at eight tomorrow morning. I don't think you do that if you're connected the way we think he's connected. You evade and get off the phone. So, I bailed on the call myself, told him I'd be back in touch with him shortly. After that, some of my contacts let me know that Mitchell's team was digging around like crazy on Jill Becker, in search of more information on my story. Nicks has already called my cell back twice since our first call. But I haven't answered."

I shook my head. "I don't know, Natalie. It's the only theory we've got right now that makes any sense. Plus, I found his name written down on a notepad inside her apartment. How else did it get there?"

"Not sure. It could mean a number of things. But I don't have the answer to that yet."

Her cell phone buzzed again. It had buzzed multiple times during our conversation. I was used to it going off all the time while we were dating. That was Natalie's world. This time she looked oddly at her phone screen, then held up a text message. No name was listed.

Is the Duke with you?

Tommy, I told her. I quickly replied with, Yes, I'm here. Another text from Tommy.

Where you been? Trying to get in touch with you for an hour. .

Tossed my phone. Sorry.

Well, your boy, Jeremy, went live an hour ago. Working under an alias, but I got him. He's still online right now.

I texted back. You got an address?

Atlas Arcade, 1236 H Street NE

Thanks, Mav. Headed there now!

"Let's go," I said, grabbing Natalie.

THIRTY-SEVEN

Monday, 12:51 p.m.
Washington, DC
Eleven hours, nine minutes till Election Day

Atlas Arcade was in a bright-orange building on a strip in a seedy part of northeast DC. It was billed as the best retro arcade bar in the city, featuring classic arcade games from the eighties and early nineties: Donkey Kong, Golden Axe, and Double Dragon II. Natalie parked her Cherokee a block up the street. It had started to drizzle.

I pulled my hood over my bald head. We pushed through the front door.

I knew what Jeremy Lynch looked like; Natalie had found a year-book photo, so I was searching for a skinny guy my age with brown hair, maybe glasses. There were about ten guys in a small, narrow room who matched that description. Along the redbrick walls on the right were a dozen full-size arcade games. On the left side, deeper into the arcade, was a small bar. Several guys were seated at the bar, where you could drink a beer and play video games at the same time. I had hung out in places just like this ten years ago.

We strolled by, studying the faces. Guys were huddled around the arcade machines in small packs. I did not spot Jeremy. Maybe he'd changed his appearance, like me. I asked the bartender if he knew where I could find him. The bartender shrugged.

We moved farther toward the back, by the restrooms and a dartboard.

That's when I spotted a guy sitting on the brown-tile floor, back up against an arcade game, huddled over a laptop in front of him. He matched the picture from the yearbook, even wearing what looked like the same glasses from the photo. Plus, he was the only guy in the arcade bar at the moment who was using a laptop computer.

"Jeremy?" I asked, standing over him.

He peered up, startled. His eyes were completely bloodshot.

When he saw us, he slammed his laptop shut, scrambled to his feet, and darted right past us. Others turned to stare as Jeremy raced clumsily past them and out the front door, me in pursuit. Jeremy pushed through the glass door and sprinted up the block. I was out the door right behind him. There was no way he was getting away, but he sure was going for it. He ran past a strip of four two-story buildings, took a left at the first alley, passed two metal dumpsters, a parked van, and ran into a tall chain-link fence. He jumped on it, tried to climb up, but I had a hand on his jeans within seconds and yanked him to the pavement.

He was still trying to get away as I pinned him to the ground.

"Jeremy, stop," I urged him. "I'm here to help you."

He peered up into my eyes. The guy was really scared. I could see it.

"I promise," I said, my voice softer.

He finally stopped struggling.

THIRTY-EIGHT

Monday, 1:08 p.m.
Washington, DC
Ten hours, fifty-two minutes till Election Day

We sat with Jeremy Lynch at a booth inside a Popeye's fast-food restaurant.

The rain was coming fast and furious now outside the windows, pounding the dirty pavement.

Although Jeremy was no longer hysterical, his hands were still shaking. Natalie had purchased him a box of chicken strips and a drink. He was scarfing them down like he hadn't eaten in weeks.

"How did you find me?" Jeremy asked.

"It's not important," I assured him. "Do you have the video, Jeremy?"

He peered up over his chicken. "What video?"

"Don't play games."

He shook his head. "No, I don't have it."

"Did you watch it, Jeremy?" Natalie asked.

He nodded. "But only after I found out Rick was dead."

"I didn't do it," I assured him.

"I know that," he said. "This is *much* bigger than you."

"What happened?" Natalie asked. "I spoke with your girlfriend. She said you just disappeared. No one has heard from you."

"I watched the video. But before I could download it, it just disappeared. Poof. Gone. Someone else was tracking it online. They pulled it down before I could get it. I tried to go hunting for it, but I kept getting blocked. Twenty minutes later, someone takes a shot at me in the parking garage by my car. I swear, the only reason I'm still alive is because I'm a clumsy idiot. I dropped my phone, bent to pick it up, and felt a bullet fly right past me into my car window. I ran. The guy took two more shots. I dove over the wall of the two-story garage, landed on an awning from a store below, nearly broke my back. I don't know how I got away. I just kept running."

"And you've been hiding?" Natalie asked.

"Yes! I have no idea who I can trust. I knew the minute the video got pulled from the server that there was much more to the story than some random political tracker killing my cousin over drugs. Maybe Rick knew that, too. And that's why he sent it to me in the first place."

"It's possible," I said, looking at Natalie. "Maybe Rick knew I was chosen for the job?"

"Why didn't you get the CIA on this?" Natalie asked Jeremy.

"When you work for the CIA, you quickly learn to trust no one, especially when all hell breaks loose. I wanted to find out more on my own first."

"Have you found anything?" Natalie asked him.

"Not much yet. I'm trying to be careful. I'd just pinpointed a location for the cyber attack when you two showed up at the arcade."

"Where?" I asked.

"Local. A remote location outside of Chesapeake, Virginia."

Chesapeake? That sounded very familiar. My mind was cycling through images that I'd stored away in my head. It finally landed on the ID security badge that I'd found inside Greg Carson's wallet back in Austin. The military training facility.

Chesapeake, Virginia. Redrock Security.

THIRTY-NINE

Monday, 1:19 p.m.
Washington, DC
Ten hours, forty-one minutes till Election Day

The bullets came in successive fashion.

The first bullet hit Jeremy right in the left temple. His head whipped back, and bright-red blood sprayed the fast-food table.

The second bullet hit the cup in Jeremy's hand, spewing Coke everywhere.

The third one clipped my shoulder. I had Natalie on the dirty floor of the restaurant within seconds. There was a scream from one of the Popeye's employees, who was wiping a table down nearby. She dove to the floor. Jeremy had fallen over, limp, still in the booth. His eyes open, blood pouring down over the seat and pooling onto the floor right next to us.

The shots had come from out front, through a window. I didn't have time to calculate from exactly where. My guess was the car parked on the curb. There was more yelling and screaming from people who were eating in the restaurant. They had hit the floor, too, ten feet from us. I heard yelling and frantic scrambling behind the counter.

Two more shots. They landed in the wooden booth inches behind us, causing the wood to splinter.

More screams. More yelling.

We had to get out of there. We needed cover, though. We couldn't just run for it.

I caught the eye of a guy on the floor ten feet from me.

"Do you have a lighter?" I asked.

"What?"

"A cigarette lighter!" I repeated.

He nodded, dug in his jeans pocket, and slid it across the floor to me. Right beside me was a plastic trash container inside a painted wooden box. Like you'd find in every fast-food restaurant. I reached up, opened the lid, pulled out the trash can from inside the box.

"What are you doing?" Natalie asked.

"Getting us out of here."

Another shot whizzed right past me, hit the wall. More screaming.

I found a paper bag on top. I flicked the lighter, lit the paper bag on fire, and then put it back inside the trash can. Within seconds, flames erupted as the fire quickly spread to the other thin paper contents inside the trash. I shoved it toward the front of the store. Smoke began pouring out the top, filling up most of the room and, most important, clouding the windows in front. I grabbed Natalie by the hand; we stood and rushed behind the order counter, where I found two gals in uniform huddled closely together, frightened out of their minds.

"Back door?"

They pointed. We moved.

Two seconds later, we pushed through the back door of the building into an alley. I knew better than to take for granted that we were safe. They could have circled, as they had before, anticipating an escape. I peered both ways. Rain was still coming down hard, and I could hear sirens. Someone had dialed 911. The police were close. We could not hang around.

We stepped out into the rain, splashed our way down the alley, and ran.

I told Natalie to text Tommy and then dump her phone.

My shoulder was throbbing. Blood was soaking my sleeve.

FORTY

Monday, 4:20 p.m.
Washington, DC
Seven hours, forty minutes till Election Day

We huddled in a motel room near the DC-Virginia border.

I sat on the bed with my shirt off, medical tape wrapped around my shoulder, blood seeping through. The bullet had clipped me good. It hurt like hell, but the damage wasn't too bad. We'd cleaned it up pretty good, and Natalie had done a valiant job playing nurse. She mentioned a hospital visit, but both of us knew that was not an option. Tommy Kucher was in the room with us on a laptop, pecking away. Natalie was on the phone with her editor. Tommy had brought us both new phones. The curtains were pulled tight.

Natalie got off the phone.

"What did he find?" I asked.

"Did you follow the Ankara debacle in the news last year?"

"The embassy bombing in Turkey?"

"Yes."

"Sort of. Not closely. Fill me in."

"If you'll remember, several embassy staff were killed that day along with US Ambassador Thomas Patterson. Islamic terrorists. Lots of finger-pointing from both sides of the political fence about the breakdown of communications and security. There'd been heated debate about who knew what and when. And why more wasn't done from the top to protect the embassy. Redrock Security was also there with private agents. They'd been given a lucrative contract to provide additional security to dozens of embassies around the globe. So, Redrock has been taking *a lot* of heat about their security services and practices. A congressional investigative committee is currently being formed to investigate deeper. Redrock stands to lose *billions* of dollars in future government military contracts should they somehow be made the scapegoat and shoulder the blame on Ankara, which some politicians seem bent on doing."

"But I don't get it. Roots is spending all of that super-PAC money to beat Mitchell. You said a dozen prominent TV ads in prime time the past two weeks and an hour-long documentary. *Not* to elect Mitchell. So, why would Mitchell's team contract out Redrock Security guys to protect Mitchell on the campaign trail? Isn't that a contradiction?"

"My guess is they didn't know they were Redrock guys. They thought they were Stable Security guys out of Dallas. Only now we know by digging deeper that Stable is a subsidiary of Redrock. I think Redrock has dozens of these private outfits around the country. You'd never know it. A lot of smoke and mirrors with these guys. There's more," she said, punching on her phone and then showing it to me. "This was taken at an intimate high-dollar political dinner in San Antonio just four nights ago."

I studied the clear digital photo. Lucas McCallister was smiling and shaking hands with a distinguished-looking man in a black tuxedo. They looked like old pals. I recognized him but wasn't sure from where. "Who is he?"

"Victor Larsen, founder of Redrock."

"You think McCallister's team is in bed with Redrock Security?"

"Redrock's headquarters are in Virginia. It's very big business in that state. Lucas McCallister's father is a senator from Virginia, and my editor says he's a private ally of Victor Larsen. There's a very strong connection there."

"You think it was quid pro quo? Secretly help get Lucas McCallister elected using this super PAC, or whatever means necessary. In return, Lucas gets appointed to the congressional committee investigating Redrock and shows political favor?"

"Yes. My inside congressional sources say it's a split house right now regarding opinions on Redrock and whether the United States should continue contracting with them. It could go either way for them next year. Victor Larsen is clearly not satisfied with those odds. I think the so-called domestic threats made toward Congressman Mitchell recently were a ruse created by Redrock, geared at getting the Mitchell campaign to hire more independent security guys. So, they went to their standby, Stable Security in Dallas, where Square Jaw and Elvis were waiting. I think they were intentionally planted by Victor Larsen and McCallister on Congressman Mitchell's team as eyes and ears into the Mitchell campaign."

"But then the game completely changed when I showed up and caught McCallister with his pants down."

"Yes, their objective changed. Some of these guys are ruthless. There are stories of assassinations by Redrock guys all over the globe, including the slaughter of fourteen innocent civilians in Afghanistan three years ago. It's not a big leap for some of these guys to go from private-security contractor to shadow assassin. Redrock also has a highly trained cyber team. A team that my sources say has been contracted out regularly by the United States military, the CIA, as well as other government entities around the globe. A team completely capable of the attack Tommy mentioned."

My mind was so tired, I could hardly keep up. "But then, what's the connection to William Alexander and the gray-bearded man?"

"I still don't know. That's a missing link for me."

I dropped back on the bed, grimaced, my shoulder throbbing. I had just gotten off the phone with David Benoltz, who strongly urged me to come in. Even though he admitted that the FBI had a stacked deck, he still insisted he could get me out of this mess. But he said it wasn't going to be easy. As much as I liked him, I wasn't ready to put my life in someone else's hands.

I stared at the ceiling. "If Redrock really has the video, wouldn't they have destroyed it by now? Gotten rid of the evidence?"

"Doubtful," replied Natalie. "Think about it, Sam. If you're Victor Larsen, that video has just become your ultimate blackmail, as long as it remains only in your possession. It's a lethal source of powerful leverage against Lucas McCallister. A way to get McCallister to do whatever Larsen wants. I'm sure Victor Larsen is now hoping to ride McCallister all the way to the top."

"Good point. It's not just about this election. Now it's about future elections, too."

"Right."

"So, we really need to change the outcome of this election, before it ever gets started. And we've only got a few hours to do it. No pressure there."

Natalie sat on the bed next to me. "How's the shoulder?"

"I stopped feeling anything twenty minutes ago. I'll probably need the arm amputated."

She gave a curt smile, knowing I was being overdramatic. "You're going to need a serious vacation when this is over, aren't you?"

"And so will you."

She nodded.

"Great, go ahead and book the reservations. The beach, maybe Aruba, a tray of fruity drinks with little umbrellas, you in a bikini next to me. Sounds perfect."

"I think I got it," Tommy suddenly announced from the small desk.

We bounced up, hurried over, studied the laptop in front of him. The gobbledygook on the screen made absolutely no sense to me.

"You seriously found it?" I asked.

"Yes, it's there."

"How do you know what's what?" I asked.

"Trust me, Duke. This is my world. I'm inside the private server at Redrock headquarters. Chesapeake, Virginia. Just a surface hack. But I'm sure it's there. All of the online threads confirm it, I promise. I identified its exact location on the server. You said it was five minutes and twenty-seven seconds in length, right? I got that bad boy."

"You're incredible, Tommy."

"Can you get it?" Natalie asked.

Tommy laughed. "Sure, it's possible. If I had six months. And if you could fly me around the world on a secure private jet to avoid being hunted and somehow keep me from being shot. This thing is protected by the most sophisticated antipiracy software I've ever seen in my life. Better than the latest I've seen from the Chinese military. Plus, it looks like it's even linked to a supercomplex GPS system."

"What does that mean?" Natalie questioned.

"It means that even their own people can't access it remotely. You have to be on-site."

"You mean inside Redrock headquarters?" I asked.

"Yep. Inside their computer center."

"So how do we get it, Tommy?" Natalie said.

"We can't. Unless . . ."

"Unless what?" I asked.

Tommy shrugged. "Unless we go get it from the inside."

"I'm a dead man."

FORTY-ONE

Monday, 7:12 p.m.
Chesapeake, Virginia
Four hours, forty-eight minutes till Election Day

The global private-security empire was on four thousand remote acres in southern Virginia. It was heavily wooded, swampland. Perfect for an exclusive, private military base. Along with a headquarters building, it was supposed to include some of the highest-level military-training facilities in the United States. Shooting ranges. Obstacle courses. Bombing sites. The works. I'd learned that Redrock got its start two decades ago training Navy SEALS for special operations.

It was hard to find much information about Redrock's property. There were press photos of the headquarters building, which looked like any other corporate office. A stone-and-glass-encased building with a spacious parking lot. It wasn't like Redrock had built its facilities underground or anything crazy like that. While its product was unique, this was still a business with accountants, salespeople, and administrative assistants. Although, the tanks in the parking lot did stand out in the press photos.

Perhaps that was only for the media. I hoped.

We knew that a tall chain-link fence with barbed wire circled nearly the entire four thousand acres. The photos also showed men with machine guns and security dogs roaming the property. We were working with two opposing theories. The first was that this place was like Fort Knox, locked down to the highest level, protected from any possible type of terrorist attack, foreign or domestic, with tanks at every corner, snipers in every other tree, and a dozen unmanned drones flying overhead. The second theory was that it was not overly secure, being that it was hidden deep in the Virginia woods and that Redrock had a certain reputation. Only a foolish man with a clear death wish would even consider trying to break into a property belonging to such a lethal agency with more than one hundred trained killers living onsite.

I was going to be that foolish man.

It was ridiculous. A twenty-five-year-old law student was going to break into one of the most badass places on the planet and steal top-level secrets. But what choice did I have? My attorney had made it pretty clear that without the video, I was rolling the dice with poor odds, a reckless gambler. With the video back in my possession, I likely had my get-out-of-jail-free card. It was the necessary proof and linchpin connection behind all my other crazy stories about what had played out over the past three days.

So, there you go. It was a no-brainer. I was going after that damn video, even if it meant getting shot at by snipers, blown up with a grenade, or taken out by a missile from a Black Hawk helicopter in the process.

Tommy suggested the only way to bypass so many complex outer layers of cyber-security walls, at least on our rushed timeline, was simply to go physically inside of them. OK, so it wasn't going to be simple. Not in the least. But he said there was no way the military cyber techs working inside the computer center would have to jump through as many security hoops as a hacker on the outside.

Tommy suggested that *if* I could somehow get inside Redrock's computer center, and *if* I could somehow log in to the main system, it might simply be a point and click of the mouse. Drag, drop, download, and run like mad.

Those were big *ifs*. But that was my plan at the moment.

Which was why I found myself perched on top of a hill overlooking a guarded security booth in the distance below, near a gated entrance into the property. I mean, this wasn't the first time I'd broken into some kind of secure facility. I'd slipped into shipping warehouses, loading docks, and even into shopping malls in the middle of the night. But they were usually not patrolled by Navy SEALS or former marine snipers who took shots from a mile away at Al Qaeda targets in Afghanistan.

We had bandied about two different approaches to accessing the property. They could not have been more opposite. The first included wearing army fatigues, painting my face in camouflage, hiking through the woods for miles, maybe swimming across a swamp, digging a hole under the barbed-wire fence, crawling across minefields, perhaps doing hand-to-hand combat with a few marines who came across my path, and basically doing my best Jason Bourne impression. Maybe have a chopper fly in and pick me up on top of the building when I'm done. It was a complex approach. The second was much more simple. I was going to walk straight into the building and grab it. And then calmly walk straight back out.

The first approach required much more skill.

The second approach required serious balls.

I chose the second. It was more my style. I was not Jason Bourne.

Natalie wasn't so sure, but I reminded her that the only reason I ever got busted stealing cars as a teenager was because I was doing it in the dark of night, while wearing all black, and in a way that the police expected. They were looking for a guy behaving just like me. However, I never came close to being busted when I simply had the courage to drop into unlocked cars that were left unattended momentarily with the keys still in the ignition and drive calmly away. No one expected that.

Behind me, parked just off the road, was the black 1997 Honda Accord I'd snagged outside of Chesapeake. I wore my hoodie with no cap. Just my shiny bald head. It was go time. I couldn't sit here all night. I grabbed the small, clear case from the driver's seat, opened it, found the tiny flesh-colored earpiece inside. I squeezed the end, as instructed, then slipped it deep into my right ear. Hidden from plain view.

"Hello?" I said. "Anyone out there?"

"Gotcha, Duke," said Tommy into my ear. "Loud and clear."

"How's the view?" Natalie asked.

Both were a mile up the road, huddled inside an empty café in front of Tommy's laptop computer, using GPS surveillance software that Tommy was somehow very comfortable working. One quick instant message on his laptop and Tommy had high-tech surveillance gear delivered to a random café in southern Virginia within twenty minutes. The minuscule earpiece was delivered by a young Pakistani guy with bleached white hair whom Tommy called Smokes. Tommy and a small group of his buddies could probably take over the government of Sweden within twenty-four hours, if they wanted.

"Pretty simple so far," I replied. "One guard, one guard booth. No dogs. A few cars have gone through. They're getting past easily. Just stopping at the gate, having their security cards scanned, and the guard opens the gate for them. I think I've got this."

Natalie said, "The building you're looking for is deep inside the property. Near the back. You'll have to pass through all of the training centers and practice grounds first." She had checked in with a colleague who had recently covered a press event at Redrock to get an overview of the property.

"You mean, past the guys with machine guns and grenade launchers?"

"Yes."

"Fantastic. No sweat. So, are we ready?" I asked.

"Ready, Duke," Tommy said. "Let's go do it."

I dropped into the Accord, started her up, pulled back onto the road.

I looped around the hill, took a left at a crossroads, and made my way back up toward the security booth, feeling a knot in my stomach. The young security guard wore military fatigues and had a gun at his belt. There was only one guard. It wasn't like they had several men out front with machine guns tonight.

I pulled up to the booth, lowered my window.

The guard walked over with a digital tablet of some kind in his hand. "ID, sir?"

I handed him the Redrock Security ID I'd stolen from Elvis. The photo on Greg Carson's ID was now a picture of me. Tommy had put the ID back together seamlessly. Tommy had also been able to check Redrock's system and felt assured that Greg Carson had not yet been deleted. Redrock had thousands of private contractors in and out of the program at all times. I was counting on the guard not knowing Carson. I figured, if needed, I could somehow outmaneuver this one lone soldier guy and still hightail it out of there. This first security clearance would also let us know just how far we could get with Elvis as my guide.

The guard swiped the ID like a credit card on the side of the tablet.

He studied the screen. I tapped the steering wheel with my fingers, trying to appear cool.

"Stop tapping," Natalie whispered into my ear. I settled my fingers.

Two seconds later, he handed the ID back to me. "Thank you, sir."

He walked back to the booth, pressed a button. The gate eased open.

"We're in," I whispered. "Elvis has *not* left the building."

I pulled the Accord through the gate. So far, I was happy with the method we chose. This was much easier than a covert swim through a swampy lake followed by an army crawl through the mud. The paved road weaved for a mile through the wooded property until I finally came upon some cleared land with several buildings. Most looked like military-style buildings, warehouses, workshops, interspersed among training facilities and fields. I gave Tommy and Natalie a play-by-play of what I was seeing. It was at this point that I noticed a few men in military fatigues with machine guns walking about. Not sure if they were guards or just doing night drills. Either way, in my current position, it was not encouraging seeing men with these types of weapons hanging over their shoulders.

If at any point this thing went south, I was going to have a very difficult time getting out. I followed the paved road and passed a row of bunkhouses, at least six of them. Then I passed an asphalt lot next to a massive hangar with a half dozen military helicopters parked out front. Some of them had Redrock's bull-shaped logo printed on the outside. Tommy had been able to pull property and building surveys from somewhere online. There were guys outside the first few bunkhouses, smoking, some drinking beer.

A quarter mile past the bunkhouses, I drove up to the main parking lot. There was another security booth and another soldier to clear, just like at the front of the property. He swiped my ID card on a matching digital tablet, waited, then nodded, pressed a button, and I watched another gate slide open. The headquarters building looked just like the photographs. The two-story building had a large glass front lobby and well-lit landscaped grounds surrounding it. I parked the Accord in the third row. Counted the number of cars still in the lot. None were anything fancy. Hondas, Nissans, Chevys, Fords. Maybe two dozen of them in total. But no tanks.

Sitting in the car in the dark, I stared at the building. The computer center was on the second level. It was a large room with a dozen cubicles. Each cube was loaded with high-tech computer gear.

I took a deep breath. "Hey, Maverick, you going to send in a rescue team if you're wrong about all of this?"

"Sorry, Duke. Just you, me, and the girl on this one."

"I was afraid you were going to say that."

I got out of the Accord, shut the door quietly behind me.

I checked my watch. It was nearly seven thirty.

Two men in matching white polo shirts were exiting the front doors of the building and walking toward the parking lot. The Redrock logo was on their shirts. I hoped I didn't stand out because I had no Redrock gear. I stopped breathing for a moment, but I was determined to do it this way. I was convinced hiding right out in the open was the best way to attack a military corporation with men trained and focused on literally digging deep into dark and hidden desert caves for assailants.

"Have a good night, guys," I said, approaching them.

"You, too, man," one of the guys said without hesitation.

"You sound good, Sam," Natalie assured me. "Confident. Like you belong there."

"Kind of like the night we first met, huh?" I replied.

"Not even close. Your voice cracked numerous times during our first conversation."

"Ouch," said Tommy.

"Don't believe a word of it, Tommy." My eyes narrowed. "Walking through the front doors now."

I entered the glass doors. My eyes did a quick survey. The spacious lobby was well lit. An open stairway was off to my right. An elevator right beside it. A man and a woman were talking outside the elevator. A security booth was to my direct left, two hulking guards in military fatigues standing behind it. I spotted a sign by the security booth that read REDROCK EMPLOYEES MUST SCAN IN AND OUT EVERY TIME YOU LEAVE THE FACILITY. I saw a stand with some type of fancy scanner on it. I knew I couldn't hesitate for long, as it would look like I didn't know where I was going. I stepped over to it, held out my badge, and put the bar code under the scanner light. Nothing happened the first time it scanned. My eyes drifted over to one of the beefy guards behind the booth. His eyes were already on me. I felt sweat on my back. On the second scan, the light turned green.

Hitting the stairs, I calmly moved up one step at a time, resisting the urge to take three at once.

"Headed up," I whispered, my lips barely moving. I was a ventriloquist with no puppet.

Upstairs, there were hallways in both directions leading to multiple conference rooms. I passed a group of four men coming out of one, giving the appropriate head nod. Most were casually dressed. They reciprocated with a polite nod but no curious stares.

I kept moving. "Almost there," I whispered.

Turning the corner, I headed to the computer center that was supposedly up ahead on the left. I stopped in front of a solid black-metal door. A plaque with the number 204 hung on the wall beside it, confirming I'd found the right place. I grabbed the metal handle and tried to open the door. It was locked. Of course. Quickly, I examined the area around the door and noticed a scanner beneath the plaque. There were scanners everywhere. I wondered if I would go four-for-four with Greg Carson. I pulled out the ID, swiped it through the reader. Nothing. I swiped it a second time. No access granted on the third try, either. *Crap.* I knew I couldn't keep swiping or it would probably set off an alarm somewhere.

"It's not working," I whispered.

"Hold on a sec," Tommy said. I could hear his fingers clicking away.

I was so close, I could taste it. I listened to see if I could hear any noise from inside the room. I thought I could hear dialogue. I examined the security scanner again. There was no way I could dismantle it. I'm sure security sirens would go nuts if I messed around with it. The only way into the room was with appropriate security ID clearance.

"You lost?"

A voice. Behind me. I spun, feeling a chill rush up my spine. It was a young woman in a gray skirt and white blouse. She held a container of yogurt in one hand, a plastic spoon in the other.

"Sorry?" I replied.

"You're just standing in the hallway," she clarified. Then she smiled. "You look like you're lost."

"I'm Greg," I said, reaching out a hand. "Just started last week."

"Kate. Very nice to meet you." She took my hand. "I'm in the PR department. You look really familiar. Have we already met?"

I felt my heart hammer away. She'd probably just seen me on CNN. "I don't think so. I think I would have remembered."

As I flashed my most charming smile, my eardrum nearly exploded.

"Are you flirting with her?" Natalie said loudly. I heard Tommy laugh.

"They have any snacks left in the kitchen?" I asked. "I'm starving."

She shrugged. "I saw some bananas, but I think the boys from Bunkhouse D have been in the building again. Looks like everything was wiped out. The fridges are nearly empty."

I shook my head. "Figures. Have a good night, Kate. Good to meet you."

"You, too."

I stepped past her, like I knew where I was going. I felt her eyes stay on me.

"What now, Tommy?" I whispered. "I can't keep roaming the halls."

"Ground floor," Tommy said. "Take the elevator down to the basement."

"Why?" I said quietly, passing two more people huddled near an office door.

"I'm going to get you inside the computer center."

I circled the floor, returned to the elevator corridor. I stepped inside an empty elevator and descended to the basement, which was much more industrial. The hallway lacked the decor of the rest of the building. Just plain white walls, gray carpet, and bad lighting. No people. There were three doors on each side of the long hallway, labeled ELECTRICAL ROOM 1, ELECTRICAL ROOM 2, ELECTRICAL ROOM 3, all the way up to ELECTRICAL ROOM 6. Each room had the same white-metal door.

"What now, Mav?" I said. "I got six options."

"Electrical Room 4," Tommy instructed.

I hurried forward, found the door on my right, put my hand on the knob. It was locked. But there wasn't a scanner box on the outside of the door. It looked like this door only had a basic lock-and-key system.

"Any idea if this room is wired, Tommy?" I asked.

"Nope. Only one way to find out."

I sighed, looked both ways, all clear. I didn't hear another soul in the basement. I reached into my jeans pocket, pulled out two paper clips, dropped to one knee, and went to town, scraping and wiggling the clips. The lock clicked, and the doorknob turned thirty seconds later. No sirens went off or lights flashed. I exhaled.

I was inside a dimly lit room that sounded like a massive beehive; there was so much electricity pulsing through it. The room had a large metal cube in the middle, like a ten-by-ten square column, floor to ceiling. There were a dozen different gray-metal boxes attached with metal tubes coming out of the top that stretched into the ceiling and disappeared from view.

"What next?"

"The boxes should be labeled. Find T2 and T3."

I carefully circled the column, found the boxes side-by-side opposite the door.

"Got them."

"Open them up," Tommy said. "Tell me what you see."

I grabbed the handle on T2, lifted. The metal box panel raised up. I did the same for T3. The guts looked nearly identical. A dozen small white boxes. Red, green, white, blue, and black wires running in and out of them, all over the place. I told Tommy what I saw.

"Good," he replied, excitement in his voice. "That's perfect."

"Glad you think so. Now, what am I doing here?"

"I want you to pull the red wire out of the third white box from the very top. Then pull the yellow wire out of the fourth white box and reverse them. Plug them both back into the boxes. But do it very quickly."

"You want to explain to me what's going to happen?"

"By switching the wires, you're clearing a path that allows me to put a minor virus into the system. That virus will give access to whoever swipes a security card at the computer-center door in the next five minutes, regardless if they have actual security clearance."

"You're a genius."

"I know."

"Kiss him on the lips for me, Natalie."

"I'll kiss you both on the lips if you just get out of there safely with the video, OK? Now get moving already."

I reversed the wires. "How's that?"

Tommy said, "Sweet. We're in, bro. Good job. Now go. Hurry. Don't waste any time. They'll be on us in a matter of minutes now."

I did not like the sound of that. But I was on the move, out of the room, back into the elevator. The elevator doors parted on the first floor, not the second floor. The muscular security guard who'd eyeballed me upon entrance stepped into the elevator with me for the ride up. He was about six foot four with a neck the size of my thigh. He gave me a menacing glare without a hint of friendliness. I stepped to the side and made room. The doors slowly shut. I was sweating profusely. The silence was awkward. I needed to break the ice, create some safe space. I didn't need this guard eyeballing me around the second floor. My eyes searched like crazy. His military fatigues were rolled up to the elbows. Tight. Neat. But I spotted it on his thick forearm.

"Is that the Macho Man?" I said.

The guard turned. I nodded toward his forearm, where among a hybrid of other ink, he had a small tattoo of the legendary wrestler and showman I recognized as Randy "Macho Man" Savage. In the tattoo, he was jumping off the top ropes dressed in his familiar wrestling headband and garb. I knew about Macho Man from a video game a few guys used to play back in the day.

The guard looked at his arm, nodded, but said nothing. I needed more. The nugget came from a conversation I'd overheard one time, between two old shelter roommates, while they played that dumb video game for hours. Just popped into my mind, clear as day.

"I was at Turning Point in '04 with my cousin. Saw him beat The Kings of Wrestling."

The guard turned, softened. "You're kidding?"

"Nope. A classic."

"That was his last match."

"Yep."

We'd connected. His guard came down. "That's really cool, man."

The elevator door opened. The security guard actually said, "Have a good one," and allowed me to exit first. We were buddies now. I stepped around the corner, watching him out of the corner of my eye. Thankfully, the guard didn't follow me. He peeled off in the opposite direction, probably headed to the kitchen.

"You've got two minutes, Sam," Tommy whispered in my ear.

"Don't need it. I'm here."

I was back in front of the computer-center door. After looking both ways again to make sure no one was coming, I scanned Carson's ID badge. The door clicked open. I smiled with relief.

"It worked," I whispered. "I'm in."

I opened the door, poked my head in carefully, found a large open room that seemed to match the size shown on the floor plan. Enough space for twelve cubicles in the middle of the floor. I could hear at least two other men talking on the opposite side of the cubicles. I knew Tommy had a plan once I got inside the computer center. He told me any open computer would work.

As expected, each of the cubes held hefty computer stations with three large screens. The first three cubes weren't being used. The screens were dark. I chose the fourth cube, the one that felt the farthest away from the conversation that was going on between the two men.

I quickly pulled the tiny flash drive out of my pocket.

"Tommy, are your boys ready?" I whispered, barely audible.

"More than ready. They've been waiting. Let's do it."

Tommy had a team of hackers on call. The "best of the best," he called them, about six guys living all around the world but connected through cyberspace. Tommy had recruited them to help with what he called Project Indiana Jones. Once I plugged the flash drive into a port on the computer, it would open up a cyber doorway for them to go to work. Like Harrison Ford's character in *Raiders of the Lost Ark*, they would each send their own Indiana Jones cyber character into this very dangerous system to go hunting for the priceless treasure, which was, of course, the video. They all knew they had maybe sixty seconds tops to get in and get out before the cannibal natives killed them with spears.

Or killed me.

My life was in the hands of six brilliant hackers.

I said a quick prayer and plugged the flash drive into a port on the computer. Immediately, something began to happen that I couldn't fully understand. A dozen password boxes popped up on the largest computer screen. They weren't simple username and password prompts. Numbers and letters started flashing and rotating like crazy inside each of the boxes. The computer geeks were going to town, hacking the system with blazing speed, when suddenly the screen went live! They'd done it.

"We're in the system, Sam!" Tommy whispered. "We're on the hunt."

"Go, Indy, go," I whispered back.

"Keep your eye on the light, Duke."

A small traffic light appeared in the right corner of the main screen. At the moment, the yellow light was blinking. Tommy said if the light went to red, it was bad news, that I should grab the nearest machine gun and start blasting my way out. He thought that was funny. I did not. If the light went to green, I was good to go. Unplug and get out. As long as it was blinking yellow, Indiana was still alive and on the hunt. The light was still blinking yellow.

"Hey, Lewis, you running a test or something?"

It was a male voice, from the opposite side of the cubes. Looking for someone named Lewis. My eyes surveyed the cube. Then I spotted a certificate on the wall. Lewis Tasker. I was inside his cube, on his computer. I stayed silent. I bet they could tell I was logged into Lewis's computer system, so they assumed I was Lewis. My eyes were locked in on the yellow blinking light. *Come on, Tommy. Make this fast.*

"Yo, Lewis, you asleep already?" said the man again, even louder.

"Maybe he's passed out on that vegan drink he loves so much," I heard from another male voice over by the other man. "That stuff was disgusting."

"Just getting a report for Mr. Waters," I said, loud enough to be heard over the walls. I, of course, didn't know if Lewis Tasker had a deep voice or high-pitched voice, so I tried to stay neutral. Anything to buy a few extra seconds. Reginald Waters was listed on the corporate website as VP of Strategy. I'd memorized that website.

"Waters?" the voice replied.

"That guy has never said two words to me," the other guy added.

"What kind of report, Lewis? And why did you change your passwords? You know we're not authorized to do that until Friday. Markson's going to be pissed."

I didn't reply. What could I say? I stared down at that blinking yellow light. We were nearing sixty seconds.

"Lewis?"

"Buy time, Sam," Tommy said into my ear. "My boy in London is close."

"Markson authorized it, guys," I replied over the walls.

The squeak of a chair made my mouth go dry. Was I about to have to take a swing? If the guy came around that corner and that yellow light was still blinking, I was breaking noses or whatever I had to do to secure that video. I heard footsteps on the carpet. He was on his way around. I stood and flexed my fist. A bearded man turned the corner and stopped in his tracks. Ten feet from me. As we connected eyes, I did my best to block the computer screen with my body.

"Who are you?" the man asked, surprised.

"I'm Carson. Greg Carson." I said it casual, like he should know.

"Wait, how did you . . . why are you on Lewis's computer?"

I peeked down. Still blinking yellow. "Didn't they tell you I was coming tonight?"

The man's eyebrows bunched. "Didn't who tell me? Coming for what?"

"Peterson. He sent me over."

Nick Peterson was VP of Development. I had all kinds of names and faces flashing through my mind. I was throwing it all out there.

"Almost there," I heard Tommy say. "Ten seconds."

"No, no one told me anything!" the guy exclaimed.

"Sorry, I thought they cleared it with you."

The man was suspicious. "But how did you get in here?"

I shrugged. "Came through the door. Just like you. Relax, man."

A look down at the blinking yellow light. London boy needed to step it up or I was toast.

"This isn't right," the man suggested. "I'm calling Markson."

I tried to look nonchalant. "All right, man, but I already talked to Markson tonight. He said he was calling you."

"You did? He didn't call up here." The man tried to peer around me at the computer screen. "What are you . . . what is it you're doing?"

I turned. *Green light!*

"We got it!" Tommy whispered. "Get out of there."

I casually reached down, pulled the flash drive out, and shoved it in my pocket. I held my hands up to show surrender. "Look, I don't want to cause any problems, OK? I'll clear it up with Peterson and Markson and come back tomorrow. No big deal."

I pivoted, moved quickly to the door. From the corner of my eye, I could see the bearded man step into Lewis's computer station behind me, eyes intently on the screen. I heard an audible curse. This was not going to end well. I was only three steps into the hall when the ear-piercing sound of an alarm and flashing strobe lights announced there was an intruder.

"Go, Sam, now! We'll cover you!" Tommy yelled. "They found us!"

FORTY-TWO

Monday, 7:47 p.m.
Chesapeake, Virginia
Four hours, thirteen minutes till Election Day

The sprinkler system erupted above me. Water started spewing out of spigots, flooding the hallway. Tommy and his boys were working their magic. A few people stepped frantically out of offices, looking around curiously. They were covering their heads with jackets, binders, paperwork, even sofa cushions, anything to keep from getting soaking wet. My legs kept moving toward the corner of the hallway. My head hurt from the siren of the alarm. I made a beeline back to the stairs. Then I heard yelling behind me.

"Someone stop that guy!"

I turned. It was the bearded man from the computer center. He was pointing at me. There were three men standing in the hallway in front of me, near the elevator corridor, looking at one another, getting wet. They looked like accountants, not soldiers, so they probably weren't comfortable accosting a stranger just because a guy was yelling and pointing. Where was the soldier? Macho Man? And the other guard? And how many trained snipers would be in the building within minutes? One of those questions was answered a second later, as the guard with the wrestling tattoos stepped out from a corner beyond the elevators. His eyes focused on me while he grabbed the gun off his waist.

"I got trouble, Tommy," I said, backpedaling.

"The other way," Tommy instructed. "Go! There are more stairs at the back. Opposite end of the building."

I turned, sprinted back toward the bearded guy, ready to put an angry shoulder into him. He cowered as I neared, ducked back into the computer center. The hallway carpet was slick from the dousing of sprinkler water overhead. More employees were scrambling out of their offices, all bewildered at the sudden commotion, clearly not sure what to do to escape it. Tommy was in my ear, giving precise instructions as he tracked me on his GPS, left, right, straight. I was darting through a maze of office hallways, water squishing in the carpet beneath my shoes. Finally, I came to a door with an Exit sign above it. I put my hand on the knob.

"It's locked, Maverick!"

"One second."

I turned. Macho Man was barreling down the wet hallway. Thirty feet behind me. He raised a fist, gun in it.

"Go, go, go!" yelled Tommy.

I pushed through a newly unlocked door into a stairwell. Gunfire rang out. Two shots. The bullets hit the edge of the thick metal door as I shut it. I saw the military guard lift a walkie-talkie to his mouth. I felt the electronic door lock reengage. There was a bang on the outside as the guard tried to open it. Tommy or one of his boys had shut it down. I spun around, bolted. There were no sprinklers inside the stairwell. I found the ground floor, pushed through another door. Tommy was again in my ear, giving me instructions on how to get back to the front of the building. Back to my car.

The sprinkler system suddenly shut off above me. A series of metal security gates began descending from the ceiling. Redrock was locking down the entire building. This was no ordinary corporate facility, after all. I was about to be trapped in the middle of a hallway.

"Tommy?" I yelled.

"We're on it!"

The metal gates paused with about three feet of clearance. I sprinted forward, rolled on wet carpet under three consecutive gates. Another shot rang out behind me and ricocheted off a gate. The other military guard had found me. I rolled one last time. When I'd cleared the last gate in the hallway, I heard the gate reengage and seal all the way to the carpet, locking the military guard inside. I stumbled into the main lobby. There were a half dozen people standing around, soaking wet. I burst straight through that small crowd toward the front glass doors. There were no guards at the booth. The glass suddenly exploded right in front of me. I dived again, rolled through the glass and onto the concrete outside the front doors. I felt tiny shards stick in my hands. I peeked back. My buddy, Macho Man, was racing forward, again in hot pursuit, gun in hand, aiming at me.

I heard Natalie screaming in my ear. "Sam, are you OK? Sam?"

I picked myself up, bolted toward the parking lot.

Another shot rang out. The headlight of a car in front of me shattered.

I jumped, slid across the hood, cleared, landed, kept running. The Accord was up ahead. I opened the driver's door, jumped in, shoved the keys into the ignition. The Accord revved to a start. I pushed the gear into drive, pressed my foot to the floor. The tires squealed as I whipped the wheel to the left. The security gate to the main parking lot was shut. It was a big, heavy, metal number. I couldn't burst through it. The Accord would be totaled.

"Tommy, the security gate!"

I heard Tommy yell, "Come on, fellas! Stop jacking around!"

The gate suddenly parted. I punched the gas. The guard at the gate stepped out, his gun aimed at me. I ducked and heard my windshield take four consecutive bullets. I had just enough space to clear the gate past the guard, who took two more shots and hit the back window, which shattered. But I was clear from the parking lot and back on the main property road.

Natalie was still screaming in my ear.

"I'm here, I'm here," I replied, short of breath, my eyes straight ahead. "But how am I going to get out of here?"

"There is a back road, Sam," Tommy said. "Right past the bunk-houses. Turn right, and hightail it all the way to the very end."

The Accord was up to eighty miles an hour already as I flew past the chopper hangar. I saw a group of men who were already scrambling toward two parked military Jeeps. No doubt coming after me. The bunkhouses were ahead of me.

"Turn right!" Tommy yelled.

I slowed enough so as not to flip the Accord, ripped the steering wheel to the right. The Honda kept two tires on the pavement, made the turn. I pushed the gas pedal down again. I cleared a half mile in a flash. Headlights were now shining behind me.

"Where am I going, Tommy?"

"There's a dirt road, right outside a back gate. About a hundred yards from the property line. You can't drive to it. You're going to have to run for it on foot."

I saw it up ahead. The massive chain-link fence with barbed wire. The road just stopped suddenly. I slammed on the brakes, put the car fully into a ditch, behind some trees. Jumped out of the car. The head-lights were getting closer. It looked like multiple sets of headlights. I sprinted through the trees toward the chain-link fence.

"Fifty feet to your left," Tommy instructed.

I kept running, through the tall grass. "I see it."

I ran up to the fence, found a heavy metal gate, but it was securely locked with an electronic system. There was no card swiper or keyhole for picking.

"Tommy, unlock this already."

"We need twenty more seconds."

"Twenty seconds! I could be dead in twenty seconds!"

I looked back again. The headlights were close now. Men with machine guns were about to be swarming me. I looked up at the top of the barbed wire. The fence was probably twelve feet tall with huge rolls of sharp barbed wire on top of it. It was impossible to climb.

"Tommy? Now or never."

"Now!" Tommy replied.

I saw a light on the gate lock blink green. I turned a handle. It opened. I was outside the property. Not that it would stop them from hunting me, but I still had a chance. I was running through the thick woods, nearly blind, only the light of a clouded moon above guiding me forward through rain-soaked Virginia hills. And Tommy was in my ear, yelling about a dirt road somewhere up ahead.

I ascended the side of a hill. My hands dug into the moist ground to help pull me up. I looked back. Men with guns were at the gate. I counted at least six of them. They spilled out onto my side of the fence, searching frantically for me. I pushed ahead, through more trees, deeper into the woods. Then I heard another sound in the distance. A loud rumble with a repeated thump, thump, thump.

Helicopters.

FORTY-THREE

Monday, 7:56 p.m.
Chesapeake, Virginia
Four hours, four minutes till Election Day

I turned around again, searched through the trees. I spotted them. Two Redrock choppers were headed my way with powerful spotlights already penetrating the ground, creating massive circles of exposure. Bright as daylight. They would be on me quickly.

"I'm so dead," I said to no one in particular.

"Not if you keep running," Tommy suggested. "The dirt road is right over the next hill."

"But what am I going to do when I get there?"

"Jump in the car with Natalie. She's en route. She should be there any second."

This pumped more adrenaline into my veins. *Natalie.* I pushed off, cleared the hill, stumbled through a ditch, and found the dirt road. The choppers were gaining quickly. Then I spotted headlights. I could only hope it was Natalie. The car swerved around a corner, the tires spewing out gravel. It was her Jeep Cherokee. She skidded to a stop. I opened the back door, dived into the backseat. Natalie punched the gas, the Jeep propelling forward.

"Helicopters are coming," I said.

"I know. I see them. But if we can get to the highway, I think we can make it."

"How far is the highway?"

"A quarter mile."

"Punch that gas, babe."

The Jeep Cherokee lifted off the ground several times as we raced straight ahead along the bumpy dirt road. I stared through the back window. I could see the floodlights pouring down from above. They were still looking for me in the wooded hills. We had a chance. We reached the highway. Natalie skidded right. There were other cars and trucks out on the main highway. We were positioned in between an 18-wheeler and an old Ford truck. Natalie slowed to a normal speed, tried to blend with traffic. Light from above suddenly swept over us. The choppers. They were wreaking havoc on the highway, blinding drivers, flying really low and reckless. Clearly desperate. Clearly willing to do whatever was necessary to stop us. Cars were already slowing and pulling over in both directions. It was chaos.

"Stay down!" Natalie yelled at me.

I ducked behind the seats. One chopper was hovering overhead, shining its floodlights into other vehicles ahead of us. They blinded the guy driving the 18-wheeler directly in front of us, who swerved severely and honked his horn, obviously irritated at the intrusion from above, until he couldn't take it anymore and started to slow and pull over onto the shoulder. Most cars were now pulling over as the choppers made their intimidating presence felt. But not Natalie. She whipped around the 18-wheeler and kept going, picking up speed. There was no way we could stop. As we raced out ahead of everyone else, we exposed ourselves. Both choppers were coming after us now, since we were the only ones traveling at full speed and accelerating. The powerful spotlights were on us. Would they shoot us from the sky?

I was up again, hanging in between the seats. Now there was no reason to hide.

"The tunnel?" I asked.

Her fierce eyes were straight ahead, both hands strangling the steering wheel. She nodded. "We can make it. It's our only chance."

I peered ahead through the windshield. The Chesapeake Bay Bridge–Tunnel. It was a bridge-and-tunnel system about twenty miles long that crossed the Chesapeake Bay from Virginia Beach to Virginia's eastern shore. The road went completely underwater for long periods of time at two different points. Completely hidden from sky view. We had a chance to get lost. The Redrock choppers could not hunt us forever. There had to be police already en route. We were almost there.

I looked down at the speedometer. She had the Cherokee up to 102 miles an hour and still climbing, the engine redlining as we raced past slower-moving vehicles on the road. We blazed through a toll check without even slowing down. We were on the bridge now and over the bay. I could see ships in the Atlantic. Within seconds we would be underwater, inside the tunnel. We debated just parking there and waiting for the police to arrive.

I saw the sparks before I even knew what was happening. They appeared on the road ahead of us and all around the Cherokee. Then I heard multiple pops against my door and the back window, shattering glass. They were shooting at us. From the sky. I peered up through the window, the two Redrock choppers on both sides of us, flying really low, men with machine guns hanging out of open windows and taking aim.

"Sam!" Natalie screamed.

"Keep swerving—we're almost there!"

Natalie whipped the steering wheel back and forth as bullets skipped up all around us, even as we sped past other cars. We ducked as low as possible in our seats. The island was up ahead, the entrance to the first underwater-tunnel section. We were so close. The Cherokee almost flipped entirely, but Natalie did an incredible job of holding it together. We were within fifty feet. Thirty feet. Ten feet. Before a bullet could hit us square, the protection of the tunnel suddenly swallowed us up as the two choppers veered off out of our sight.

Unfortunately, we had no time to exhale. There were headlights right on our tail. I knew it wasn't just another driver on the highway. They were after us. I peered through the shattered back window. It looked like a Chevy Impala. It was a much faster vehicle than Natalie's old Jeep Cherokee.

"We've still got trouble," I said, turning to Natalie.

Natalie nodded. "I see them. What do I do?"

"Keep going. We've got to be running into police soon. They can't chase us forever."

"I'm going as fast as I can."

When the other lane was clear from traffic, the black Impala swerved into it, started speeding up beside us.

"Don't let him pass, Natalie!"

Natalie turned the steering wheel, veered into the lane, cutting the car off. It swerved back behind us again, then made another pass. Natalie swerved again. We flew past slower vehicles in the open lane, then returned to our lane. But we were no match for the speedy Impala. This time, the vehicle juked us, swerved right, then left, and then made a clean pass. When it was a few feet in front of us, the Impala veered directly into our front bumper, crashing against us. Glass shattered, metal crunched, and sparks flew everywhere. It was a blur. The Impala was relentless, pounding us into the wall of the tunnel until both vehicles finally came to a screeching and sudden halt. I smelled nothing but smoke and gasoline.

In the collision, I had flipped upside down in the backseat. I think there was blood on my forehead. I was dizzy. My hearing was muffled. Tommy was no longer in my ear. I'd lost him somewhere in the wreck. I quickly righted myself, reached for the door handle, then spilled out onto the hot pavement. I was coughing and fuzzy-headed. I heard Natalie yelling something, still sitting in the front seat. She had on her seat belt. The authority in her voice let me know she was OK. But I couldn't tell what she was saying, my head was pounding so badly. She looked frantic, yelling my name over and over again.

Then I looked up, realized why. Square Jaw was approaching. He'd been the driver of the Impala. My nemesis was standing right over me, gun in hand. There seemed to be a deep sense of satisfaction in his eyes as he lifted his gun, ready to end me. Something he'd wanted to do three nights ago.

But the satisfaction didn't last. His head whipped back. Once. Then twice. Then blood. Lots of it. Pouring out over his face, his eyes glossing over, his legs buckling, the gun in his hand dropping to the pavement beside him. He fell to his knees, then flat on his face. Square Jaw was dead.

In the chaos of the seconds earlier, I hadn't noticed another set of headlights. Another vehicle that had pulled in right behind our wreckage. Before I could even process what had happened, I was face-to-face with the gray-bearded man. Two feet apart. His clear-blue eyes barreling directly into mine. He spoke to us for the first time.

"Sam, Natalie, come with me. Hurry."

He held out a hand, lifted me to wobbly feet. Then he hurried over and pried the door open for Natalie to get out.

"We don't have much time," the man said. "You have to trust me."

I could hear police sirens now. Somewhere in the distance.

I stared down again at the pavement, looked over to Natalie. How could we say no? He'd just saved my life. Again. She nodded, as if in agreement with whatever I was conveying with my eyes.

The gray-bearded man ushered us over to a black Suburban with tinted windows. He opened the back door for us, and we climbed inside. My eyes went to the driver. I was shocked to see the blond banker, William Alexander, CIA agent, sitting behind the steering wheel. He gave me a quick nod of recognition. The gray-bearded man quickly climbed into the passenger seat as the Suburban pulled around the wreckage. We passed a row of police cars racing into the tunnel from the opposite direction. Soon we were out of the tunnel and back onto the bridge. As I peered up into the night sky, there were no Redrock helicopters anywhere to be found.

FORTY-FOUR

Monday, 10:06 p.m.
Washington, DC
One hour, fifty-four minutes till Election Day

We rode in silence back to DC. The gray-bearded man promised we would have all the answers we wanted as soon as we returned to the city, so we just sat back and waited. I had no desire to argue about it. I was just thankful to be alive. My girl beside me. The flash drive with the video snug in my fingers, undamaged in the wreck. Natalie was texting back and forth with her editor the entire way. Natalie's colleagues had been digging like crazy. Of the dozen companies that gave to Tolstoy & Peters, which in turn gave to the Roots super PAC, Natalie's editor had already connected six of them directly back to Victor Larsen and Redrock. An aide inside Senator McCallister's office had confirmed that he'd overheard private discussions between the senator and Victor Larsen about the best channels to get the younger McCallister onto the congressional investigative committee immediately upon election. The story was coming together.

The Suburban pulled up to the curb in front of the historic Hay-Adams Hotel, directly across from the White House. The gray-bearded man guided us inside through side doors, up the elevator, and down a long hallway to a door labeled FEDERAL SUITE. He swiped a card and led us inside the spacious room. Someone was waiting for us near the patio doors to the balcony overlooking the White House. Natalie and I exchanged a quick, confused glance.

Lisa McCallister.

Wife of Lucas McCallister.

Lisa wore a conservative dark-blue dress, her blonde hair pinned neatly back. She looked dressed for a high-class dinner function. I noted the sadness in her eyes.

"Are you two all right?" Lisa asked. She seemed sincere.

"I've had much better days," I replied, "but I think we're OK."

"Please, have a seat," she insisted.

We sat on a sofa. Lisa chose to remain standing. The gray-bearded man stood off to the side. Lisa pressed her lips together, as if she was gathering her thoughts, her eyes drifting between the older man and us. Then she started. "I'm sure this must be very confusing to you, being here with me right now. I assume you know who I am?"

"Yes, Mrs. McCallister," said Natalie.

"Please, call me Lisa."

"OK," Natalie replied. "I assume the reverse is also true, that you know who we are?"

Lisa nodded. "Yes, I know all about you, Natalie. And you, too, Sam. Of course."

OK, that was a weird comment.

"Why are you here?" Natalie asked. "I mean, the election is tomorrow."

Lisa nodded again, eyes toward the balcony. "Yes. My husband thinks I'm on a plane right now headed back to Texas to meet him in Austin. But you need to hear the truth."

"The truth about what?" I asked.

Lisa sighed. "The truth about why you were standing outside that motel-room window in Boerne three nights ago."

And there it was. I was on the edge of my seat.

Lisa began by saying that she needed to give us some background. Otherwise, none of it would make any sense. We might still have a hard time with it even after hearing it. But truth was truth, no matter how hard it was to hear.

She said that the first few years of her marriage were magical. She and Lucas were college sweethearts at SMU. They'd married during his second year at Harvard Law, had the kids early, back-to-back, and she really enjoyed being connected to a very influential political family. Life was fun and exciting, with lots of adventure. It was a whirlwind. She got to meet interesting, famous people from all over the world. For a small-town Texas girl, it felt like a real-life princess story.

But then a few years ago, things started to take a darker turn. Lucas changed almost overnight, started drinking more and even experimented with drugs. All while beginning to dip his toes into the family business of politics. Lisa urged him to stop, especially with two young kids at home, but he became dismissive to her. And then abusive. First, emotionally. Lots of yelling, lots of screaming, lots of cursing and name-calling, even in front of the toddlers.

Then came the physical abuse. First, grabbing and slapping. Then it turned even more violent at times. To the point where Lisa was struggling to keep it hidden. And the affairs. There were several girls. Lisa begged him to get help, but he wouldn't listen. Finally, at her end, she threatened to leave him, to divorce him. She just couldn't take it. She wouldn't take it.

And that's when things went from bad to worse.

The first threat of divorce was almost three years ago, right in the middle of Lucas's father's presidential exploration. Lisa's mother-in-law, Gloria McCallister, visited her one night at the house. She and Gloria, who was always standoffish, had never had a close relationship. Lisa had tried early on to build a bond there, but her mother-in-law always kept her at a distance. Even after they'd had children. It was never hostile. They were at least cordial with each other. But that night, alone together, Gloria was anything but cordial. She said she'd heard about the talks of divorce between Lisa and Lucas. That her son was distraught. She encouraged Lisa to back off that kind of talk. Lisa had made a commitment to her son—to their family, really—and they took that commitment very seriously. Divorce was not an option.

At that point, Lisa felt the need to divulge the full truth. The drinking, the drugs, the emotional and physical abuse, the string of sexual affairs. The nightmare that had become her life over the past year. She'd not yet told anyone about her awful secret life at home. She felt alone and isolated. Her parents had passed away ten years ago. She was an only child, so she had no siblings or family confidante to lean on during those difficult days. She'd hoped that her mother-in-law would at least understand and sympathize.

Her mother-in-law did understand. But she didn't sympathize. Instead, she made excuses for her son. She said life in power and under the spotlight was pressure packed and very difficult. You don't abandon your man during those challenging seasons, she said. Their roles as wives were to support their powerful men through those tough times, regardless of the personal sacrifice. Did Lisa really think her mother-in-law hadn't experienced something similar at different points during her marriage? All great women in power did, she said. You deal with it. You don't run away. Lisa said she didn't want to deal with it. She couldn't deal with it. She would no longer allow Lucas to treat her that way. She had to protect the kids.

At this point in the conversation, her mother-in-law began threatening Lisa, said she wouldn't let some small-town Texas sorority girl ruin her husband's legacy or his chance at the White House by creating some unnecessary family drama. She wouldn't stand for it. They could have the kids taken from Lisa. She would rarely see them. Who did Lisa think the courts would believe in a custody battle? Her mother-in-law assured her it would go very badly for Lisa.

Lisa believed her and was horrified. She dropped the talk of divorce, hunkered down, tried to endure it all for the sake of her precious kids. There were months where she thought Lucas was getting better, but then he'd revert back. Lisa felt more alone and isolated as Lucas's political aspirations grew. Everyone called him a rising star for the party. That made it worse. She felt trapped. She'd cried herself to sleep every night for the past two and a half years.

But when Lucas told her he was running for Congress, something reignited in her. A newfound courage. She decided she could not turn out like her mother-in-law. She knew she had to get out. Somehow. Some way. Before the stakes became even greater, if that was possible. She had to escape. But it was clear she couldn't do it the conventional way. She couldn't simply hire a lawyer and file for divorce. They would destroy her and take her kids. They'd made that very clear. She would have nothing. So, she began to devise an intricate plan. A plan that even a powerful family like the McCallisters couldn't squash under the public scrutiny of it all. She would exploit her husband's extramarital affairs at the worst possible time. Create a media circus. To protect her kids, she would ruin him and his career. She would get out clean in the middle.

But Lisa needed help. She couldn't do it alone. Her life was under constant scrutiny. She felt like she was being watched very closely, so she called an old family friend. Marcus Pelini. He was like Uncle Marcus to Lisa. Marcus had even been at the hospital when she was born. He had watched her grow up outside of Dallas. Marcus had served with her father in the navy many years ago, said that her father had once saved his life. After his time in the navy, Marcus had spent thirty years with the CIA working in counterintelligence around the world. He'd retired five years ago. In a private setting, she broke down and told Marcus everything. The whole truth. The anger, the fear, the willingness to go the distance to get away. Marcus, of course, agreed to help her. She was like a daughter to him.

At this point, Lisa officially introduced Marcus to us.

The gray-bearded man. Marcus Pelini. Uncle Marcus.

I was sitting there in shock. Still trying to process everything she was saying.

"How did you choose Jill Becker?" I asked.

Lisa sighed. "With his career in politics ramping up, my husband had become more discreet. I knew it would take the right woman to get him to trip up at such a crucial time. And there was only one woman from our past that Lucas had never been able to resist: Jill Clayton. He cheated on me with her three different times back at SMU, always swearing it would never happen again. That marriage would change everything. I was stupid, of course. Kept forgiving him, wanting to believe. So, Marcus tracked her down in New York City. We discovered that she was in a perfect position to accept such an assignment."

"But how did you pay her?" Natalie asked. "We were told from sources that it was somewhere around a hundred thousand dollars."

"Yes, I had to be very careful. I have a trust fund that my parents left me, for future grandkids, with a significant amount of money in it. It's the only account I have sole control over. So I accessed it in private and have paid for this entire operation out of it."

"But why me?" I asked. "I'm just a law student."

Lisa looked over toward Marcus, who stepped forward.

"I needed the right guy," Marcus said. "We could take no chances. I knew we'd have one shot at this. I needed someone who could handle the situation no matter what came up. Someone who had the skills to adapt and get the job done. You're clearly much more than a law student, Sam. I chose you specifically."

"Lucky me."

"I got it right," Marcus assured me.

"Why not just hire a private investigator, take some pics?" Natalie asked.

"Too risky," Marcus replied. "We needed this to look like it came as part of a natural process in politics. We couldn't have it look manufactured or leave a trail back to Lisa. Political trackers are a known commodity. It was an easy fit. A perfect plan. Until Lucas ruined it."

"So, the text to me that night was from Jill Becker?" I asked.

Marcus nodded. "Yes. She followed instructions."

I shook my head. "But I don't understand. I was inside Jill's apartment this morning. I found the scribbled name of Devin Nicks, Congressman Mitchell's chief of staff, on her notepad."

"I planted it there for you to find," Marcus said.

"Why?"

"To redirect. To throw you off the trail. I felt you were getting too close to Lisa."

"So, what, you were willing to throw Congressman Mitchell and his team under the bus on this thing?"

"Absolutely."

Lisa interjected. "Marcus was only trying to protect me. Things, of course, did not go as planned with Jill and Lucas. I would never in my life have gone through with this had I known what would ultimately happen to Jill. I can't sleep because of it. A woman is dead because of me."

"Not because of you, Lisa," Marcus corrected. "Because of him. You can't blame yourself."

"I don't know how to stop blaming myself."

I turned to Marcus again. "Why couldn't we have had this conversation two days ago? Right after things went haywire? You and I were together in Austin. I saw you in the alley. You could have stopped this. Why have you left me hanging out there for the past seventy-two hours?"

"To protect Lisa," Marcus said plainly and with resolute eyes.

"I'm so sorry, Sam," Lisa cut in again, gathering her emotions. "I wanted to come right out after this happened. I was horrified when Marcus delivered the news about Jill. But Marcus convinced me that he could still get this done, that he could still bring our version of the truth out, without ever exposing me. That he could still use you *and* help you to get there. He just needed a few days. I should never have agreed to it. I'm so sorry, but I wasn't thinking straight. You may have kids one day and understand better. How you'll do anything for them. I was so scared."

"You're still alive, aren't you, Sam?" Marcus asked me directly. Clearly not happy that Lisa was getting upset about it all.

"Yes." It was hard to argue with that fact. But still.

"What about the man driving us here? William Alexander?" Natalie asked. "He's CIA?"

"Yes, an old associate of mine, off duty," Marcus answered. "Simply working with me on private contract."

Natalie asked Marcus, "So, is it safe to assume that you know who is behind the men who have been trying to kill Sam the past three days? The men who killed Rick Jackson and Ted Bowerson and Jeremy Lynch? To make sure Lucas gets elected?"

"It's safe to assume, yes. I likely don't know as much as you. I'm not a journalist. And my focus has been Lisa. But I know enough."

"Is this in *any way* connected to Congressman Mitchell?" I asked Marcus.

He shook his head. "Leonard Mitchell is a saint. A choirboy."

Natalie turned to Lisa. "So, they still don't know about you, Lisa?"

"I don't know, Natalie. I don't think so. Marcus believes he has the trail covered. They have not yet gone looking into Jill Becker's situation. Marcus thinks they believe she truly was in San Antonio on business, that this encounter really was random in nature and not at all orchestrated by someone else. My husband is just a cheating idiot who couldn't keep his zipper shut, and it turned from bad to much worse. So they've only been looking to stop the damage from that one perspective."

"You mean stop me." I looked at Marcus. "How have you followed me so closely?"

"I'm very good at what I do, son."

I didn't even want to know. There was probably a GPS chip implanted somewhere inside me.

"Do you know what they did with Jill Becker?" Natalie asked Marcus.

"Yes. I can help locate the body."

This comment about a dead body brought a deep sigh out of Lisa.

"So, why expose yourself now?" Natalie asked Lisa.

"I had to stop it, Natalie. Too much damage has already been done. I couldn't let it continue any further. I asked Marcus to end it. Even if it meant I had to come out and come clean. So be it. I couldn't live with myself if more innocent people were harmed. There's been too much death already. I don't think I'll ever be able to sleep again, may God help me."

I stared at Marcus. "Where is my mom?"

"She's safe, Sam," Marcus assured me. "In this hotel. She's been very well taken care of, I can promise you that."

"I don't understand. Why did you have to take her?"

"To protect her. And to protect you. I had the luxury of having months to do my homework on you. I knew all about your mother and her situation. They did not. Not yet, at least. And I wouldn't chance them finding that piece of leverage and somehow using it against you. Or harming your mother. It may feel like I'm cold and calculating, but I promise you that I'm not. Your mother is doing well."

Even though I was pissed, a rush of relief washed over me at this revelation. My mom was OK.

"Do you have the video, Sam?" Lisa asked me directly.

I reached my hand into my pocket. Held it out.

"Good." Lisa nodded. "No matter what happens with me, at least he won't get away with it. I can't stomach that thought."

"Will you go on record?" Natalie asked Lisa.

"Marcus wants me to disappear tonight. Says he has the network to give me and the kids a brand-new life with new names on the other side of the world, where they'll never find us. But I just can't do it. Not after all that's happened. Not after what I put you guys through. I'll tell you anything."

I turned to Marcus. "Can I go see my mother now?"

FORTY-FIVE

Monday, 10:31 p.m.
Washington, DC
One hour, twenty-nine minutes till Election Day

When Marcus opened the hotel-suite door, I found my mother inside wearing a thick, white hotel robe over silk pajamas and sitting comfortably on the sofa in the living room, watching an old movie on the large television. There was a tray of freshly sliced fruit on the coffee table with a pot of coffee and creamer, the whole nine yards. My mother looked shockingly well. Better than she'd looked in six months. I couldn't believe it. The color was back in her cheeks. She looked ten years younger. Like she'd had a makeover or something. I knew then that Marcus was telling the truth, that they'd indeed taken very good care of my mom over the past two days.

"Samuel!" she exclaimed, getting to her feet.

I rushed over, hugged her tight. "It's so good to see you, Mom."

"I've missed you."

"Same here. I'm glad you're OK."

"I'm more than OK, Samuel. This place is incredible. Your friends told me to order whatever I wanted, so I've been wined and dined the past two days. The best food I've had in years. Crab cakes, red snapper, duck breast, scallops. I think I've put on ten pounds in two days. I've never eaten so much. I've had people come up to the hotel suite to do a facial, even got myself a Swedish massage. Never had me one of those before. It was wonderful."

"That's great."

She smiled wide. "Thank you."

"For what?"

"Well, the man said you set this whole thing up for me."

"Oh, yeah. Right. You're welcome, Mom."

She hugged me again. I felt my heart begin to settle for the first time in three days.

"Is it finally over, Samuel?" she asked.

"Almost, Mom. It's almost over."

FORTY-SIX

Monday, 11:27 p.m.
Washington, DC
Thirty-three minutes till Election Day

We were in a boardroom on the fourteenth floor at *PowerPlay*'s small
office headquarters, a stone's throw from the Capitol Building. I could
actually see the bright glow of the giant dome from the window. Natalie
was at the table with her laptop, pecking furiously away. It was a hell of
a story. A congressional candidate killing his mistress four days before
Election Day? With a four-point lead? The son of a sitting senator.
A battered wife desperately trying to escape. And the powerful secret
player behind the scenes pulling the strings on the election and sending
out a team of military mercenaries to cover their tracks. It was a bomb
of nuclear weight that would shake this powerful city to its very core.
Especially when there was an eyewitness video attached. It was possibly
the biggest breaking-news story on the eve of an election in history. And
I loved watching Natalie work.

Her editor and boss, Nick Montague, a burly man with a ponytail,
was skating in and out of the boardroom, barking orders, gathering

research, info, and photographs. Two more editors and three other young blog reporters were also scrambling about the small newsroom. It was an exciting moment for them, for Natalie. Montague had also called in the blog's lead attorney, Judd Lambert, a man of fifty with silver hair.

David Benoltz returned from the office kitchen with a large cup of coffee for me.

"Thanks," I said. I needed one more surge to get through this ordeal.

"I just got off the phone with them. He'll be here any minute."

"Fantastic."

"You'll be fine, Sam. That video is your life preserver; I promise you that."

"I hope you're right."

"Just tell the truth. Let me handle the rest."

"Whatever you say. You know I can't pay you for any of this, right?"

He winked at me. "I'll take fifty percent of the book deal."

"Yeah, sure."

I walked over to Natalie, whose eyes were glued to the screen.

"How're we doing, babe?" I asked.

"Almost there. Working as fast as I can."

"Well, print out what you've got, because I think it's showtime."

I peered through the interior boardroom window into the small newsroom. A group of six imposing men in trench coats had just entered from the hallway. The one in the middle was the most intimidating and made me want to piss my pants: FBI Director Luther Stone. He was short and squat with a box-shaped head, hair shaved up tight, military-style, perpetual scowl. Forty years ago, he'd won the NCAA wrestling championship for Army. The others were just his support posse. David had insisted on going straight to the top with this. We could not play around with junior-level guys. We needed to speak with the big dog himself. David got him there by sending a teaser clip of the video of Lucas McCallister up the right channels.

David Benoltz, Nick Montague, and Judd Lambert met Director Stone and his FBI team inside the newsroom; they spoke for a few minutes, eyes glancing in my direction several times, and then the director and one of his men came inside the boardroom with us. David quickly introduced Natalie and me. There was no shaking of hands. Just appropriate head nods. My heart was starting to race again. It was the director of the FBI. Standing right in front of me. Looking at me like a lion waiting to eat its prey. How could I stay calm? I needed six weeks sitting on a quiet beach somewhere to get my heartbeat back to a normal rhythm.

"Well, let's have it," Stone said, turning to David. "I didn't come down here for small talk and bad coffee."

David turned to Montague, who turned to Natalie.

"Printing it out right now," Natalie said.

Montague snapped his fingers. Another editor left the boardroom and returned ten seconds later with freshly printed papers in his hands. He handed the small stack to Stone.

"What is this?" Stone demanded.

Montague answered. "A draft of a story that we'll want you to comment on. It will be going online shortly implicating Lucas McCallister in the death of a woman named Jill Becker. And the ensuing cover-up by Victor Larsen and Redrock Security using former military operatives as assassins to control an election that Larsen was determined to have McCallister win by all necessary means."

David chimed in. "The same night my client was wrongly implicated in the death of one Rick Jackson, which the FBI has been investigating."

"One of two deaths, if I recall correctly," Stone said, glaring a hole in me.

"Yes," David replied. "One of two *incorrect* implications of murder toward my client."

Stone looked put out by having to get his reading glasses out of his pocket. He sat down at the table, slipped them on his thick and crooked nose, squinted at the words on the pages. To his credit, he never flinched. He took a few minutes to review the story and then set the papers down on the desk in front of him.

"OK, so where's the damn video?" Stone said.

Montague picked up a black remote control, pointed it at the large flat-screen TV on the far wall. The five-minute-and-twenty-seven-second video began playing. It was surreal to watch it unfold on such a large screen. And it never got any easier to watch. I could still feel the charge of adrenaline when I heard Jill's screams, still taste the numb dryness in my mouth at the sight of so much blood, still clearly see the hollowed look in Lucas McCallister's eyes, still recall the panic in my chest as I raced across the parking lot. It started, it played out, then it was over.

And the air was sucked from the room.

Stone just stared at the black TV screen for a second. Then he let out a soft whistle.

Natalie slid over a piece of paper. "This is the location where you will find Jill Becker's body in Texas."

"How do you know this?" Stone asked.

"Sources."

"I'd like to have those sources."

"Yes, I'm sure you would," Natalie replied. It was fun watching her measure up against one of the most powerful men in Washington. She was in her element. It was sexy.

"So, where can I find Mrs. McCallister?" Stone asked.

"She's waiting for you at the Hay-Adams Hotel," Natalie answered.

Stone turned, snapped a finger. The agent raced from the room.

The director's eyes shifted over to me again. He put a thick finger on the news story on the table in front of him. "This all true, son?"

"Yes, sir."

"Sounds like you've had a helluva few days."

"Yes, sir. I'm just glad it's over now."

Stone chuckled. "Oh, we're just getting started. I can promise you that."

Thankfully, my lawyer jumped in for me. "Director Stone, I'm sure you and your team will have a lot of questions. We'll need to sit down in a room together over at FBI headquarters and go over every detail together in a proper way. You know, after we're all lawyered up and whatnot. To get it all down on the official record. My client is willing to cooperate fully with you—in the right setting. After he is protected fully. So if you don't mind, let's save the rest for now."

Stone stood. "My guys will escort him over to headquarters. I never liked Victor Larsen." He actually said that last line with a beefy grin.

"Can I quote you on that?" Natalie asked, smiling.

"No, Ms. Foster. My assistant will get you a proper quote."

Then he marched back out of the room, his men in tow.

I huddled with David again.

"He's a fun guy," I said, catching my breath.

"Don't worry about him. I got it covered."

"What's next?"

"We need to do what he said. Head over to FBI headquarters. Do this properly."

"How long will that take?"

"Probably all night, I'm afraid. With the breaking news, the FBI will hold a quick follow-up news conference here shortly, where I believe they will officially drop you from the investigation and announce a new series of arrests and targets. But then we'll need to tell your story to the world. So, we need to get it right. After the past three days of your name and face being recklessly defamed across CNN and Fox News and every other news outlet in the country, we'll need to do something serious to clear the air and get you your life back."

"And how do you figure we do that?"

"I've already got calls in to the *Today* show and *Good Morning America*. In about an hour, I promise that both of them will be begging for you. So you choose."

"You've got to be kidding me."

He smiled. "Nope," he replied. "But that's for tomorrow, Sam. First, the FBI."

I frowned. "Can't wait."

David answered another call on his cell, patted me on the arm, took off down the hallway. I watched Natalie for a second. She looked up, gave me a quick smile, then eyes back to her laptop. She was so focused. It felt so right to be there with her. Like home. I felt safe and at peace. I no longer wanted to run. For the first time in a very long time. It felt good.

I turned back to the window, stared at my reflection.

I couldn't help but see a scared ten-year-old boy staring back at me.

I wanted to hug that kid and tell him to hang on. It'll get better. I promise.

SAM, AGE TEN

Denver, Colorado

I sat alone in the back of the police car, watching the chaotic scene.

I'd counted six other police cars on the street, red-and-blue lights still flashing, but the sirens had stopped a few minutes ago. Cops were everywhere. Two ambulances were in the middle of it all. I wasn't under arrest or anything. The cops were just protecting me. Amy was in the police car behind me. One of the female officers had collected our things from the house.

I hoped Amy was OK. She wouldn't even respond to the police officers. She hadn't said a word and had barely moved. Just stared at me with hollow eyes. They had to pry her fingers out of mine, as she'd been clutching my hand ever since I'd pulled her out of the house.

This made me angry all over again.

The street was lined with neighbors, all jostling for a look at the crime scene. All undoubtedly now whispering about the ten-year-old foster kid who might have actually killed one of their neighbors. Several officers in uniform kept them all at bay at a block perimeter. However, I could still see their stares at me through the police-car window.

Pointing, gawking, whispering.

At this point, I wasn't sure if Carl was alive or dead. No one would tell me anything. I wasn't sure if I cared. A big part of me hoped he was dead. Monsters like him should be killed. He'd collapsed in the front yard of our neighbor, Margie, right as the first police car arrived on the scene. I'd overheard two officers talking about him being barely conscious. Medics were working on him now. There was a big huddle of them around Carl when they'd guided me to the back of the police car a few minutes ago. I couldn't actually see Carl through the mass of medics. Which was fine. I never wanted to see that man again.

I saw several of the medics lift a rolling cart into the back of the first ambulance. Then the medics shut the doors, the siren blared once, and the ambulance eased through the crowd of people, who all turned and did more gawking. The ambulance wasn't in a hurry. I didn't know if this meant Carl was OK and stable, or that he was already dead and there was no reason to rush to the emergency room.

For the first time, I spotted my foster mom, Judy, standing on the sidewalk. She looked dazed and confused. She was still in the uniform she wore at the truck-stop diner. Someone had obviously called her. Two police officers were interviewing her. I liked Ms. Judy. She seemed like a good person. She treated us well. In that moment, I felt bad for her. One of the police officers nodded toward me in the back of the police car. I perked up when Judy looked over. I expected a look of sadness or grief. But all I got was an angry look, as if this was all my fault. I couldn't handle her unexpected glare, so I sank way down in the uncomfortable backseat of the police car.

Would other adults think this was my fault, too? Would they believe me? If Amy never talked again, there was no one else to corroborate my version of the story. Especially if Carl died. Not that he would tell the truth, anyway. I started to panic. I wondered if I was about to go to juvie for a really long time. Or prison.

My heart started beating faster again. Tears formed in my eyes.

I stared at the blood on my hands. I felt more tears hit my cheeks.

Don't be a crybaby, I scolded myself. But I couldn't help it. It was like the dam was bursting open, all the pent-up emotions from the past hour flooding out. I closed my eyes and tried to force the tears to stop. But all this did was start the film reel in my mind. A horror movie. I could feel the rage again, see myself flying across the room with my knife in my hand, hear the tear of his flesh throbbing in my ears.

I peeked outside the car window.

I could feel so many suspicious eyes on me. The cops. The neighbors. Judy. All staring my way like I was the monster. I sank down again, out of view.

I felt so alone, so afraid, so lost.

And I suddenly felt so guilty that I'd even caused this mess.

I just wanted to crawl out the other door and run away. Save them all the trouble of having to deal with a kid like me. Just run. This world had nothing for me.

No hope. No purpose.

No one to love me. No one for me to love. I wanted to run.

Run away and never look back.

FORTY-SEVEN

Tuesday, 12:17 a.m.
Washington, DC
Election Day

We had a few minutes alone. That's all the FBI would give us.

Before the world started spinning like crazy.

We headed to the roof of her office building. We'd spent many nights up there, sitting in two lawn chairs, drinking wine and watching the bright lights of the city below us. We had the Capitol Building to one side of us, the White House on the other. There was such incredible power in this town. And such unthinkable depravity. There seemed to be a very thin line separating the two for some people. What did Lord Acton once say? *Power tends to corrupt, and absolute power corrupts absolutely.* I had experienced the full measure and ramifications of those words the past three days.

And I'd lived to tell about it.

The sky was dark, the city lights spectacular. Natalie's big story was set to release on *PowerPlay*'s political blog at twelve thirty. It would hit the digital wire, and we knew from there it would go viral within minutes. By morning, nothing else in the world would be reported. It was Election Day. Twitter might explode.

It was done. I let out a deep breath. My first in seventy-two hours.

"You OK?" Natalie asked.

"I will be."

We stood by the railing, gazing down toward the Potomac River. I watched the wind push Natalie's hair around.

"So, where do we go from here, Natalie?" I said.

She shook her head. "It's going to be a very busy few weeks. There will be a lot more stories. Daily. A lot more excitement. It will die down eventually."

"No, I mean us. You and me. What now?"

She turned, considered her words. "You know, you really hurt me, Sam."

"I know. And I'll spend my whole life trying to make up for it. I promise."

She nodded. "I believe you."

"But?"

"But I can't just let you off the hook that easy. You have to win me back."

"I'll do anything."

"I propose a contest."

"What kind of contest?"

"Well, I'm thinking ten pitches each, at fast speed."

I smiled. "Really? I'm not sure that's fair."

"For you or me?"

I laughed. "OK, fine. What does the winner get?"

She twisted her mouth up, her eyes dancing. "I think the winner should get to choose the beach destination."

"We may have to take a skinny twenty-year-old cyber geek with us."

She smiled. "I can handle that."

"Good." I pulled her in close, kissed her. "You got a deal."

ACKNOWLEDGMENTS

When you write for nearly twenty years before finally publishing your first novel, there are *a lot* of people to thank. I'll do my very best to do that here, but I'm sure I'll miss someone important. Please forgive me if I do.

To Katie, my wife, who stood by in support and love through the roller-coaster years. This has been a wild and challenging ride, and it wouldn't have happened without you. You were my steady rock, wise counsel, and perfect partner when I needed it most.

To my mother, Nancy, who never stopped believing, supporting, and praying. You kept wind in my sails in so many ways. To Doug and Nancy, the best in-laws on the planet. To my whole family (on both sides!), thanks for the many years of unbridled encouragement. I wouldn't be here if it weren't for all of you.

To Thomas Aitchison, for listening to my publishing frustrations for more than a decade and never allowing me to lose hope or give up. To Sam Patton and John Wilson, who've both given me a lifetime of encouragement. To Mark Groutas and Chris Larsen, for always picking me up with a positive word when I needed it most. To Alex Alexander, Jeremy Self, and Lee Rutter, for graciously giving me the space and freedom to chase after this for so long, along with my whole supportive family at CLT. To my forever family in Simonton, thank you. You gave me the foundation.

To David Hale Smith, my agent and the best in the business; and Liz Parker, for jumping in at just the right time. To Karyn Marcus, for breathing new faith into the book in a key moment. To Will Roberts, for helping set the foundation for the story. To Christopher Reich, an incredibly generous and fantastic writer, for going above and beyond. To so many others in publishing who were there for me in a perfect moment, with a simple word of encouragement, or with key contributions at different points along my journey: Brita Lundberg, Beth Vesel, Steve Fisher, William Callahan, David Gernert, Molly Friedrich, Seth Fishman, Lisa Erbach Vance, Taylor Stevens, Fred Burton, Matthew Quirk, Matthew FitzSimmons, and Owen Laukkanen. To Crystal Watanabe, a tremendous editor. To Mike Woodard, who always comes through for me in the clutch.

To Alan Turkus, who made the most important connection of my career. I will be forever grateful. To Gracie Doyle, who opened the pages and took a chance. To Liz Pearsons, who passionately advocated on my behalf and helped make all my dreams come true. To Sarah Shaw, for showing me the ropes. To the entire team at Thomas & Mercer, my wonderful new publishing family. Thank you!

To all my early readers—you made this happen with your passion!

To Anna Ryan, Madison Lane, and Lexi Elizabeth, my precious daughters. You girls are the biggest reason that I never gave up on this dream, because I never want you to give up on yours. Reach for the stars—I believe in you! And finally, to Jesus, the perfect author of my story. Here, words fail me. Thank you.

ABOUT THE AUTHOR

Chad Zunker studied journalism at the University of Texas, where he was also on the football team. He's worked for some of the most powerful law firms in the country, invented baby products that are now sold all over the world, and even helped start five new churches. He lives in Austin with his wife, Katie, and their three daughters and is hard at work on the next novel in the Sam Callahan series. For more on the author and his writing, visit www.chadzunker.com.